THE
TIME
TIDER

To the memory of Jean E. Hogan –
student, teacher, shining light.

LITTLE TIGER
An imprint of Little Tiger Press Limited
1 Coda Studios, 189 Munster Road, London SW6 6AW

Imported into the EEA by Penguin Random House Ireland,
Morrison Chambers, 32 Nassau Street, Dublin D02 YH68

www.littletiger.co.uk

A paperback original
First published in Great Britain in 2023

Text copyright © Sinéad O'Hart, 2023
Illustration copyright © Abigail Dela Cruz, 2023

ISBN: 978-1-78895-330-6

MIX
Paper | Supporting
responsible forestry
FSC® C171272

The Forest Stewardship Council® (FSC®) is a global, not-for-
profit organization dedicated to the promotion of responsible forest
management worldwide. FSC defines standards based on agreed principles
for responsible forest stewardship that are supported by environmental,
social, and economic stakeholders. To learn more, visit www.fsc.org

10 9 8 7 6 5 4 3 2 1

SINÉAD O'HART

THE
TIME
TIDER

LiTTLE TiGER

LONDON

*The Time Tider's Handbook, Introduction:
Recognizing Warps is a basic skill,
instinctive to most Tiders...*

Chapter One

"Evening, sweetheart!" Mara looked up at the sound of a woman's cheery voice. The woman, a volunteer, was pouring soup into cardboard cartons, her bright yellow City Homeless Outreach bib pulled tight over her thick, patterned cardigan. Mara shook her head at the soup, and the woman gave a friendly wink before setting the carton down and pouring another. As soon as the woman was distracted by the next person in the queue, Mara quickly swiped three bread rolls from the pile at the end of the table, squishing them into one of her deep pockets. There were already two hygiene kits in there, one for Mara and one for her dad, and there was space for plenty more contraband if Mara had the chance to grab it. This city was unfamiliar, but every queue like this was exactly the same. Mara knew what to expect.

She glanced up at the volunteers at the next station. They were stacking tubs full of hot food on to the table in front of them – Mara didn't know, or care, what the food was. She moved up and waited her turn.

"You on your own, little one?" said a young woman, placing a tub along with plastic cutlery wrapped in a napkin into a thin bag. "You got a grown-up with you?" Mara glanced at her but said nothing. The volunteer wore a purple beanie over her long black locs, as well as a concerned expression.

As Mara took the bag, she saw the woman turn to speak to a colleague. She didn't give them a chance to ask her anything else. Dropping her gaze, she darted away, grabbing two more tubs of food from the far end of the table. She ignored the volunteer at the last station, who was handing out some sort of leaflet, and hurried out into the drizzle, stuffing the extra tubs into the bag.

"Hey!" came a voice. Mara didn't look round; she knew better than that. "Sweetheart! Please – stop!"

Mara pressed down her panic and focused. She didn't know this city, but she didn't need to. As her pace quickened, she opened her mind to a noise she'd been trying to block out ever since she'd neared the top of the queue: a noise like a distant electrical crackle, or a radio signal from a dying star. The gentle swish of buzzing filled her ears. There was a soft place nearby and Mara let it draw her.

Taking a right at the next corner, Mara plunged into a dark side street. Alleys split off to the left and right. Straight ahead was an entrance to a multi-storey car park, locked up and shuttered. Ahead and to her left, a narrow alley opened out; nearby, a street light glowed, throwing down a cone of orange light into the alley that let her see the outline of a large wheelie bin. Anything past that was drowned in shadow. Inside her head, the crackling noise intensified.

"Little girl!" came a voice from behind. Mara jerked, instinctively facing the speaker. The woman with the patterned cardigan was there, squinting into the darkness, a brightly lit mobile phone in one hand. "Please, darling! I just want to help!"

For a moment Mara was frozen with indecision, out of sight in the shadows. Then the woman's colleague came from behind her, a young man with round, owlish spectacles. "Is she here?" His voice was low. The woman put the phone to her ear and began to speak. "Hello? Is that Store Street police station? It's Angela Addo, with the City Outreach. We've got a child endangerment issue here…"

Mara's muscles finally kicked into action. She turned and ran, breaking her cover. Behind her, the adults shouted again, telling her to stop, but her father's voice rang in her head. *You must avoid the police at all costs.*

The buzz from the soft place was like the whispering sea,

gently calling her forwards. It was a small one, and calm. It probably wouldn't last long. Mara ducked into the alley, feeling her teeth chatter with cold and fear, and then – she felt it. She *saw* it. Right behind the wheelie bin, a greyish-silver wrinkling in the air. She saw its edges, the extent of its spherical shape as it waited. Without hesitation she ran into the soft place and it folded around her.

Mara closed her eyes. The cold was gone and the fear along with it. She breathed, slow and deep, her pulse settling. In this soft place, it felt like she was floating – like something else was bearing her weight, setting her free, letting her rest. Sounds from outside reached her ears through the still-crackling static buzz but Mara couldn't properly hear anything. She knew that if she opened her eyes she might see the misty, indistinct outlines of the people searching fruitlessly for the child they'd seen running in here only moments before – but she didn't want to do that.

She wanted to wait until the soft place was ready to let her go.

Finally, like waking up from a deep sleep or a bubble making its way to the surface, she was back in the dark, cold alleyway – but she kept her senses on full alert. The adults from the Outreach were gone, but she could still hear their voices. She breathed slowly, letting the world settle back around her once again.

...istorm

"This is my favourite Sinéad O'Hart so far. *The Time Tider* crackles with lives lived on the edges and precious time running out. It's spine tinglingly good."
Nicola Penfold, author of *Where the World Turns Wild*

"With its rich, vivid writing and creative handling of the concept of time, this fast-paced and warm-hearted adventure story is one that's sure to stay with readers long after they've turned the last page. I loved it!"
Sophie Cameron, author of *Our Sister, Again*

"*The Time Tider* is a read-past-bedtime, utterly gripping thriller.
My new favourite of [Sinéad's]!"
H.S. Norup, author of *The Hungry Ghost*

"*The Time Tider* is an exciting and warm-hearted novel about family, and growing up that had me on the edge of my seat... A unique and magical take on our relationship with time and with each other..."
Katharine Corr, co-author of *The Witch's Kiss*

"An explosive, thought-provoking adventure in book form. Beautifully strange."
Eve McDonnell, author of *The Chestnut Roaster*

"Fast-moving, mind-bending and thrilling. Recommend!"
Lou Abercrombie, author of *Coming Up for Air*

"...ate and intense, *The Time Tider* is an adventure story like no other.
...s the momentum builds, you'll be hanging on to every second."
Rachel Delahaye, author of *Mort the Meek*

"This is a wonderful, rip-roaring adventure, packed with non-stop action and laced together with friendship, heart and wisdom. I absolutely loved it."
Sharon Gosling, author of *The Diamond Thief*

"An intelligent and tightly plotted adventure with a time-stopper of a concept. Reading this book will make you lose track of time –

"C..." Victoria ...Gazelle

Mara didn't know what these soft places were. All she knew was they'd often saved her skin, giving her somewhere to hide if she needed it, or a place to just *be*, away from everyone. She couldn't remember when she'd first started noticing them, but she'd always known they were there.

She got to her feet. Her muscles ached with tiredness and she was cold through. There was a bad smell in the air too, not just the stink from the wheelie bin, but something more pungent. Something *rotten*, and it was close by. Mara had been around soft places long enough to know that sometimes, when you found one, you'd find something dead not far away, but she never let herself think too deeply about the connection. She put her sleeve over her nose and mouth to block the stench as a sudden, freezing splash landed on the back of her neck, almost making her yell in surprise; instead, she just turned, looking up. A drainpipe came to an end above her, its yawning mouth leading up into total darkness, and she quickly moved out of the way.

She walked to the end of the alley, looking both ways before she stuck her head out. The voices of the volunteers were gone now, but she had to be careful – they might not have gone far. Moments later she emerged on to the wide road she'd left behind as she'd run from the Outreach. She approached the corner and peeked round it. To her left she could see the brightness of the Outreach station, and parked in front was a police car, its lights flashing;

the woman with the cardigan was speaking through the window with the officers inside. Mara glanced up at the clock above the portico. It had only been eight minutes, and she frowned thoughtfully. It had felt like she'd spent much longer than that inside the soft place, hours and hours, but she knew enough about them now to know that was how they worked. When you were inside one, time didn't seem to run the way it normally did – what felt like forever would turn out to have been only a few minutes by the clock. She shrugged, pushing the thought away, and looked back at the police car.

An officer had opened her door and was standing beside the vehicle, taking a statement from the Outreach volunteers. Mara knew that was her cue to disappear. She pulled up her collar and was gone into the darkness, hoping she'd make it back to her dad before the food got much colder.

The Time Tider's Handbook, 1/B/ii: The tools of the Time Tider are three – the Stitch, the watch, and the hourglass. Most important is the hourglass, which must never be surrendered to another, even on pain of death...

Chapter Two

Her dad was bent over his work when she got back to their van. The door's rusted hinges creaked open and screeched shut but he didn't lift his eyes from the pool of light at his table.

"Food," Mara said, dumping the plastic bag down on to her bunk.

Her dad grunted, his attention unwavering from the deconstructed watch that lay in pieces on a white cloth in front of him. On a shelf above his work desk, his apparatus – that was his own word for it – was set up, consisting of three small glass vessels connected by narrow glass tubes. A thick, colourful fluid flowed noiselessly between the vessels, swirling strangely as Mara glanced at it. She'd been curious about this apparatus and its contents all her life, but when she asked her dad about it his answers were vague or confusing. She'd long ago stopped asking, though her curiosity remained.

"Dad, I said *food*." Mara turned to the cupboards behind her and pulled out a pair of cracked plates. She stowed the plastic cutlery the Outreach lady had given her in their "silverware drawer'" an old wooden box crammed with whatever knives, forks and spoons they owned, and pulled out their only pieces of proper stainless steel cutlery, mismatched and stolen from who knew where. She turned back to her father.

He hadn't moved. He hadn't even glanced at the food. Mara sighed.

She laid the plates on the floor, glancing up at her father as she did so. His eyes were hidden behind his magnifying goggles, and he made no indication he even knew she was there. She pulled open the lid of the first tub and breathed in the steam that billowed out. *Spicy*, she thought with a grin. Some of the sauce splashed on to her fingers as she dished it on to her dad's plate. She licked it off, her senses tingling. It was tasty.

She forked out half of the second tub on to her own plate and sealed up the rest, hoping it would keep until the next day. Then she placed her father's plate and cutlery at his elbow, careful not to disturb his delicate work, before settling herself on the floor with her back against her bunk and her knees against the edge of her dad's. She'd almost finished eating her meal when she remembered the bread rolls. Shifting to one side, she slid a hand into her pocket and pulled one out. Tearing it open, she used half to mop up the sauce.

As she swallowed the last mouthful, Mara looked up. Her father had put away the timepiece he'd been working on and now held his own pocket watch: a beautiful silver thing in a polished case. He was looking at its face but Mara couldn't read his expression. Once in a while, he would let her look at this watch and the crest it bore, along with the words engraved above it – a motto, he said, though Mara wasn't sure whose, or what it meant:

Time and Tide May Wait for None; But They Will Wait for Me.

"Dad?" Mara said gently. She pushed herself up on to her bed, looking at the table. Her dad hadn't touched his food. It sat beside him, congealed on his plate. Mara pressed her lips tight. "*Dad,*" she repeated loudly.

Finally he turned to her. "Mara," he said, his voice sounding hoarse. She saw him blink once, his eyes looking insect-like and strange behind his watchmaker's lenses, before he flipped them up and looked at her with his ordinary eyes. They were tired.

"You haven't eaten." She glanced down at the food.

Her father followed her look and blinked again,

surprised. "So I haven't." He met her eyes again. "Sorry, love."

"You were busy when I came back."

Her father closed his eyes and rubbed them with his free hand, pushing his glasses up. "I'm always busy, Mara."

"You shouldn't be too busy to eat," she said. "Go on. It's still warm enough."

Her father took in a breath and slowly let it back out. Then he slid his watch into a pocket and tucked his hourglass, which he always wore around his neck on a length of thin leather, into his collar. He took off his glasses, with his loupes still attached, and left them carefully on his desk. Finally he was ready. He pulled the plate towards him, picking up the cutlery with a faint *click*.

Mara watched him as he ate. When he was finished, he handed her the plate with one hand while he reached for the stack of road maps in a cubbyhole over his desk with the other. "Let's get moving as soon as we can. Right, love?"

Before Mara had even risen to her feet, her dad was absorbed in a map, plotting their route with a ruler and pencil. They often travelled at night, when it was quieter, taking back roads – her father did his utmost to avoid motorways. And they never used anything but paper maps to find their way. Her dad didn't even own a mobile phone, let alone one that was connected to the web. This wasn't just down to the fact that they drove – and lived in – an ancient, clapped-out van; mostly it was because he was paranoid about being followed. Mara paused at the van's back doors, looking back at him. Once again her father was absorbed in his work, the light like a halo around him in the darkness of the van's interior. It glinted off the streaks of grey in his hair and his scrubby beard, and Mara sighed internally as she watched him.

Who on earth would follow us, Dad? she thought for the millionth time. *Nobody knows or even cares who we are.*

She pushed open the protesting door and hopped down to the ground. The spigot sputtered a bit as she turned it, fed by the water collection tank on the van's roof. The water was cold, and her hands were numb by the time she was done rinsing the plates, but she filled her palm and took a long drink before flicking the spigot off.

She stacked the plates back in their cupboard, fastening the door with a home-made wooden lock. She hoped it would be enough to stop the doors swinging open as they drove, and that nothing would get too rattled about. Her dad had already packed away his apparatus, the glass vessels safe in their storage box. Mara looked at it, sharp cornered and emblazoned with his initials, *GD* for Gabriel Denbor, as she checked the table and stool had been folded flat. They didn't own much, and what they did have was easy to secure. They needed to be ready to move at a moment's notice – or so Mara had been raised to believe.

Her dad pulled open the drapes on the van's windows and tied them in place. Wordlessly, Mara settled herself into the passenger side and put her seat belt on.

"Don't you want to get some rest?" her father said as he set the engine roaring into life.

"Not sleepy," Mara said, reading the clock on the dashboard. It was almost quarter to one in the morning, and she squished her lips tight to avoid a yawn.

"Mmm," said her dad, throwing her an amused sidelong glance. Mara gave him a half-hearted grin as he shifted the van into gear. With a roar, they lurched forwards, the dim street lights guiding them down narrow, deserted alleys, all the way out of the city. Her dad avoided using the headlights until he absolutely had to, and eventually, they *pinged* to life, scattering the darkness in front of them.

On and on they drove, the van's wheels eating up the night, and very soon Mara was asleep. Curled into the worn leather of the seat, she dreamed of things she wouldn't remember when she woke. Somewhere at the heart of her dreaming walked a cat, sleek and shiny eyed, who went where she pleased, completely unafraid.

The Time Tider's Handbook, 1/B/iii: You must avoid being seen when using the Stitch, as effects on onlookers cannot be predicted...

Chapter Three

Mara awoke in her bed, warm in her blankets. She stretched, blinking as she looked around. Daylight seeped into the van through the cracks between the drapes, though the tinted back windows were dark, as usual. The van's interior was thick with shadows, and all she could hear was the trill of birdsong that trickled in through the vents. She knew, without having to listen for her dad's breathing, that she was alone. *He's on a job.*

She closed her eyes again as a familiar weight began dragging her down into a well-worn memory. Once, when she was little, her dad had left her in a playground by herself while he'd gone on a job. Mara remembered the girl her own age who'd played with her and the girl's mum who'd looked after her – but who'd grown worried and impatient as the minutes ticked by and there was still no sign of Mara's father. She recalled the argument the adults had when her father finally reappeared and how she'd clung to the other little girl in fear. Most of all she remembered how it had broken her heart to feel her dad pulling her away from her new friend – who'd told her all about school, and horses, and music lessons, things Mara couldn't even imagine – while her mum, anger pinching her pretty face, had threatened to call the police.

"What *is* your job, anyway?" the woman had shouted at Mara's father, as he'd dragged her, weeping, out of the playground. "What sort of job makes you *leave* your six-year-old alone for all this time?"

Mara opened her eyes, realizing they'd been squished tight, and blinked hard as she looked around. What *was* her father's job? He would never tell her the specifics. She knew he worked with watches – but that didn't explain anything about their life and why they lived it this way. It didn't explain what his "apparatus" was for, or the odd-looking contents of his glass vessels, or why he never seemed to take a day off. All she knew was that he and Mara spent their lives going from place to place, never stopping long enough anywhere for her to meet anyone, *know* anyone, or do anything besides exist inside this van…

Wiping her nose on her sleeve, Mara pushed off her blankets and sat up, placing her feet squarely on the threadbare rug between the bunks. She counted her breaths, feeling her heart rate settle as she pushed her thoughts down into her belly. Then she scraped her greasy curls back into a tight bun and hauled herself out of bed. Crawling into the front seat of the van, she checked the clock – 7:10 a.m. – and peeked out beneath one of the drapes to see what sort of place her dad had chosen to stop in for the night. The city was long behind them. All she could see outside the window was a tall, brambly hedge, overgrown and untended, down some country lane in the middle of nowhere.

Moments later, Mara emerged from the van holding her hygiene kit from the City Outreach – wipes, toothpaste and brush, and a bar of soap – along with her own old washcloth. Quickly, she used the spigot as she brushed her teeth and scrubbed her face, and then she vanished into some long grass behind the van to take care of the rest of her needs. When she emerged, she looked all around. The narrow road had a line of green growing up the middle, the tarmac shattering into gravel at the edges. Somewhere, she could hear the faint *swishswishswish* of tyres on a motorway. The poles holding up the power lines were leaning to one side, thick with ivy.

With a shrug, she tossed the hygiene kit back inside the van and began to walk. The hedgerows were heavy with fruit and soon she had a tummy full of blackberries. She had no idea how long her dad would take or where he even was, and—

Mara stopped in her tracks as a noise reached her ears. Silently, she hopped off the road and on to the grassy verge. Then the noise came again. A man, laughing.

Stepping over brambles and choosing her footsteps carefully, Mara edged her way towards a gap in the hedgerow, an entrance to an overgrown field. In the gap was a car, parked so that it was hard to see from the road. Mara crouched, peering through the greenery, keeping out of eyeshot. A man, tall and well-dressed, leaned against the car with his arms casually folded, talking to someone. Mara stretched forwards, craning her neck to see who his companion was – and froze. *Dad.* She gasped, even though deep down Mara knew this was what she'd see. She curled herself up tight as she tried to think. She knew her father wouldn't want her to watch – he'd never allowed her to see him at work.

So that's why I've got to take this chance, Mara told herself, unfolding her body and getting back into position.

Gabriel stood, wearing his long, many-pocketed coat, in the muddy entrance to the field.

"So what've you got for me this time?" the man said. Mara couldn't help but notice how well-made his clothes were, and how shiny his shoes. His car was brand-new, a top-of-the-range model. "The sooner we get this deal done and get out of here, the better!" He took in a deep breath, pulling a face. "I'm not really made for all this fresh air."

Mara saw her father give a short, polite smile. "I've got what you asked for," he said. "Exactly as you ordered, Mr Gormley – three weeks, fully complete, down to the last second. And it's at the most cost-effective price I could manage, though you must appreciate the difficulty in sourcing the product."

Mara frowned. Whatever her dad was selling to this rich man, it certainly wasn't a watch. But what else did he have to offer?

"Let's see it, then," Mr Gormley said, stepping forwards. Gabriel reached into one of his pockets and pulled out a small glass vessel – same as the ones he used in his apparatus. Mara watched closely, her heart thumping hard. The jar was full of that strange, swirling fluid, which had always reminded her of honey – except, unlike honey, this fluid seemed to move strangely, almost like it was being stirred from inside. Mr Gormley grunted with approval as Gabriel held up the jar. "And you're sure it's the best you could do?"

Gabriel began to put the jar back into his pocket. "If you'd prefer to cancel—" he began, but Mr Gormley shook his head impatiently.

"No, no," he said, irritated. "My old man swears by you, and he'd never let me hear the end of it if I didn't keep up the family tradition." He reached into his own pocket and pulled out his wallet. "I'll give you your price, though I don't see why you can't offer me a discount." He began to count out some notes from a thick wad. "Like frequent flyer miles, or whatever." Gabriel's mouth twitched upwards at the joke.

"I hope you can appreciate that the price is reflective of my work and effort," Gabriel said. "I don't overcharge, Mr Gormley. I assure you."

Mara watched intently. She still had no idea what was in the glass jar but she guessed it had to be something bad. Something illegal, even. Why else would their business be conducted here, in an empty, isolated field? *And what's my dad been doing with this stuff all these years?* Her thoughts were fast and sharp.

Mr Gormley checked the notes one last time, and then handed them over. Gabriel smoothly passed him the glass jar at the same time. "Pleasure doing business with you, Mr Denbor." Mr Gormley gave a wide, self-satisfied smile as he examined the contents of the jar. He flicked the glass with his fingernail and it gave a rich-sounding *hum*. "I assume it's the same process as usual?"

Mara's father nodded, tucking the money into his pocket. "If you could take it now, I'd be grateful for the return of the vessel," he said. "They're always in demand."

Mr Gormley shrugged. "Sure, sure," he muttered, twisting the lid of the jar – but he must have been careless, as some of the contents oozed through an opening. But instead of spilling out, like a liquid would, drops of the colourful "fluid" rose into the air like tiny balloons before vanishing. "Whoops!" Mr Gormley said, putting his mouth to the gap. He tossed the rest of the contents back. Inside the now-empty jar, Mara could see a stick, slowly spinning. It widened a little at the end, like a paddle.

"Excuse me," Gabriel muttered bad-temperedly and reached out for the jar. Mr Gormley nodded, wiping his lips and raising his eyebrows apologetically as he handed it over.

Mara stared at her father as he opened the jar with a twist of his hand. Then he cleared his throat, closed his eyes – and *vanished.*

Mara gasped, loudly enough for Mr Gormley to straighten up and look around. "Who's there?" he said. He glanced past Mara's hiding place, his eyes worried – but before he had a chance to come looking for her, there was a ripple in the air and Gabriel reappeared. He was holding the resealed glass jar, this time with a tiny amount of fluid in it. Mara guessed these were the drops Mr Gormley had spilled a few moments before – but none of the rest of what she'd seen made any sense. Her heart was thundering so fast, she felt she was going to be sick.

"I think we'd better get out of here," Mr Gormley said, taking the jar. "I'll give this back next time I see you."

"Is there a problem?" Gabriel settled his coat around him.

"I think – we might not be on our own," Mr Gormley said, nodding towards the hedge Mara was hiding behind. Her father turned to look and their eyes met.

Mara got to her feet and ran, her panic making her steps noisier than she'd like, but she didn't get far before she heard her father calling her name. She stopped, turning round just as her dad came striding out of the field, his arms wide. "What's the rush, little one?"

"I – um. Dad, I'm sorry. I know I'm not supposed to—"

"This is your girl, then?" Mr Gormley said, appearing behind Gabriel. He tucked the glass jar into his jacket as he spoke. "Pleasure to meet you," he said to Mara.

Gabriel turned to shake hands with Mr Gormley before joining Mara on the road. He put his arm round her shoulders as they walked on. A soft purring roar made Mara turn to look back – it was just Mr Gormley's car taking off. He gave them a friendly wave as he drove away.

"Now, now," Gabriel began, his voice low. "Who's been a nosy parker, then?"

"I was just walking," Mara said. "I heard you talking. I didn't mean to spy."

Gabriel chuckled, pulling Mara close. "No matter."

Mara swallowed hard. "Dad – what did you do? What happened just now?"

Gabriel gave her a strange look. "What do you mean?"

"I mean, you disappeared. You *vanished.*"

Gabriel shook his head in fond disbelief. "Don't be silly, sweetheart. People don't just vanish, do they?"

"*You* did," Mara said, pushing hard against her nerves, fighting to settle herself. *Didn't he?* For a moment, Mara wasn't sure. Had she really seen what she thought she'd seen? It seemed impossible. Ridiculous, even.

Gabriel shrugged. They'd reached the van and he took off his coat as he spoke. "Fair enough. I'm not going to get into an argument. You're probably hungry, right? That can make you see things." He winked at her as he tossed his coat on to her bunk and closed the van's back doors. "Let's get going, and we can pick up something nice on our next stop."

Mara's anger flared up. "What? Paid for with the money you just took for – *whatever* that stuff is?" She gathered her strength. "It's illegal, isn't it? Whatever you're selling?"

Gabriel gave her an incredulous look. "Illegal, no. Unregulated, perhaps you could say. I'm not breaking a single law, Mara, not in any jurisdiction in the world. I promise you."

"So what is it?"

"It's none of your business," her father said, pulling open the driver's door and hauling himself into the van. Mara strode around to the passenger side and yanked her own door open, listening to her father whistle as he did up his seat belt.

Moments later, the van roared into life and pulled out on to the road again, travelling in the opposite direction to Mr Gormley's car. Gabriel hummed as he drove, drumming out a rhythm on the steering wheel, and Mara's head boiled over with questions. *Could* she have imagined it all? It was true what her father said: People didn't just disappear. And Mr Gormley hadn't seemed bothered by anything unusual going on. Surely, if someone vanished before his eyes, he'd think it was a bit unusual, wouldn't he? Or completely terrifying? Mara closed her eyes, feeling her head begin to pound. *I don't understand any of this.*

She glanced sidelong at her father. He seemed unusually cheerful. Mara kept her breaths even as she turned back towards the view outside the window, replaying what she'd seen in her mind. *I didn't imagine it,* she told herself. Her dad *was* keeping something from her – perhaps many things, perhaps more things than Mara could bear. Whatever had been in that jar, Mara knew, was the reason their lives were so strange – and she knew she was tired of pushing her questions down, leaving them unasked. She had to find out what the vessels contained and what it had to do with her father, and with her.

And she realized that if her dad wasn't going to tell her the truth, she'd have to get to the bottom of things herself.

The Time Tider's Handbook, 1/A/iv:
Trust that Time will lead you in the burial
of your tools. Just as you have discovered them,
so you will leave them for another to find,
as Time decrees...

Chapter
Four

The rain had started barely half an hour into their journey. Mara sat with her legs tucked beneath her, balancing a sketchbook on her knee. The world passed by outside the van, streaked through with watery tendrils, and as she drew, she did her best to pretend she was completely, entirely alone. Besides the fact that she was in a moving vehicle not being driven by her, Mara felt there might as well be nobody else on earth.

"Nice to see you drawing again." Her dad's voice dredged her up out of her thoughts.

"Mmm," Mara replied, glancing down at her work. She'd drawn a screaming face, wild-eyed, with cracks running over its skin. She flipped the book closed before her father could ask to see it, running her fingers over her own childish handwriting on the front cover. *Mara Denbor*, she'd written, years before, when her dad had begun to teach her letters.

"We're coming into a town," her dad said, glancing at the road sign as they passed it. Mara read its name – Newtownbarry. It meant nothing to her. "Do you need a break? Or food?" Mara shrugged, straightening up in her seat, and her father sighed. "Well. I could do with a bathroom stop, so if it doesn't inconvenience you *too* much, we'll do it here."

Mara stared at the side of his face. "Makes no difference to me where we are." She picked at a frayed edge on the cover of her sketchbook. "My entire life makes no difference to anyone," she muttered.

Her father sighed again. "Are you still being dramatic about earlier?"

Mara swallowed hard against the words she wanted to say. "No," she finally managed.

"Good. I'm glad we've put that behind us. Once we've had something to eat, I'm sure you'll feel better."

Mara made no reply as they drove into a small, pretty village, bursting with full window boxes and neatly trimmed verges. A narrow canal ran through it, trickling down the main street, and Mara noticed a cluster of shops, cafés and a pub festooned with flags on the far side of the road. Picnic benches were set out in front. She peered out of the van's windows as her dad pulled up the squealing handbrake and turned the engine off. People walked their dogs, children were running home from school. A car drove past, its radio pumping.

Mara turned to her dad. He was gazing thoughtfully at her and when she met his eye he smiled, looking wistful.

"I remember once, when I was a kid, you told me you'd never lie to me," Mara said. Her father's eyes widened slightly.

"You're still a kid, pet," he responded softly. "At least, that's what twelve-year-olds were in my time."

Mara pressed her lips tight. "You know what I mean," she muttered.

Her father scratched at his hairline. "Yes. All right. And it was true, what I said."

"But you *do* lie," Mara said. "Not telling the full truth is a type of lying. Isn't it?"

Her dad paused before answering. "I suppose," he said, not meeting Mara's eye. "But parents also have a duty to keep their children safe, Mara. Sometimes, not being entirely honest is part of that." He looked back at her. "It's not the same thing as lying."

Mara turned away from her dad. Outside, two ladies, one with an energetic dog on a lead, had stopped for a chat outside the pub, their umbrellas bobbing as they moved. "So, if I asked you to tell me exactly what happened in that field, what would you say?" She looked back at him, fixing him with a stare.

He sighed wearily. "*Nothing* happened in that field, Mara. At least, nothing beyond me doing my job, which is not something you need to know the ins and outs of. Trust me."

Mara chewed the inside of her lip, turning away again. She could hear the ladies still chatting.

"Right," Gabriel said after a silent moment, tapping his fingers on the steering wheel. He nodded to a café beside the pub. "I'm heading to that greasy spoon there to try to stomach a cup of coffee in exchange for the use of their bathroom. If you want to come and join me, I'd be glad." Mara said nothing. "Well, I'll leave the keys in the ignition. In case you get cold or you want some music or whatever," Gabriel continued.

She turned back to her dad. "Aren't you scared I'll take off?"

"I'll trust you this time," he told her. "Just make sure to lock the van if you're leaving it. And watch the road. Right?"

"Yes, Dad," Mara said, looking away.

Gabriel said nothing else. Mara felt the van shake as he climbed out of his seat and picked his coat up from her bunk. The back doors creaked as he opened them and a gust of cool, rainy air filled the van. Mara didn't look around, even when he sighed wearily before shutting the door again with a *thunk*.

Mara watched her dad check the road before jogging across. The ladies and their dog gave him a wide berth. Gabriel didn't even seem to notice, giving them a friendly nod as he ducked inside the café, but Mara could see the mistrust on their faces. Sometimes, Mara forgot that most dads – most men her dad's age – didn't wear combat trousers, battered boots and long, ex-army coats, and didn't let their hair and beards get so long and dirty. She realized, again, that they looked, both of them, like relics from another age.

She focused on the dashboard in front of her, suddenly hating it and this van and everything in it. *At least I now know where he's getting money for coffee and cakes*, she thought. *But I need to find out what's in those glass jars. What is he selling?* She knew the answers to her questions had to be in the van. There was literally nowhere else for them to be.

She let her legs drop, sitting forwards so sharply that the seat belt cut into her shoulder. She unclicked it and turned in her seat, taking in the van's interior.

The back doors were shut, their darkened windows giving nothing away. In front of those doors, against the side wall, was her bunk. Her dad's bed, facing it, was folded up. Mara let her gaze roam, trying to see her tiny home like she'd never seen it before. Their folding table, with her dad's shelves above it. The stool, collapsed and flat, tucked in beneath it. Facing that, the wall-mounted cupboards with their locked-shut doors, and beneath them the hob and the battered sink.

Finally her eyes fell on the storage box for her dad's glassware, strapped down beside the table. Was she imagining it, or did the light gleam on its metal fittings?

Mara tossed her sketchbook and pencils on to her bed and clambered out of her seat, dropping to her knees beside the glassware box. She *oof*ed with effort as she loosened its straps and picked it up, settling it on her lap. It seemed so innocuous – just a box, with a handle in the lid and a large lock on the front. *But how do I get it open?*

She put the box back on to the floor, fixing its strap fast out of habit, and climbed into the driver's seat. Her father's keys were hanging from the ignition. Unless her dad had the key to the box with him, chances are it was included in this bunch – but as Mara tried to reach out for them, she drew her fingers back.

She stretched up to see out over the dashboard, imagining how it would feel to have the freedom to go where she wanted, when she wanted; to have friends, to attend school, to do *any* of the things she dreamed of. She rested her forehead on the bottom of the steering wheel, her eyes squeezed tight. *Just go. Get out of here. You'll never find answers with Dad breathing down your neck.*

Mara lifted her head, her jaw clenched tight. Keeping one hand on the steering wheel to anchor herself, she felt around beneath the seat for the lever which, when pulled up, made the seat slide forwards. Her dad had taught her to drive as an eighth birthday present, but it had been a long time since Mara had found herself behind the wheel. The seat was pushed right back to accommodate his long legs.

But instead of the lever, her scrambling fingers found something unexpected. Something soft and cool, like leather – and then the coldness of metal. She leaned down as far as she could and *yanked* on this strange, hidden thing. Eventually it came free, and Mara sat up again, blowing stray hair out of her eyes, the object in her right hand. It was a bag, softened with age and ripped along the seams. Its metal buckle was tarnished and the cracks were thick with ingrained dirt.

She blinked at it in confusion. Whatever she might have been expecting to find beneath her father's seat, this was not it. *Maybe it was Mum's,* Mara thought, sudden sadness taking a bite out of her, but then she noticed a small, circular design embossed into the leather right above the buckle. The dirt had dug itself in here too, making the design hard to read. She scratched at it gently with her nail. After a minute she felt sure the design showed two long-barrelled guns, crossed like an X.

A sudden chill jabbed through her and Mara looked up, stretching to peer over the steering wheel once more. Her dad was sitting at the café window; she could see his elbow and the sleeve of his patched jumper and she let out a breath. *Come on, then*, she told herself, settling back into the seat. *Let's see what we've got here.*

Mara's fingers quivered as she pulled at the buckle. The leather was stiff and she had to work hard to get it through the fastening. Finally it came undone.

Inside was a battered-looking metal tin and a large glass bottle. They both looked *ancient*, like things which had been hidden a hundred years before and completely forgotten about. Mara chewed her lip as she stared at them. She picked up the tin and shook it gently. She couldn't hear anything moving around inside it, and the tin was light, though not light enough to be empty. *Is this where he keeps his cash?* She wondered whether it would be worth the effort of trying to force it open – with a knife, maybe, or a screwdriver. Her dad had both of those, but… She glanced back at the café. Gabriel was reading a newspaper, his forehead wrinkled, but the plate before him on the table was empty. *Not worth the risk*, she told herself. *He could be back any minute.*

She turned her attention instead to the bottle, picking it up carefully. It was made of greenish glass and stoppered with a cork – but the seal around the cork had been opened.

Inside the bottle, Mara could see something like rolled-up sheets of paper.

She glanced back at the café window. Her dad was still there. *Do it.*

She put her thumbs beneath the flare of the cork and pushed. Gritting her teeth, she pushed again, harder, willing the cork to move. Slowly, it began to creep upwards, dragging itself reluctantly out of the neck of the bottle. Mara set it to one side and fished out the tube of paper, hoping it wouldn't turn out to be something boring, like a shopping list or someone's will.

She blinked with surprise as she unrolled the papers. They turned out to be rather like a book – thin and flexible, with a cover which had once been stitched on. Over the years many more sheets had been added to it – some had been stapled in and some of the staples had rusted orange. The entire thing was quite fragile.

The Time Tider's Handbook, Mara read on the cover sheet. It had been hand-drawn beautifully on the slightly thicker card binding the rolled-up book together. Gingerly, she opened the book, and a sheet came loose. She pulled it free and held it steady.

To the Finder, Mara read, her heart pounding. *Whosoever may happen upon this message, and who finds himself compelled to dig up these objects and read these words, I send you my heartfelt greetings, and my even more heartfelt sympathy. Once, many years ago, I felt a similar pull to the one which drew you here. Once, as a young man, I dug in a foreign field, using nothing but my hands to unsettle the soil, and I found a box containing that which I now bequeath to you. The watch, the hourglass, and the book, enclosed herewith, which will tell you all you need to know, and everything I cannot. Suffice it for me to say: Welcome, Time Tider, to the calling of your life. May you conduct yourself with integrity, may you serve with courage, may you never forget the importance of your task. I, one who filled your shoes before you ever drew breath, salute you. Time and Tide May Wait for None; But They Will Wait for You.*

Underneath this was a signature which Mara couldn't make out, followed by the words *Royal Fusiliers, First Battalion, 1947.* Just as she was about to lift it to read what lay beneath, an instinct made her look towards the café window.

All Mara saw was an empty plate and a folded newspaper. Her dad was gone.

The Time Tider's Handbook, 1/B/iii: Time Tiders are those who are steadfast of mind and heart, courageous beyond all measure, and willing to live in the shadows, but also those who have suffered great loss. You must use that loss to navigate your path...

Chapter Five

Mara launched herself out of the driver's seat, the bag and its contents clutched to her chest. She scrambled into the body of the van and dived for her bunk. Beneath it was everything that was important to her: the stack of old charity shop books she'd picked up over the years, mostly tattered and read to pieces, her plastic box of pencils and scrounged art supplies, and her "treasure chest", an old shoebox which her dad had sworn, years before, never to look in without her permission. She pulled this out and dumped its contents on her bed before tossing the bag, the open bottle, the handbook, and the sealed tin into it. She'd only just pushed the box out of sight when her dad opened the driver's door.

"Hey, I asked the lady at the till if she'd mind you using

her bathroom. She said so long as you've got my receipt, you can go for it." He stuck his head into the van and Mara looked up. His eyebrows quirked. "You're playing with your old stuff? I thought you'd chucked all that years ago."

Mara fought to keep her breathing even. "Nah," she said.

Her dad held up a receipt. "Well? I don't know how long the offer's going to last."

Mara looked down at the toys in her hands. She was holding half a doll, its legs long gone, and a figurine from some forgotten movie, its paint mostly rubbed off. "Don't touch my stuff, Dad. OK?"

Her father rolled his eyes. "Do I ever? Come on. When you're done we'll get going again."

She dropped the toys on to her blankets and got to her feet. "How much further is it?"

"About another hour." Her dad reached out a hand to help Mara over the driver's seat. "But my business shouldn't take long. And then we'll find somewhere to camp for the night."

Mara hopped to the ground, taking the receipt from her dad's fingers, and made her way to the café. The woman behind the till didn't look up as Mara walked past. The bathroom was clean and neat, smelling of air freshener. Mara washed her hands and pulled some paper towels free from the dispenser. She dried her fingers then took some more towels, stuffing them into her pockets as she made her way back out. This time, the owner did look up. Mara handed her the till receipt and kept walking, burying her hands in her pockets as she hurried back to the van. The café door closed behind her, its *ting* altogether too good-tempered for Mara's liking.

"All right?" her dad said, as Mara pulled open the passenger door. He was already in the driver's seat, ready to go. His eyes were on the mirrors as he watched the traffic going up and down the street and his fingers drummed impatiently on the wheel.

"Yep." Mara climbed into her seat. She pulled the door shut, casting a worried glance back at her bed. She noticed she'd twisted one of the straps around her father's glassware box in her haste and hoped he wouldn't spot it.

"Your stuff's still there, never fear." Gabriel turned the engine on as he spoke, clicking the indicator lever and getting ready to pull out. He turned to look at her as they moved off. "And here I was, thinking how grown-up you were getting. I guess there's always time for fun, eh?'

Mara tried to smile. Her dad reached over and switched on the radio. Treacly sweet easy listening began to pour out of the speakers.

"Where are we going?" Mara asked, as they left the pretty village behind.

"Whiteharbour," her dad replied. "We're taking the old road. It's a nightmare for traffic, but so be it."

They travelled along narrow, winding roads, passing through several towns at a crawl – Gabriel had been right about the traffic. Finally the road widened and grew busier. Mara saw her father shift in his seat, scanning the mirrors uneasily every few seconds. She knew he hated larger roads, and she hoped they were nearly at their destination.

WHITEHARBOUR 5 KM read a road sign, and she breathed a sigh of relief.

They passed what looked like a large old hospital on a hill and then the town of Whiteharbour opened up to their right. Roofs and spires and cranes rose in a jumble of layers, like they were in a pop-up book, and Mara saw a wide-mouthed river opening to the sea. Its silty banks were flat, shining in the sunlight, and as they passed she was sure she caught sight of a hazy wrinkle in the air, hovering right at the water's edge. *A soft place*, she thought, watching it as long as she could before it slipped from view. Another weird thing about her life that she'd never thought of as being all that weird before – until now.

The road passed over a long bridge, its arches letting the river flow through. As her father drove, Mara looked out to sea, her heart thudding heavily. On the horizon she saw the shape of a ferry sailing away, full of people with ordinary lives. Mara chewed her lip as she turned back to the road. Her father was indicating left and when the lights changed they drove down towards some quays, with several tall-masted boats tied up at anchor. Gabriel navigated the van into a parking bay on one of the quays and as soon as he turned the engine off, he slumped with theatrical relief.

"Glad that bit's over," he said, looking at Mara.

"We'll be leaving soon, won't we?" Mara said. Gabriel nodded as he released his seat belt and pulled open his coat. Something was concealed in his inside pocket but Mara got enough of a glimpse to recognize its shape. *Another glass thing, like the one in the field,* she thought. *Full of – what?*

Gabriel settled his coat closed again, meeting Mara's eye. He smiled, quick and tight-lipped. She didn't return it. "I have to make a drop-off and then we'll be on the road again," he said. He patted the central console, the compartment between the driver and passenger seats where anything and everything ended up. "I bought a couple of chocolate bars in the café – they're here if you get hungry." He dipped his fingers into another of his pockets as he spoke, to pull out his pocket watch.

Curled inside the watch's lid were two locks of hair, one carefully braided, and the other loose, tied only with a rubber band at one end. The braided one had belonged to Mara's mother and the loose one was Mara's own. Her mum's one was dusty looking and faded now. She'd died when Mara was two.

Gabriel raised his eyebrows inquisitively, looking at Mara. "Now that I notice it, maybe it's time for another lock of yours to go in here." He gestured with the watch. "The one I've got is going a bit scraggly."

Mara sighed, turning for the glove box. They kept their understocked first-aid kit in here, complete with their only pair of scissors. In no time at all Mara had the compartment open, the scissors pulled free from its plastic sheath, and a lock of red-brown hair curled on her palm like a comma. She handed it to her father.

"Perfect," he said, fishing out an elastic band from his odds and ends box in the van's central console. He tied the hair together, then clicked the watch open again and set it in place, nestled against the others. He closed the watch with a decisive nod. "I'm all set."

Mara replaced the first-aid kit and clicked the glove box closed. "One day, you will tell me what you need that hair for. Right?"

Gabriel gave her a level look, though his eyes were kind. "Right. One day." He smiled briefly. "Stay out of trouble until I get back."

"I'll try not to join a gang or get a tattoo or whatever," Mara muttered. Gabriel huffed out an amused breath, and then with a quick kiss on her forehead, he was gone.

Mara watched him walk up the footpath that skirted the quays until Whiteharbour had swallowed him. Once he'd disappeared from sight she let five full minutes tick past on the van's clock before she moved out of her seat.

The Time Tider's Handbook, 1/A/ii:
Include as few outsiders as possible in your
work, and none at all if you can. Yours shall
be a solitary life, by necessity...

Chapter Six

Mara dropped to her knees beside her bed and pulled her treasure chest out from beneath it. She prised off the lid and quickly placed the rolled-up handbook, the bottle and the tin back into the bag, before raiding the toolbox her father kept tucked beside the fire extinguisher, pulling free a small screwdriver. She unlocked the back doors of the van and warily hopped down – but nobody gave her a second glance.

Whiteharbour's quays bustled with activity – fishing boats were being unloaded, people walked dogs, delivery riders whizzed by on bikes – and Mara's head swam. The near end of the quay, by their van, seemed quieter. The closest moored ship seemed deserted, nobody going aboard or coming ashore. The boat simply bobbed up and down with the water, and all Mara could hear was the gentle *swish* and slap of the waves on its hull, speckled through with the shrieks of seagulls overhead. She took a few steps away from the van, her tummy prickling with anxiety, and then her eyes fell on a set of stone steps leading from the quayside to the water below. Checking left and right, Mara hurried towards them, tucking herself on the third step down. The steps ended underwater, the bottom treads dark and covered in algae, the upper treads worn smooth by the passage of time.

Giving one more glance up and over the edge of the quay, Mara opened the bag.

The handbook was curling and brittle from its years inside the bottle, and Mara unrolled it as carefully as possible. Its cover bore only its title but as she opened the book to reveal a neatly laid out contents page, she saw at least three styles of handwriting, in different languages, inks and pens. The writing was in the margins and even between the lines. The book wasn't long – fewer than ten pages, Mara thought – and each page was thin and fragile. Mara's fingers shook as she handled them, her mind whirring as she thought about who might have handled them before her. Judging by the efforts at translation scribbled in every blank space, this little volume had been all around the world.

The contents page noted that the handbook was divided

into parts and sections, and an introduction. Quickly, she scanned the handwritten scribbles all around, but very little of it made sense. There were diagrams and equations, all labelled – one looked like a heavy ball in a blanket, with numbers describing the curves and angles formed by the ball's weight. Mara didn't understand any of it, so she turned the page.

Introduction, she read, neatly printed, in very faded ink. Her gaze was caught by some handwriting in the right-hand margin, which had been made with ballpoint pen. For a second Mara stared at these handwritten words. *Dad's writing*, she thought, feeling numb.

She glanced up over the quayside, in case her father was making an unexpected early return, but there was no sign of him. Then, she looked back at the handbook. She couldn't help but read her father's notes first but as she read she felt as if she were wading through heavy quicksand, growing more unsteady with every step.

The Time Tider, her dad had written. He'd underlined it three times. Mara's pulse quickened as her eyes skipped on, taking in the next few lines. They were laid out like a list.

Always a man. (Why? Can/Will it ever change?)

Doesn't necessarily pass from father to son. Chosen at random?

How does a Tider know when it's time to bury the tools, and where?

How many have there been? I think: every c.30–50 yrs, a Time Tider emerges. Can be anywhere in the world – wherever he's needed most. (Who, or what, decides this?)

No Tider is ever capable of harvesting every Warp. Some will remain. Key is: to get as many as possible. Do your best.

Beneath this list was a sketch of a watch, done quickly and carelessly in the same ballpoint pen. It had three faces, and Mara recognized her father's pocket watch. Beside it was drawn a diagram of the hourglass he always wore around his neck. The contents were merely a scribble, but from it her dad had drawn an arrow, with the words *Control? Record-keeping? Memorial?* Mara sucked her lips tight as she read this. She had no idea what was inside her dad's hourglass – it looked like millions of tiny beads, or marbles, but she'd never examined it closely. She stared at the words her dad had written, and the question marks.

"You sure seem to be asking a lot of questions, Dad," she whispered. "I hope you've figured out the answers by now."

She turned to the printed words, drew a breath and began to read.

For the Attention of the Newly Appointed Time Tider, Mara read. She sucked her cheeks in and kept going.

Time, to most, is something taken for granted: a simple aspect of the world in which we live. But Time is not merely the appearance of hands on a clock or the celestial bodies in the sky. Instead, Time can be visualized as a substance, perhaps a fluid, which must be allowed to flow freely in order to function correctly.

When the flow of Time is impeded, the role of the Tider becomes clear.

Mara's head ached but she continued.

A Time Tider's primary duty is the eradication of Warps, which are anomalies in the flow of Time, formed when a person dies before they are supposed to. As far as we understand it: each person is born with an allocation of Time, but when they die before their Time has been used up, their unused Time forms an immovable 'bubble', anchored on the second of their death. This disrupts the flow of Time and is called a Warp. When many such deaths occur, as happens in the case of war or other disaster, the collective weight of unused days, months and years creates a large anomaly, like a boulder in the flow of Time. Warps such as these are detrimental to human existence.

Time subject to a Warp will stretch and twist, disrupting lives and causing unexplained disappearances, trapping the people caught within it and threatening the stability of Time itself.

Recognizing a Warp is a basic skill, instinctive to most Tiders. Time Tiders are usually aware, from childhood, of places where things seem 'wrong', where the senses do not work properly, and where Time doesn't flow as it does in the everyday world. Some report hearing noises or encountering a particular smell to alert them to the presence of a Warp. When a Warp is encountered, it (or rather, the excess Time which has gathered to form it) must be contained, ideally within glass or metal, and safely stored. To do this, a Time Tider must master the art of using the Stitch – the mental technique which allows him to pinpoint the precise moment in the flow of Time where dangerous Warps have formed – and this is discussed further in Section 1/B.

Mara saw that her father had drawn a diagram in the margin beside these words – a drawing of the glass jar she'd seen him holding, the glass jars that he used in his apparatus. She saw the stick inside the jar, which he'd labelled a 'spindle', but something like damp had mottled the ink where he'd written the name of the jar itself. All she could see now was the arrow pointing away from the jar towards a bluish blot. She frowned at it and then looked back at the words.

Major Warps, if left unattended, will eventually grow so large that they rip the fabric of Time and Reality itself. In this situation, Time will stop, leaving humanity trapped in an unbreakable stasis. Even smaller Warps can lead to disorientation; they can be terrifying to experience, which can leave anyone stumbling into one with severe side effects, if indeed they manage to escape (though Tiders appear immune to this). Smaller Warps tend to be attracted to one another and can eventually form larger Warps, which means they must be neutralized as early as possible.

A Time Tider's work is secretive, unsung and solitary, but know this to be true: they are all that stand between humanity and its destruction.

The Time Tider's Code: Trust in Time to lead you. Guard your truths. Keep your secrets. Tell no tales. Walk your own path. Do not fear the truth. Never underestimate the importance of your role. Be steadfast. Do not shrink from your duty. Be ever wary.

Mara looked up. She closed her eyes, listening to the water rising and falling beside her, and tried to close her mind around all the information it was now being asked to contain. After a moment she opened her eyes again and her gaze fell on one word: *Warps.*

"They're not Warps. They're soft places," she whispered, her voice shaky.

The Time Tider's Handbook, 1/A/i: Guard this handbook and any further instructions you may find with it, for in it is contained all the knowledge necessary to fulfil the role of Tider. If it is lost, chaos will ensue...

Chapter Seven

Mara read the introduction twice, her brain thumping with each word, before flicking through the rest of the handbook. Her father's notes in the margins, she found, were mostly questions: *Time needs something to be aware of it??* he'd written at the top of one page. *Time allocated: unique to individual, or standardized?* One hastily scribbled note was particularly confusing. Her dad had been trying to work something out – *Two minutes' dark with five minutes' summer Time (how much July does it take to lighten January?)* There were lines upon lines of what looked like equations or ratios and at the bottom of the page he'd scribbled: *Is effective Blending even possible??* Mara had no way of answering any of it. Finally she closed the handbook and rolled it up tightly.

Warps, she thought, recalling how it felt to be inside a soft place. *And I knew there was some sort of connection with…* She recoiled. *With dead things.*

She unrolled the handbook and looked again at the one line which seemed to poke her attention the hardest. *Recognizing a Warp is a basic skill, instinctive to most Tiders.* She swallowed hard, her eyes focusing so intently that she was surprised the paper didn't burst into flames.

"I've been spotting soft places forever," she whispered. Instantly, her eyes clamped shut. She wrapped the handbook and the loose sheets included with it into a tube again – they weren't as neatly arranged as before but she did her best. *The letter talked about digging stuff up. Like you're chosen to be the Time Tider or something. And they're always men – which, y'know, is wrong, but it means … it means, it can't be me. Right? I found this stuff. I didn't dig it up. I wasn't called by some mystical force or whatever. It was just bad luck.*

She slid the handbook back into the neck of the bottle and tried to push the stopper into place but she couldn't quite drive it right down to make a tight seal. She gripped the bottle between her palms and tried to press the cork down with her thumbs but it didn't budge. Eventually she gave up. *I'll put it back properly before Dad sees it*, she told herself, placing the bottle carefully on the step beside her.

Then she turned her attention to the tin.

It was rectangular, a little bigger than her outstretched

hand. The metal had rusted a bit around the edges and there were several bashes and scrapes on its surface. There didn't seem to be hinges – the lid just popped on, too tightly to be shifted – and there were no markings to tell her what might be in it. It felt almost light enough to be empty but Mara knew she had to look inside.

"Come on, then," she muttered, picking up the screwdriver. The tip of her tongue between her teeth, Mara wiggled at the seal around the tin until, rather unexpectedly, the lid popped off. She clamped her grip down hard on the tin and its contents, catching the lid before it went clattering down the steps. After a moment Mara lifted her palm away, and her eyes opened wide.

The interior of the tin was fitted with a piece of foam. In it was a cylinder-shaped depression, just the right size for a glass jar to be popped in and held securely in place. Mara saw its spindle, empty now of whatever it was supposed to contain. But behind the jar, distorted a little by the glass, was a photograph. Mara reached in and pulled the glass jar free. Sliding the photograph carefully out, she pushed the jar back in place and put the tin down on the step beside her.

The photograph was of a woman. She was young, her hair a profusion of curls. She looked away from the camera towards something in the distance, her head slightly turned to one side. Her eyes were green and crinkled at the corners, her laugh animating her entire face. Her front teeth were crooked and she had a mole on one cheek. All along the lobe of her ear she wore a collection of rings, some with gemstones and some without, in lots of different sizes. Around her neck was a scarf made of light, thin fabric, a burst of reds and blues and greens.

She wasn't *beautiful*, not exactly, but there was something about her that Mara couldn't stop looking at. Maybe it was her happiness. Or maybe it was the freedom that sang out from the image like the sound of a distant bell.

Finally Mara flipped the photograph over. On the back was written a single word in block capitals. The pen that had been used had leaked a little. The word was *THEA*.

"Thea," Mara said, her heart gathering pace. She looked back at the image, blinking hard. "But that's Mum's name."

Mara stared at the photo for ages. A huge, painful sob built up and she let it loose, right at the same time as her eyes overflowed with tears. One plopped on to the photograph and she wiped it away, leaving a smear across the woman's face. Mara had only ever seen a couple of small photographs of her mother before – her dad had told her there weren't any more. She remembered seeing one taken from a distance, a shot of her mother holding her by the hand when she was learning how to walk, but Thea's face hadn't been clearly visible. There had been another of Mara as a baby being held in her mother's arms but all you could see of her mum – of Thea – had been her hands and a few strands of her curling hair, framing Mara's newborn face. She'd never before seen her mum so young, so alive, so *happy*.

"Hi, Mum," Mara whispered, trying to smile through the ache in her chest. She sniffed, wiping her nose with her hand, and hiccupped a laugh as the breeze blew a curl into her face. She pushed it back behind her ear. "Thanks for the hair, I guess."

A car horn blared suddenly, making her look up and over the quay. Her father was crossing the road but something had distracted him enough to make him walk out without looking. The car horn that had disturbed Mara had been beeping at him and she watched him shake an angry fist at the driver. Mara jumped, her heart kicking up a gear. Quickly, she shoved her mother's photograph and the glass jar back into the tin and pushed on the lid, hearing it click into place. She turned to pick up the bottle, cursing herself for not finding time to settle the seal properly – but as she moved, her elbow knocked against it. Mara gasped and made a grab for the tumbling bottle, but it was too late. She watched with horror as it landed in the water with a *sploosh*.

"Oh no, no, *no*," she moaned, as the bottle was sucked down into the depths. It vanished so quickly that Mara could hardly believe it. *The handbook*, she thought. *All*

Dad's notes… They're gone!

Mara knew she had no time to think about it any longer. Shoving the tin and the screwdriver back into the bag, she scrambled up the steps and hurried back towards the van, hoping she'd make it before her dad looked up and spotted her.

The Time Tider's Handbook, 1/A/ii: Keep secret the workings of the Stitch and the details of your calling. Do not boast, do not lose your self-control, do not place your burden on the shoulders of another...

Chapter
Eight

Mara scrambled through the passenger door of the van and flumped into the driver's seat. She could see her father through the windscreen, only a few metres away, his face tight and distracted. Fumbling the bag into place beneath the seat, and hoping she'd put it back where she'd found it, Mara threw herself across the central console just as her father pulled the driver's door open and hauled himself inside. Mara got ready to speak, to defend herself, to explain what she'd been doing, but her father hadn't seemed to notice any of it. He yanked the door shut and shoved the key into the ignition. It took him several tries as his hand was shaking.

"Are you ready?" he finally said, turning to her.

Mara swallowed her words and nodded, pulling the

seat belt around to click it into place. "What's wrong?" she asked.

"Wrong?" Gabriel ran his hand through his hair and Mara got the sense he was trying to seem calmer than he really was. He met her eye and gave a quick smile, one that barely lifted his cheeks. "There's nothing wrong. I just remembered something I've got to do, so we need to get moving again, that's all. We'll camp somewhere else for the night. And tomorrow we'll have to visit one of my old friends, I think."

"A friend? Where?" Mara shivered as her dad set the van in motion. They reversed out into traffic, forcing the oncoming cars to stop and let them out. Then her dad set off along the quayside, past the fish stalls, sunlight glinting on the surface of the sea as Mara watched it. Her thoughts turned to the lost bottle, gone forever, the handbook turned to mush beneath the water, and every metre they travelled was taking them further and further away from it – but she couldn't tell her father what she'd done. *So, Dad, I was poking through your personal stuff and it seems I've managed to wreck the most important thing you own...* Then a flash of anger surged through her and she frowned at her father, who seemed oblivious. *And what's with the photo of Mum? Were you ever going to tell me about that?*

"We're not far from Lenny and the gang here," Gabriel said, throwing her out of her thoughts. Mara watched him

72

scanning a junction for oncoming traffic before urging the van, its engine roaring, up a narrow street to their right. Whiteharbour was full of winding, haphazardly laid out streets but her father appeared to know them somehow. "We haven't seen him in a bit. He's probably wondering what we've been getting up to."

Mara watched the colourful shop fronts and higgledy-piggledy houses flick past the window as her dad drove. She vaguely remembered Lenny, a small man with a scruffy beard, his glasses silver-rimmed. "What do you need to see him for?"

Her dad shrugged, checking his mirrors. "Oh, you know. This and that. He keeps some things for me, I do him the occasional favour in return. It's no big deal." He shifted uneasily in his seat. "What did you do while I was gone, then?"

Mara opened her mouth, wondering where she could even begin to tell him. "Nothing much," she finally mumbled.

Gabriel glanced at her. "Sorry I took so long, love. Things got a bit … heated, at my meeting. But it's all OK now."

"Dad, is it dangerous? Whatever you're doing? I mean—"

"It's nothing for you to be concerned about." Gabriel cut her off in a firm tone. "It's my business and it's how

I earn enough to keep fuel in this thing and food in your tummy, so let's not worry about it. All right?"

Mara stared at her dad, her eyes feeling hot. Her lips were pressed tight around all the things she wanted to shout at him but he appeared not to notice. "It's *not* all right," she finally managed to say.

Gabriel met Mara's eye as he checked the mirrors. "Well, I'm afraid that's just tough luck, then," he said. He drew the van to a gentle stop at a set of traffic lights, tapping his fingernails against the wheel.

"I found your stuff," Mara said into the silence. Her voice was low. "That's what I was doing while you were away."

Gabriel stared at his daughter, his eyes round with surprised anger. "What stuff?"

"Your *stuff*," Mara continued, her voice raising. "Your … handbook! The tin, with Mum's photo in it. I found them both!"

Gabriel opened his mouth to reply but before he could, a horn sounded behind him. Both he and Mara looked up at the traffic lights – they had changed to green without them noticing. Gabriel put the van into gear, the mechanism grinding as he did so, and set off, waving apologetically to the driver behind as they moved away. "You had no right to pry into those things," he finally said, once they were in the flow of traffic. "No right, Mara!"

"I did!" Mara retorted. "I *did*, Dad. I wasn't looking for your bag – I found it by accident. But I was looking for answers. Like what you *do* when you're not with me. Why we live in a *van*!" Mara wiped her nose. "I *deserve* to know the answers to those questions. You have to see that."

Gabriel scrubbed his left hand through his hair. "I always said I'd tell you when you were old enough," he said. "Can't you trust me? Don't I keep my promises?"

"When am I going to be old enough?" Mara said. Gabriel made no reply, refusing to meet her eye as he focused on driving. "I saw what happened in that field, Dad," Mara continued. "You *did* vanish. And then you *lied* and tried to make me think I imagined it." She paused, settling her breath. "You've always lied to me. Every single day, you've lied. And I don't want you to lie any more."

"It's not that easy, Mara," Gabriel said, his voice softer now. "I can't…" He paused, searching for the right words. "You know, sometimes, explaining the answers to these questions is hard. Harder than I know how to handle."

"You could've *tried*," Mara said.

"That's not fair," Gabriel replied sharply. "And watch your tone. Whatever you think you know, I'm still your father – and I'm in charge around here."

"Don't!" Mara shouted. "Don't try to change the subject and make *me* feel like the baddie. Please, Dad!"

"That's not what I'm trying to do!" Gabriel roared,

his anger forcing Mara back into her seat. For a moment, there was silence, broken only by the sound of Mara's soft sobbing. "Sweetheart, I'm sorry," Gabriel began, reaching out a hand to hold Mara's, but she shuffled away out of his reach. "Mara. Please, darling. Don't cry." He thumped the steering wheel gently, making Mara jump. "This is *not* how I wanted this conversation to go," he muttered.

"I need you to tell me the truth," Mara said. "That's all I want, Dad. I'm old enough to know. You've got to tell me."

"Look," Gabriel replied after a moment. The van complained as he changed gear clumsily. "We've both had a bit of a shock, right? Let's find somewhere to make camp and then we'll talk." He threw Mara a worried glance. "I promise you, love. I promise. And then tomorrow, once we've spoken to Lenny, you and me are going to find a café and have a sit-down with tea and lemonade and the stickiest buns you've ever seen." He smiled at her, so briefly it was barely there. "I'll tell you everything I know. You can ask me anything you want. You've got my word on that."

Mara wiped her cheeks with the heels of her hands. Her dad's eyes flicked between the road and her face, growing more worried by the second, until finally Mara nodded. He looked as though someone had poured relief all over him.

"OK," Mara said, her voice barely there. "OK, Dad."

Then, with one last roar of their over-taxed engine, their van trundled off, leading them away from Whiteharbour and towards who knew where.

The Time Tider's Handbook, 1/A/iii: Do not allow yourself to grow close to anyone. Excessive attachment is as dangerous as any Warp...

Chapter Nine

Mara watched the leftover curry as it bubbled. She was using their only saucepan, which was propped above their campfire. It was a lot more awkward than using their old one-ring hob but there was very little gas left in their tiny tank, as usual. She hadn't even tried to get it to light.

"Grub's up," she called, lifting the pot free. "Get it while it's warm. Ish."

Gabriel sat cross-legged on the floor of the van, its back doors thrown open. They'd stopped for the night in a field some distance outside Whiteharbour and the countryside all around ached with silence. The sky overhead was a perfect sweep of stars and the moon was bright, surrounded with a scudding of clouds. As Mara got to her feet, the pot of food held steady, she heard the shriek of a barn owl from somewhere in the darkness. As always, the sudden scream made her catch her breath in surprise.

"Thanks, love," Gabriel murmured, pushing himself forwards and tucking his notebook into his pocket. He picked up the plates from where they'd been lying near the fire and Mara spooned the food out on to them. They used the stale bread rolls to scoop up the curry, eating in companionable silence as they breathed in the night air.

"I'm sorry," Mara said into the stillness.

Her father started, throwing Mara a strange look. "What for?" He took a large mouthful of bread roll and curry, his eyes on Mara as he ate.

"For … sneaking," Mara said, with a shrug. "Poking about. And … the rest of it," she finished, in a near-whisper.

"The rest of what?" Gabriel's words were muffled, his mouth still full.

Mara looked at her dad. She was glad of the darkness. "I lost it, Dad," she said. "The bottle fell – or, well, I dropped it. Into the sea. By mistake. I hadn't sealed it properly and it sank."

Her father chewed thoughtfully and then swallowed. "The handbook's gone," he said tonelessly.

Mara took in a deep breath and slowly released it. "Yep," she said.

For a long moment, the crackling of the fire was the only sound. "What's done is done," Gabriel finally said, wiping his mouth on his sleeve.

Mara glanced at him. "I thought you'd be angry."

Gabriel shrugged. "What's the point in that?" He put his plate to one side and drew his legs up, hugging them to his chest as he gazed into the fire. "I've read that handbook a million times – I can rewrite it, word for word. Plus, you were right. What you said, back in Whiteharbour. I should have explained all this stuff to you years ago. I should never have left you in a position where you felt you had to go searching to find the answers to your questions." He looked at her and the firelight warmed his eyes. "I'm the one who should be sorry."

Mara shuffled over to sit at her dad's side. He stretched out an arm to hold her close as they watched the flames licking the night air.

"Tell me about Mum," Mara finally said.

Gabriel's voice was warm when he spoke again and Mara looked up to see him smiling, though his eyes stayed focused on the campfire. "Well ... ah, Mum was ... she was remarkable," Gabriel said. "The most remarkable woman I'd ever known. That's why we ended up together, I guess." Mara looked back at the flames. A log settled, throwing sparks into the air, and she huddled closer to her father.

"Tell me about how you met," she said.

"Right," he replied quietly. "Well. I met your mum at a protest rally, of all places."

Mara wriggled around to stare at him. "A *protest* rally?"

"Don't sound so shocked!" Gabriel chuckled, as Mara snuggled back down. "Yes, a protest rally. It was many years ago now, probably twenty or more. There was a war, which nobody agreed with – except the politicians who'd led us into it, of course." Gabriel stopped, thoughtful for a moment. "Your mum and I both found ourselves marching, and we ended up carrying either end of the same long banner, right at the front. We were all so sure we were going to change the world." He paused again, giving a rueful chuckle.

"And did you?" Mara whispered. "Did you change the world?"

Gabriel looked at her, his eyes shadowed and sad. "The war didn't stop, sweetheart," he said. "There was a lot of suffering. So many poor people, taken away before their time." He paused, clearing his throat. "Anyway, we gathered in a city park after the rally, all of us, singing songs and sharing stories and that sort of thing, and your mum and me … well. We just sort of belonged to one another after that."

"Thea," Mara whispered.

"Dorothea, actually," Gabriel said, and Mara looked up. His gaze was far away. "Dorothea Furlong. But she liked to be called Thea."

Mara felt her heart swell. *Mum's real name*, she thought.

"She liked music," Gabriel began, without any prompting. "Old music, from years before she was born. She loved books and words and learning new things. She liked collecting stuff – teapots, elephant figurines, thimbles." He chuckled gently. "She was the kindest person I'd ever known. We'd be walking down the street and suddenly I'd turn to her and she'd be gone, running off to give someone money or offer help with something. I wouldn't even have noticed but your mum noticed. She saw everything."

"And me?" Mara said, her voice barely a whisper. "What did she think of me?"

Gabriel looked down at her. "She thought you were the only good thing she'd ever done in her life," he answered and Mara's face crumpled. Her dad pulled her close, kissing her forehead. "She loved you, darling. She was better at it than I am." Gabriel paused. "She'd sing to you all the time. She made a sling out of a long shawl and she'd carry you around with her when you were tiny. And she'd talk to you and tell you stories. When you grew too big for the sling she walked with you, holding your hand, and when you got tired she'd carry you."

Mara blinked hard, but her tears came anyway. "I wish I could remember."

"I should have helped you to remember," her dad replied, his own voice tight. "I didn't want to think about your mum, but I should have thought about you instead. It's hard for me to remember her because it hurts but I shouldn't have been so selfish. I'm sorry, Mara."

She nodded, wiping her cheeks. "It's all right," she whispered. "I just – I wish we'd talked about her more, Dad. And we need to talk about her more, from now on."

"You're right, love," her dad said, his voice a rumble in Mara's ears. "We should've. And we will. And I knew these days were coming, these days when you'd grow old enough to ask me questions I didn't want to answer." He pulled back a bit, looking down into his daughter's face, wiping her cheeks gently with his thumbs. "I just didn't think they'd come quite so early, that's all." He gave her a fond grin and then gathered her into a hug again. They shuffled about, getting comfortable as they slotted together, Mara tucked against her father's chest.

Mara blinked, gazing into the flames as her eyes cleared. "What happened to her, Dad?"

Gabriel stiffened. "Can we… Maybe, can we leave that for another night?"

She looked up at him, incredulous. "What? *Why?* You've just said you were sorry for not telling me stuff—"

"Leave it, Mara. Please." His voice was low but Mara ignored the pain in his eyes.

"Dad. Come on! You've got to tell me. I deserve to know." She pushed herself away from him, dislodging his heavy arm as she got up on her knees to stare him in the face. "Why won't you talk to me?"

"Because it was my fault!" He recoiled from Mara as though she were something red hot. She watched him, open-mouthed, as he wept, the light from their fire dancing over his face. "My fault. She wouldn't have been there if it hadn't been for me."

"Been ... been where?" Mara said after a moment. She pushed herself forwards again. "She wouldn't have been where?"

"At a meeting with the Clockwatchers," Gabriel said, not looking at Mara. His face was twisted with pain, his cheeks wet. "We were there just to talk, they said – just to gather information, keep in touch, so that they knew I wasn't overstepping my duties. They wanted to see my logs, check my records, find out where I'd been harvesting and how often I'd used the Stitch, and that was all fine. But then someone asked a question I didn't like and someone else got upset at the answer I gave, and the next thing – the next thing, your mum was lying on the ground and there was someone else having a gun wrestled out of their hands, and I tried to save her but it was too late. It was too late."

Mara's head ached with confusion. "The ... the *Clockwatchers*? Who on earth are they?" Gabriel still wouldn't meet her eye. Mara put her hands to his face and forced him to look at her. "Dad? Who are they?"

"The enemy," Gabriel said, his words growling through his teeth. "*Never* let them take you, Mara. I can never let them take you from me!"

Gabriel's words were lost in weeping and Mara hugged him tight. They held each other as he cried but all Mara could do was stare into the fire, her mind burning with questions and the image of her mother's face being consumed by the flames.

The Time Tider's Handbook, 1/B/i: Always protect the tools of your Tidership. Do not allow yourself to be separated from them. Do all you can to recover them, should they be lost...

Chapter Ten

It had taken ages, but Mara had finally managed to get her father into the van and settled for the night. She'd doused the fire, washed the dishes and put them away, tidied up inside and locked the doors before finally turning in herself.

Despite the exhaustion that was making her bones feel like lead, she lay wrapped in her blankets, staring at the darkness, unable to sleep. Her heart raced in her chest and she pressed her hand against it, willing it to slow down. Her thoughts were cascading so loudly that it took her a while to notice that her dad had been silent for a long time, and then Mara heard him begin to snore gently. She felt herself relax at the sound. She closed her eyes and breathed deeply for a few minutes, trying to calm her swirling head. Finally her heart rate started to lessen its frantic pace too.

Dorothea … the Clockwatchers … I tried to save her, but it was too late…

Mara thought of her mother's face and tried to imagine what she might have looked like when she was alive. The photograph could only tell her so much; it couldn't tell her the things she really wanted to know. It was impossible to figure out, from a flat image, who her three-dimensional mother had been. What had Thea's voice sounded like? Did she get freckles in the summertime? What had been her favourite food, her favourite scent, her favourite colour? What sort of laugh did she have? How did she smell? Mara tried to press these questions into her memory, so she could ask them of her dad the next day. And who, or what, were the Clockwatchers? Mara squeezed her arms around her middle, trying to quell her fear. *The people Dad's been afraid of all these years?*

"He promised me," Mara whispered to herself. "He said I could ask him anything. So I will."

Beneath her blankets, Mara was warming up. She rubbed her feet over one another, back and forth and back and forth, the same way she'd always done to soothe herself to sleep, and somewhere in the depths of her mind she remembered a song. It was about stars shining and night breezes whispering and sycamore trees, and a beautiful voice sang it right into her ear…

Mara jerked awake, her heart thudding, her senses on

high alert. The light inside the van was different – she knew, straight away, that time had passed. There was a hint of brightness creeping in beneath the drapes on the windscreen. *Nearly dawn*, she thought, frowning. So at least four hours had slipped by since she'd gone to bed. But what had woken her? She listened. Everything seemed still and silent, but her heart kept on racing.

She pushed herself up on one elbow and leaned into the gap between the bunks, opening her mouth to whisper to her dad. She reached out to shake him gently but before she could call his name a brick came crashing through a back window of the van.

Mara ducked her head, gasping in shock. The brick sailed right past her, smacking hard on to the floor and skidding forwards until it became wedged beneath the passenger seat.

"Mara!" It was her father's voice. In the dim light, she could just about see him throwing off his covers. They reached for one another.

"Dad, I'm OK. I'm OK! But what's—"

"Get in the driver's seat, sweetheart. Start the van."

"Dad – what? I don't—"

"Mara, do as you're told!" Her father's voice was ragged. Mara could see his bared teeth and his wide eyes but he wasn't looking at her. He was staring out through the broken window. Somewhere, Mara heard the sound of an engine. Voices too. The cool breeze of early morning carried the noises right to her ears.

She scrambled out of her blankets, tossing them aside as she clambered up the van and into the driver's seat. The floor was covered with shards of glass, metal and plastic. Mara was sure something sharp had become embedded in her sock, but she told herself not to care. *Sort it out later.* Her fingers shook as she struggled to undo the drapes and pull them back.

"Come on," she muttered, yanking the last tie. Then, with one final *swish*, the windscreen was clear. There was nothing in front of her but empty land and an open gate a few hundred metres away. Mara pulled the seat forwards, clicked her seat belt into place, settled her feet on the pedals and turned the key in the van's ignition. For once, the old machine roared into life without any coaxing.

"Good girl," Mara whispered to it.

"Drive, Mara," her father called from the back. "Get us out of here."

Mara slid the van into gear and moved off. "Where do I go, Dad?"

"Anywhere!" Her father crouched with his eye to the broken window. "Anywhere away from here. Go!"

Mara pressed the accelerator and the van screamed a reply. The ground was bumpy and uneven and visibility was poor but they picked up speed as the gate drew nearer.

Then Mara saw something moving at the gatepost – a figure in the shadows. She squinted at it, unsure, and then she realized what was happening.

"They're trying to close the gate," she called to her dad. "What do I do?"

"Keep going!" her father shouted. "Don't stop, Mara, not for anything!"

Mara drove on, urging the van to go faster. She flicked the headlights on, drowning the people at the gate in bright light. They threw up their hands to avoid the sudden glare, giving Mara a precious second or two. She screamed as the van crashed through the half-closed gate, the impact sending the people behind it sprawling into the road – and then, with a screeching of tyres and some more panicked shouting from Mara, they were out and through. She struggled with the wheel as she fought to straighten the heavy van but once she'd managed that, she was away. The needle climbed as her speed increased. Third gear, fourth, fifth and they were going as fast as Mara had ever driven. Her heart thundered so hard, she felt sure her ribs would shatter.

And then, in her mirror, she spotted the headlights of a pursuing vehicle.

"Dad, they're after us!" Mara fought to keep the panic out of her voice.

"I know, love," her father replied. Mara turned her

head; her dad was beside her, between the seats, holding on to her headrest as he peered through the front windscreen. She looked back at the road again.

"Who are they? What do they want?"

"They want me, sweetheart." Mara felt her father's hand against the side of her head as he pulled her close enough to kiss her on the cheek. She felt the scratch of his beard and his greasy hair brushing against her skin and the warmth of his breath. "Keep going, Mara. Don't stop until you've thrown them off. Then get to Lenny. OK? All the maps are in the van; you know where I keep them. I know you'll be able to find your way." Mara felt something being placed into her lap. She freed one hand from the wheel to grab at it but what she felt didn't make sense.

"What?" Mara sobbed, flicking her gaze between the road and her father's face. "What are you talking about? Where are *you* going? I can't find Lenny on my own, Dad! I haven't seen him in years. I probably won't even recognize him!"

"He'll know you, Mara. Trust me. He'll look out for you. And I'll come back and find you, I promise. I *promise!*"

And then he was gone. Mara twisted in her seat, trying to see. "Dad!" she screamed.

Her father was at the rear of the van, his hand on the back doors. He turned to her, and his face was a frantic mask. "Drive, Mara! Just go! Once they've got me, they won't keep following you. Get out of here!"

She turned back to face the road ahead. Glancing in the central rear-view mirror, Mara saw the lights of the vehicles behind them, getting closer and closer. The shattered glass of the broken window made the light scatter like a rainbow. It was almost beautiful. And then her father pushed open the back doors of their van – of their home, where he had lived with Mara all her life – and he jumped out through them, right into the path of whoever was following, and no matter how loudly Mara shouted his name, there was no answer.

*The Time Tider's Handbook, 1/B/ii:
Maintain the condition of your tools. Care
for and calibrate the watch as regularly as
possible. Without it, you risk being lost
among the Warps...*

Chapter Eleven

Mara drove for as long as she could bear, her hands growing numb on the wheel and her eyes blurring. Eventually she was shivering so much and her teeth were chattering so hard that she had to find a place to pull over. The back doors of the van had been swinging and banging as she drove and when they finally fell silent, all Mara could hear was the sound of her own sobbing.

At last she sat up, wiping her running nose on her sleeve. She switched off the van's headlights and took her feet off the pedals, wincing with pain. She turned to look out through the broken pane in the van door – the road behind her was deserted. Her dad had been right – whoever had been chasing them had only wanted him. As soon as he'd given himself up, they'd let her go, just as he'd told her they would.

"I'm sorry, Dad," Mara whispered to the emptiness inside the van. "I should've believed you." But who were 'they'? The Clockwatchers? And when would her father come back? She wished she knew that too but she closed her eyes tight around the swell of loss and loneliness and tried to push it away.

Mara opened her eyes again and stared down at the things her father had put into her lap, the things she'd struggled to keep safe as she'd driven. The sight of them made her more scared than anything. On impulse, she popped open the storage compartment in the van's central console and shoved the objects inside, clicking the lid closed over them, and leaned her forehead against the steering wheel for a moment or two, just trying to breathe. As soon as she could, she hauled herself out of the driver's seat and into the passenger side. She opened the glove box to find the first-aid kit, trying not to think about the last time she'd opened it, and the lock of hair she'd cut off to give her dad…

"Stop it," she muttered to herself, fighting to open the kit. She propped it on the dashboard, hoping there were enough supplies in it to sort out her foot.

Carefully, Mara peeled off her sock. A shard of plastic was embedded just below her biggest toe. Her skin was murky with blood, the wound itself lost in a sticky pool.

She got the worst of it off with spit and the corner of her sleeve, and then, using the tweezers from the first-aid kit, Mara worked at the shard, wincing and hissing as it shifted, until finally she'd pulled it free. She cleaned her foot with a mostly dried-up antiseptic wipe and bandaged it with a pad of cotton, looping tape between her two biggest toes. Finally she examined her handiwork, trying to ignore how long and dirty her toenails were. As she put the first-aid kit away her stomach growled and Mara sighed as she ignored it.

Limping a little, she scanned the floor carefully for debris and made it to her bunk, rummaging through the storage boxes underneath for her spare pair of socks. She pulled them on, careful not to dislodge the bandage, and then forced her feet into her shoes. The wounded foot felt strange, but the pain wasn't bad.

Then, knowing she couldn't put it off any longer, she looked back at the central console. *Please, Dad,* she begged, inside her head. *I hope you've left me instructions or something. Anything to help me figure out what to do next.* But she knew he'd done nothing of the sort. She knew what he'd left her. She just didn't know why.

And she also knew she had to keep the objects safe, and hope her dad would come back soon to take them off her hands. *But the fact that he gave them to me in the first place means he might never...* She clamped her mind around the thought, smothering it.

Mara limped back towards the seats. She knew she'd have to clean up the shattered glass from the floor and find something to block the window with, but she pushed all that aside as she climbed into the driver's seat and took a few deep breaths. Then she popped open the central console and pulled the lid back. She peered down into the recess beneath. The objects were still there.

Her father's pocket watch and his notebook.

Mara reached in, her hands shaking, and lifted them out one by one. She placed the pocket watch into her lap and took the notebook in her hands. It was battered and scruffy, its pages kept closed with a thick leather strap, and in the middle she could see some banknotes, creased and filthy, which her father had shoved into the pages.

She opened the popper fastening on the strap keeping the notebook closed. For a minute her fingers refused to move, curling into a fist. *I've got to look*, she told herself severely, forcing her hand to relax. *There might be something in here that can help.* Even so, her mind reeled as she glanced at the pages. This was her dad's most private thing, the notebook he kept his whole life in. Looking in it felt like a betrayal.

Not that it mattered much. Her father's scribbled notes, written in a tight, cramped hand, made no sense. She chewed her lip, her eyes skipping down the narrow, pencil-drawn columns, wondering what the references were to and what her father had been recording here. She saw dates and numbers, some of which might have been coordinates or grid references, and each page was totalled at the bottom in three columns, like the notebook was some sort of ledger. *So it can't be money,* Mara thought, frowning. *Is it ... Time? Days, weeks, months?* Her eyes skipped to the dates, down the right-hand side of each page. She noticed they'd become erratic; up to a few years before, the entries had been regular but more recently the entries skittered about without shape or logic.

Mara slapped the book shut and fastened it securely closed, trying not to think about its contents. She picked up the pocket watch instead, feeling its cool weight in her hand, running her fingertips across the crest and the inscription. *Time and Tide May Wait for None; But They Will Wait for Me.*

"Time Tider," she whispered. A sudden fear washed over her at what the inscription actually *meant* – it wasn't just a collection of pretty words. It was the motto of the Tider – her father. *And now it's mine.*

Mara popped the watch open. She glanced at the locks of hair curled inside the lid, wondering again what her father needed them for – and why, in all the years she'd been handing over her hair without questioning it, she'd never thought to ask him for a lock of his. Blinking hard, she swiped at her nose, and continued examining the watch.

The inside face looked completely ordinary – three circular displays, one large and two small, their numerals and markings black, all housed beneath glass – but that impression only lasted until you examined the largest of the three displays. It didn't have just one dial; instead, it had three concentric dials, each with the same central point but growing smaller in diameter as they went in. There were six hands, all radiating from the same spot, but varying in size and length. The largest and thickest reached all the way to the outer dial. It was made of something that shone like gold. The second pair of hands were the same size as one another, each of them a bright silver colour, and they fitted with the middle of the three dials. The smallest hands were ebony coloured, three of them thin as paintbrush hairs, and they were used to read the inner dial. Each of the dials had been skilfully marked up, black divisions against the white of the watch face, but there were no numerals. Mara frowned as she studied them. There was no indication of what they might measure and no way, as far as she could see, of working it out.

The smaller faces were more regular, though Mara frowned at them too. They were set to one side of the largest dial, one at the top of the watch face and one at the bottom. The dial nearest the bottom, the smallest of the three, looked to be an ordinary watch – she glanced at the clock on the van's dashboard and saw that it was reading exactly the same time as this small face. *So that's the time here*, she told herself, trying to understand. *The time as it is, wherever – or whenever – the Time Tider is.*

Feeling secure in her guess, Mara turned her attention to the last dial. It was still, its hands unmoving, placed exactly at noon. The markings around its face looked to be as expected – numbers from one to twelve, with thin lines to mark out each minute interval – but Mara wasn't sure what, exactly, this clock face measured. *A stopwatch?* she thought, wondering where the controls for it might be. There didn't seem to be any sort of mechanism to set this stopwatch going – if that's what it was – and Mara gave up trying to guess. *I'll ask Dad, as soon as I see him*, she told herself.

She ran her finger along the coiled hair in the watch case lid one more time, and as she did so her stomach gave another, more painful rumble. "All right, all right," she whispered, huffing out a long breath through her nose as she clipped the watch case closed. "Let's go."

The Time Tider's Handbook, 1/A/iv: It is recognized that help may sometimes be required. Ensure to choose your helpers with exceptional care. Do not think of them as friends or colleagues or confidantes; none must know the full truth of the burden you carry...

Chapter Twelve

The inside of Mara's mouth was still coated with chocolate from the half-eaten, half-melted bar she'd found in the pocket behind the driver's seat. It had given her enough strength to sweep the detritus out of the van and to find a blanket to use as a temporary fix for the broken window. She knew it wouldn't do for long, but she had no idea where she'd go to find a sheet of plywood or anything like it to make a better and more ransack-proof replacement for the shattered pane.

"Maybe when I go to get fuel," she muttered to herself, her eyes falling on the canister they used for diesel. "They might have a hardware shop at the pumps."

She climbed back into the driver's seat and pulled out her father's notebook. Carefully, she took out the money her dad had left her and counted it. "Two hundred," she said, checking it again just to be sure. Her head swam at the thought of carrying that much money around but she knew she had to. With the window broken, there was no security here – she couldn't leave anything valuable in the van, and that included the notebook and the watch as well as the money, until she managed to get the glass replaced. *No. Until Dad's back*, she told herself. *He'll fix it.*

Mara licked the chocolate residue off her teeth and took a swig of water from the bottle she'd found beside it. The water was warm and tasted of plastic, but it helped. Then she sat back and tried to make a plan. *Get some more food*, she thought. She blinked down at the console, which still contained her father's notebook and the watch. *Keep those safe. Find Lenny.*

She took in a deep, determined breath and started the van. She watched the fuel gauge, waiting for the needle to settle. There was over half a tank of diesel left and Mara felt herself relax a little. The van was old but it could run on fumes. Half a tank of diesel meant she wouldn't have to buy more for a while.

Reaching into the storage compartment in the driver's door, Mara pulled free the map she'd stashed there. She unfolded it, glancing up at the sign that stood on the far side of the road, and quickly oriented herself. "Whiteharbour," she whispered, tracing her finger along the road network until she found exactly where she was. She let her gaze continue along the map, following the road she was on until it reached a town by the banks of a wide river. The town was called Port Ross. In the middle of the river, on the map, her dad had sketched a symbol. *A pair of glasses*, Mara thought, running a fingertip over them. *Lenny.* Somewhere in that town, or along that river, she'd find him.

Mara folded the map up again, hoping that she'd also find somewhere to stash the van once she was closer. Then she'd continue on foot until she reached Lenny's place – but after that, her plan grew hazy. She had no idea what to do when she got there. "Hope he doesn't mind taking care of a random kid until who knows when," she muttered, as she put the van into gear. She remembered Lenny as a kind, friendly man, and she knew he was one of her dad's best, and probably *only*, friends – but it had been so long since she'd seen him. She hoped he'd remember her.

She pulled out, her heart *thunk*ing as she drove. There was only one road to Port Ross, a large and busy one, and the further she went, the more she was afraid of being spotted. All it would take was one bored police officer wondering why this beaten-up van was driving around with a smashed back window and the game would be up. *Can't let that happen*, she thought, her gaze hopping between the road ahead and her rear-view mirrors with the regularity of a ticking clock.

But she was in luck. There were no signs of the police anywhere as she approached the outskirts of the town. She turned with the road, the river to her left, and saw the span of a wide bridge up ahead. Mara drove over it, scanning the road once she was across, looking for anywhere she could leave the van where it might have some chance of blending in. She passed an entrance to a fancy housing estate but just past it was a derelict house, set back from the road and mostly hidden by overgrown, untended trees. Mara made her move. Moments later, she was bumping over mud and gravel as she drove slowly around the back of the abandoned house. She stopped the van and cut the engine, listening carefully for a few minutes, but there was nothing to be heard besides the distant, muffled sound of the road she'd just left.

"OK," she breathed, clenching and unclenching her fists. As she unclipped her seat belt, Mara realized she was bone-tired – too exhausted to think. She put her face in her hands for a moment or two, breathing deeply. She turned, looking at her comfortable bunk, and before she could talk herself out of it she was asleep, curled up in the shadows of her van.

She woke up to a painful cramp in her middle, hunger gurgling through her. Pushing herself up and shucking off her blankets, Mara discovered that most of the morning had passed. Cursing under her breath, she scrambled to pull her father's coat out from underneath his bunk. She put it on, reaching into the central console to grab her valuables. Into one pocket went the map and the bottle of water; into the other, the watch and the notebook. She kneeled behind the driver's seat to pull free her father's bag, taking the tin containing her mother's photograph from it. She shoved the bag back into place before sliding the tin in beside her map. Then she hopped out of the driver's door, landing heavily in the gravel before locking the van and putting the key in her jeans pocket. For several heartbeats, she stood beside it, feeling an almost overwhelming need to climb back inside again, to just hide in the darkness until all this was over.

"But I won't," she whispered. "I'll find Lenny, Dad. I'll be waiting for you."

She used the mirror to pull her curls back into a high ponytail and then she looked down at herself. Her dad's coat was too big but it was in good shape, mostly. Her jeans were old, but they looked OK. Her trainers were past their best – her big toe poked out through the mesh – but they'd have to do.

Mara turned away from the van and began to walk around the house, her footsteps loud on the weed-choked gravel. She glanced up at the house as she passed. Some of its roof had caved in and all the windows were broken. Its front door was missing a panel and the steps were soft with moss, but there was no sign of anyone living there. That didn't mean there wasn't, of course, as Mara knew too well. *Just leave my van alone, OK?* she silently asked the house as she walked out on to the road, heading for Port Ross.

Mara stopped at a busy intersection and tried to think. She looked down the wide street ahead of her – crowded, filled with cars, the hustle and bustle of ordinary life – and she knew: wherever Lenny was, he wouldn't be *here*. The people her dad knew, the people he trusted, were people who lived in the cracks and around the edges.

She sucked hard on her lower lip and glanced down the side road to her right. At the top of it, just across the road, was a small takeaway restaurant. Next door to it was a charity shop and then a laundrette. After that, all Mara could see was open land behind a tall metal fence, the grass growing out through the links. The road seemed to lead towards a car park, and on the far side was a housing estate built on a hill, the homes small and cramped together. *But somewhere down there is the river,* she told herself, closing her eyes for a moment and putting herself, mentally, back into her map. Something told her Lenny would be near the water – a half-memory, a feeling. Mara knew enough to trust it.

First things first, she told herself, as the hollow feeling in her stomach turned into another grumble. It was long past lunchtime. *The only thing you'll find, if you don't get food soon, is your face landing smack on the ground.*

Checking for traffic, Mara crossed the road. She stopped outside the takeaway to pull free some money before going inside. A few minutes later she stepped back out on to the pavement, her hands full of a hot, delicious-smelling taco. She took her first bite and began to walk, hoping the water would draw her to it like a divining rod.

The Time Tider's Handbook, 1/A/iv:
Take particular care to investigate the
motives of any who would befriend you...
Be wary, be wise, use your wits.

Chapter Thirteen

A school bell started ringing and Mara jumped at the suddenness of the sound. There was a red-brick wall beside her, topped with a metal fence. Judging by the excited shrieking that was coming from behind it, she guessed she was about to pass the school gates – and that it was the end of the day for the students. She checked the time on her dad's watch, noticing with a jerk that the hands on its largest face had shifted slightly; she let her worry slide as she put the watch away, knowing there was nothing she could do about it. Leaning against the wall, Mara tried to quell her irritation. She'd wasted so much time wandering around housing estates, being guided by a map so out of date as to be useless, that almost the whole day was gone – with nothing to show for it besides an aching foot.

A torrent of kids came pouring out of the gates – breathless, uniform-wearing, with clean hair and shining skin and new clothes, and bags filled with books slung over one shoulder. They were loud, laughing and calling to one another as they tumbled away down the street or into waiting cars. Mara held her breath as she watched, trying – and failing – to imagine herself among them.

"Oh my *God*," said a voice nearby. Mara blinked out of her thoughts and looked at the girl who'd spoken. She was tall – taller even than Mara – and looked to be much older. "Are you lost or something?" She curled her lip, her dark brown eyes unkind. Mara's heart sped up.

Another girl, shorter than the first, joined in. "They letting you tunnel weirdos into *school* now?"

Mara felt her mouth fall open. "I-I mean, no, I mean—"

"Bleuh-bleuh-bleuh!" mocked the tallest girl. She wobbled her head from side to side, making her hooped earrings swing and the beads on the ends of her braids click together. "Can't even talk, can you?"

The other girl waved a dismissive hand in Mara's direction. Her fingernails were long and painted a pearlescent pink. Mara stared at them in fascination. "Go on, then. Back to your hole in the ground, right? With all your other little tunnel rats."

At these words, something clicked in Mara's memory. *Tunnel rats!* Lenny's place was near a tunnel, she remembered. An outlet tunnel, near a pedestrian footbridge, which drained water into a river. Into *the* river, the one running through Port Ross. And right around the corner from that footbridge was a school. *This* school. The map bloomed in her memory again as she looked back up at the girls and gave a wide grin. "Thanks!" she said brightly. "It's down this way, right? The tunnel?"

The tallest girl wrinkled her nose, but her unkind eyes were confused now. "Weirdo," she muttered, looking Mara up and down. She grabbed her friend's arm as she turned away. "Come on. Let's go."

"Yeah," the second girl said, giving Mara a hard stare. "See ya 'round, rat girl."

The first girl looked back at her friend and honked with laughter, and then they were gone, walking arm in arm down the road, their voices loud and unapologetic, their colours bright. Mara watched them go, a strange ache around her heart, and then she turned away.

She hurried down the street, dodging the gathered kids and adults, all the while ignoring the smarting pain beneath her big toe, until finally she'd made it round the corner. She slowed her pace, trying to catch her breath as she passed a bus stop. A crowd of kids from the school stood around it, most of them on their phones or listening to music through small, plastic earbuds. Two boys at the far end pushed one another playfully, pretending to fight.

School bags and coats were tossed here and there. The kids fell silent and still as Mara drew near, and as she hurried through, the whispering and laughing began.

Mara felt her cheeks burning but she kept her head down as she walked. Behind her, she heard the *ksss* of hydraulic brakes and looked over her shoulder to see the bus arriving. The kids, distracted by picking up their discarded belongings, seemed to lose interest in her – until moments later, when the full bus passed her by. A *bonk* to the top of her head made Mara cry out in surprise and the next thing she knew, there was something cold and sticky running down her face and the back of her neck. She turned to see a discarded milkshake carton lying on the ground a few metres from her and she knew before she touched her head what she'd find. "Yuck!" she said, looking at the pink mess all over her hand.

The bus drove on, its exhaust fumes making Mara cough, and she tried not to hear the laughter that went with it. Once the bus was gone, the road was quiet.

Mara walked on, shaking cold pink gloop off her fingers. She wrapped her arms around herself and forced everything out of her head except for one thing: *finding the tunnel.* It had to be close. Checking the road for traffic, she hurried across and kept walking, striding along a narrow concrete footpath beside a low wooden fence which seemed to guard nothing more than long, rain-sodden grass. But with any luck, in about fifty metres or so, Mara knew she'd see…

"The bridge," she whispered, with a satisfied grin.

It was made of red-painted iron, its rivets like pimples on its rusted face, carrying a pathway over a narrow, reed-thick river. Mara stepped over the fence and into the wet grass, her trainers instantly soaking through. The river ran along beside her, much narrower and faster here than it had been as it entered the sea. Mara walked slowly, her feet sinking in the boggy, soft earth, knowing that sooner or later she'd find the tunnel – and Lenny.

She'd barely left the bridge behind when she saw the tunnel up ahead, its dark, yawning mouth letting a gush of murky water into the river. *I've been here before*, she told herself, knowing for sure this had to be the place. *Except we came by boat last time – didn't we?* She had a vague memory of a colourful narrowboat, its engine loud and dirty, coughing black clouds as they went; Lenny, his glasses shining in the sun, a hat sideways on his head; her dad, relaxed as she'd ever seen him, smiling at his friend as they tried to get the motor started again. She remembered someone on the footbridge overhead waving at them as they passed beneath and how she'd waved back.

Mara crept towards the tunnel's opening, her feet getting wetter with every step, her ears primed and ready, straining for every sound – though all she could really hear was her own nervous heartbeat.

"H-hello?" she called, blinking into the blackness inside the tunnel. "Lenny? Are you—"

Whatever she might have been about to say next was stopped in its tracks as Mara felt a hand clamping down on her mouth and an arm wrapping itself tightly around her body, pinning her arms in place.

*The Time Tider's Handbook, 1/B/iv:
Maintain your stores with dignity. Store
the harvested Warps safely behind glass
or metal, in a clean and quiet place that is
not likely to be disturbed. Guard the key,
which only you should hold...*

Chapter Fourteen

Instinctively, Mara lifted her right foot and kicked back against the shin of the person who'd grabbed her. It was a desperate move without much strength behind it, so she was surprised to hear a voice shouting in pain as she made contact.

"Ow! *Come* on, give me a break!"

Mara felt herself released and then pushed away by the person who'd ambushed her. She whirled on the spot, fists raised, ready to fight – but then she stopped, frowning, as she stared at her captor. She lowered her hands.

It was a kid. A boy, maybe her age, but shorter. His hair was shaved close to his scalp until just above his ears and then it became a cloud of springy black coils all around the top of his head. He wore clean jeans with no holes in them, good trainers and a rain jacket, bright and colourful and much too big for him, that made a *swish* noise every time he moved.

"You must've crept up on me with your arms sticking out, eh," Mara said, fighting to get her breathing back to normal. "I didn't hear your stupid raincoat once."

"It's not *stupid*," the boy retorted. "It's my brother's."

Mara wiped her nose with the edge of her hand, shrugging as she glanced at his jacket with her eyebrows raised. "Yeah. Well," she muttered.

"What are you doing here, anyway?" the boy said. He stared at Mara, his eyes a deep golden brown.

"I'm looking for someone," Mara replied. "A friend of my dad's."

"I heard you shouting for Lenny," the boy said, folding his arms with a rustling of his jacket.

"I didn't *shout*," Mara objected. "I was just—"

The boy sucked his teeth in irritation. "I heard you looking for Lenny. How do you know him?"

Mara wrinkled her forehead and stared at the kid. "Why should I tell you anything? I don't even know you!"

The boy ran a hand through his mass of black curls, scratching at his head thoughtfully for a second or two. Then he pulled his fingers free and offered his hand to Mara. After a moment, she shook it. "I'm Jan," the boy said, pulling back his hand. "I live nearby. My parents know Lenny and the crew that stay down here. They do some stuff for them now and then."

"Yann?" Mara repeated, frowning at the unfamiliar name.

The boy nodded. "It's spelled with a J. It means 'John' in Dutch. I had a Dutch granddad. I'm named after him."

Mara blinked at this information. "Right."

Jan raised his eyebrows. "So. How about you?"

"I've got no idea where my grandparents were from," she said.

Jan grinned. "What's your *name*?"

"Mara," she told him, before realizing she should have made up something fake.

The boy pushed out his bottom lip, nodding in appreciation. "It's a good name."

Mara grinned a bit at Jan's expression, but it faded fast. "It was my mum's idea. She wanted to name me after the sea, so that's why it's pronounced the Irish way, like 'morra'." Mara blinked as an image of the sea filled her mind – the surge and swell of it, rhythmic as a ticking clock, the tide rising and falling. *Time and tide…*

"So why isn't she with you?"

Mara focused on Jan again, her lips tightening for a moment. "She died. When I was two."

"Oh," Jan said, his eyes widening with apology. "Man. God. I'm sorry."

Mara shrugged. "Long time ago."

Jan nodded slowly and there was silence for a few minutes. "So who's your dad, then?" Jan finally said. "You said he was a mate of Lenny's."

"I'm supposed to meet him here," Mara said. "He ... he had to go somewhere and he told me he'd catch up with me at Lenny's place. So I'm going to wait for him here."

Jan blinked, looking up at Mara's hair as if seeing it for the first time. "You've got something all over you."

Mara rolled her eyes. "Milkshake," she said. "It's no big deal."

"What happened?"

"Some kids," Mara mumbled. "From the school."

"They tossed it?" Jan's eyes were wide. "What for?"

Mara glanced down at her clothes. "Take a guess."

Jan raised his eyebrows sympathetically. "Look. Let's get back to mine, get you cleaned up. We can come back here later if you want."

Mara gave him an incredulous look. "There's no way I'm leaving. What if my dad comes? He won't know where I've gone."

Jan gave her a troubled stare. "Look, I don't know anything about your dad," he said. "But I do know that you need that milkshake off you. And it'll be getting dark in a few hours – you can't stay here all night."

"I'm not leaving," Mara repeated in a louder voice. "My dad told me to find Lenny, and that's what I'm doing.

OK?" She turned to the mouth of the tunnel and began to walk into it. "I'll see you later."

"What are you playing at?" Jan called. Mara heard the quick *splash-splash* noises of his feet as he hurried after her. "You can't go in there." He grabbed her forearm and she felt his fingers digging in.

"Says who?" She turned towards him, shaking his hand off in a flash of anger. "*You?* I met you like ten seconds ago. I don't have to do anything you tell me."

"It isn't safe," Jan said. Mara couldn't see clearly in the darkness of the tunnel, but enough light was seeping in for her to be able to read his worried expression. "C'mon. I'm sure your dad wouldn't want you to stay somewhere that's not safe. Right?"

"You know *nothing* about my dad," Mara said, through clenched teeth. Something bubbled up inside her as she spoke, a volcano of burning frustration that finally overspilled. "I'm used to stuff not being safe. I've never been safe. Not ever."

Jan looked puzzled as he searched Mara's face. "How did you even know where to come? I mean – Lenny, right, he doesn't exactly have an *address*, does he? Nobody *normal* ever comes looking for him." His voice was soft as he continued. "Who's your dad? Is he in the network?" Mara made no reply but Jan shook his head as if clearing it. "Stupid, of course he isn't. If he was, I'd know you, right?"

His eyes met hers again and this time they widened with realization. "Just … tell me, OK, if I guess it." Jan licked his lips nervously. "Is your dad the Tider?"

Mara stared at him. "How … how do you—" she began, before stumbling back a step or two. "Leave me alone," she said, turning away again. She kept going, heading into the darkness, her heart thundering with every step – then her leg collided with something hard and she felt herself stumble against a sharp corner. She bit her lips in tight, refusing to allow anything out that might show her surprise.

"Careful!" Jan's voice sounded far away. Mara turned – he'd stayed near the mouth of the tunnel. She could just about see him, lined in daylight.

Mara looked down. She'd bashed her leg on the edge of a shelf. She ran her hands along it, barely able to see. She squinted. There seemed to be more of them, built against the walls of the tunnel, designed to keep something clear of the water. But what?

"Where's Lenny?" Mara said finally. "I really need to talk to him."

"But – doesn't your dad know?" Jan said. Mara looked back at him. His confusion seemed real. "If your dad's the Tider, why doesn't he know? Lenny's gone. The Keepers he was storing here? They're gone too. And nobody knows where."

The Time Tider's Handbook, 1/B/iv: Fashion (or have fashioned by another) vessels of glass or metal with a lid that can be sealed or otherwise fixed permanently in place... Fashion your spindle from bone or metal... Make more than you require, for the Tider after you will surely have need of them... The vessel can be any size, any shape and any colour – all that matters is that it can be sealed, that it can be stored somewhere inaccessible to any but the Tider and that none besides the Tider shall know what it is for...

Chapter
Fifteen

Mara followed Jan as he hurried down the street. She hadn't known what to do when he'd told her Lenny had vanished months ago and nobody had heard from him since. Jan said that the 'gang', the others who lived in the tunnel and who gathered around Lenny like moths to a flame, had scattered too, all of them vanishing into the cracks and crevices once their 'leader' was gone. Jan hadn't explained yet what he'd meant by 'Keepers', but Mara could take a guess. *The glass things*, she realized. *The glass things my dad keeps in his coat and in his storage box back at the van. The thing he drew, with the label I couldn't read.* She felt a momentary jolt of guilt to think of that drawing, now at the bottom of the sea. There must once have been boxes and boxes of them, stacked on those shelves inside the tunnel, as safe as they could be made. *And they're full of Time, harvested from Warps,* Mara told herself. *Time Keepers.* It was almost funny but Mara had never felt less like laughing. Had Lenny done a runner, taking the Time with him? Or had someone taken both him and the Time – but who could have done something like that? And why? Mara's thoughts hopped, her mind crowding with questions.

Jan looked back as if to check she was still there and Mara threw him an irritated glare. He turned again, shaking his head a little. Then he vanished around a corner. Mara stopped in her tracks, until Jan popped his head back around the corner and beckoned her on, impatiently, with one hand. They made their way down a narrow street, barely wider than an alley, lined with bins and rubbish bags and broken things.

"Just up here," Jan said, indicating a tall block of flats at the end of the alley. Mara counted seven storeys, the balconies hung with washing and the roof bristling with satellite dishes. "Welcome to Elysium Towers."

Jan hurried through the gate that led into the complex. It hung open, swinging on squeaky hinges. They made their way through a children's play area towards an arch in the centre of the building and Jan led Mara to the left, where an opening gave way to a staircase and a lift, an Out of Order sign stuck to its doors. Up the stairs they went, Jan taking them two steps at a time while Mara looked around at the graffiti on the walls. Buggies were parked in corners, along with discarded toys and rubbish. On a windowsill sat an old TV with inches of dust on it and a star-shaped crack right in the middle of its screen.

"Almost there," Jan said, as they reached a landing with a large number three painted on the wall. He turned to the right, pushing his way through another narrow gate – unlocked, just like the one outside – and leading Mara on to a long, wide balcony. Clothes flapped to their left, and Mara looked out over the waist-high barrier. She could see lots from up here – the river and the bridge and most of the sprawling town.

Finally Jan stopped at a green door numbered nineteen, the brass numbers screwed into the wood. He glanced furtively up and down before digging his hand into his pocket. He pulled out a key. It turned in the lock and then they were inside.

Mara was instantly hit by a wave of noise coming from somewhere close by – thumping music and the crackle of gunfire. She stumbled back a little, bashing into Jan who was behind her, trying to close the door. "Hey!" he said. "What's up?"

"You said we'd be safe here!" Mara said, staring at him. He frowned at her.

"We … are?" he replied, confused. "I mean, my parents aren't here, they're working, but my older brother Willem

is in there. You can call him Will, he hates the real thing."
Jan jerked his head towards a nearby door, standing open –
the one all the noise was pouring through. Mara peered in
to see a tall, older boy, his limbs long and thin, crouched in
front of a screen – and on the screen were explosions and
running soldiers, faces shouting, men falling to the ground
amid splatters of blood and gore. The boy – Willem –
had something in his hand and his fingers were moving
quickly as he used it, Mara guessed, to control whatever
was happening on screen.

A game, she realized. The fear that had filled her up a
moment ago began to fizz away.

"Hey!" Jan shouted. "Will, turn it down. We'll get
another noise complaint from Mrs Maybury!"

"Aw, *what*?" Willem shouted as the screen froze. He
turned to look at his brother. "What do I care about that
old bag?" His eyes flicked to Mara. "And who've you got
there?" He snorted, shaking his head in amusement. "Nice
hair," he said, and Mara looked at the ground, her cheeks
flushing.

"C'mon, let's get out of here," Jan said, turning away from
the living room. As they moved off down the corridor, the
noise from Will's game started up again – but then they heard
the door slam shut and the sounds of battle lessened a bit.

A little girl came out of the kitchen at the end of the
hallway. Her face was covered with chocolate spread and

she looked up at Jan mischievously. "Jan-Jan," she said. "You got a girlfriend?"

"This is Mara, who's my friend and who's a girl, so I guess so," he said, bending down to pick up the child with an exaggerated groan. The little giggling girl was probably five and Jan only managed to carry her a few steps before he had to put her back down. "Say hi, Annelies!"

"Hi, Annelies!" the little girl said, her giggles turning to laughter as Jan began to tickle her.

Jan straightened up, his hair askew, and looked at Mara. "Annelies is the baby," he told her, settling his curls. Mara smiled at the girl, who grinned up at her. They followed her into the kitchen. Annelies had filled the table with colouring books and scraps of paper, and there was a plastic tub full of crayons and markers, most of them missing their lids, sitting in the middle of the mess. To one side was a plate covered in crumbs and smears of chocolate spread and a half-drunk glass of milk.

"You want something to eat?" Jan said, heading for the fridge. Annelies clambered back up into her chair and resumed her colouring, humming quietly to herself. Mara looked around the room. The fridge was dotted with magnets and pieces of paper, drawings and notes and shopping lists. The counters were cluttered with things Mara couldn't even guess the uses for. The sink was piled with dishes. Jan noticed her looking around and grimaced.

"Yeah, I know. Mum's going to go crazy when she sees this mess."

"Oh, no," Mara said. "That's not what I was thinking." She felt her cheeks turn hot. "I mean, Dad and I live in a van. So..." She shrugged. "This is all pretty nice."

"In a *van*?" Annelies said, her voice squeaking with disbelief. "But where do you go to the toilet?"

Mara laughed as Jan scolded his sister for being rude. "It's fine," Mara said. "I think that's a very clever question. But the answer –" her voice dropped to a whisper – "isn't really suitable for a kitchen."

"Right, you're *both* gross," Jan said, burying his head in the fridge. Mara and Annelies shared a conspiratorial grin.

"Speaking of which," Mara said. "Could I please use your bathroom?"

Jan pulled his head out of the fridge. "Sure," he said. "It's just up the hall a bit, second on the left."

Mara passed the closed living-room door as she found the bathroom. The sounds of Will's game still boomed out behind it but they faded completely as she closed and locked the bathroom door. Mara walked to the sink, peering at her reflection in the mirror. The milkshake had dried in, leaving her with flakes of sugary-pink mess all over. She shucked off her coat, leaving it carefully on the floor. Then she took down her hair and used the taps to rinse as much of the gloop out of it as she could, before squeezing it dry and tying it back up. It looked a mess, she thought, but at least it wasn't pink.

She dried her hands on the towel hanging by the sink, pulled her dad's coat on again and opened the door.

At just the same moment, the front door of the flat opened and two adults walked in – a tall man with long grey hair that puffed around his pale face and in front of him a shorter lady wearing cornrows, carrying shopping bags in each hand. The man closed the front door behind him just as the lady opened her mouth to shout a greeting to her kids – but whatever she had been about to say died on her tongue as she caught sight of Mara, her hair dripping down the back of her neck, standing in the bathroom door.

She took a step back, knocking against her husband. "Oh my God, girl. What are you doing here?"

"I'm sorry—" Mara began, as Jan burst out of the kitchen.

"Mum," he said. "Dad. Sorry. This is my friend. Her name's Mara."

After a few moments of silence, broken only by the muffled *boom-boom-boom* from Will's game, Jan's dad stepped around his wife, putting a gentle hand on her arm to nudge her aside. He stood in front of Mara. "And you're a Denbor, unless I'm mistaken," he said, holding out a hand for Mara to shake. She couldn't help but notice how it trembled and then she shook it.

The Time Tider's Handbook, Introduction:
Guard your truths. Keep your secrets.
Tell no tales.

Chapter Sixteen

The noise in Jan's kitchen was overwhelming. Mara – her foot washed, slathered in antiseptic cream and freshly bandaged – sat huddled between Jan and Annelies, perched on a stool. Jan's dad was to her left at one end of the small dining table, his mum to her right on the other end and straight in front sat Will, who glowered at her every other minute. They were eating dinner, which Jan's mum, Helen, had cooked – lamb chops, mashed potatoes, buttered peas and carrots. Mara had never seen so much food in one place in her life. But despite the delicious meal, everything felt weird, and Mara closed herself up tight, afraid of saying or doing the wrong thing. She wondered whether, if things had been different, she and her mum and dad could have had a table to sit around and all the food they could eat too. *But instead, I got to eat off my lap in the back of a van...*

"Someone pass the salt, please," Jan's mum said, her voice barely heard over the clamour.

Will decided to take a break from glowering at Mara and instead he glowered at his father. "Dad, come *on*! I mean, *everyone* goes down the quays at the weekend. Ricko's parents have been letting him go for, like, six months!"

Jan's dad raised his eyebrows as he focused on scooping up a forkful of soft potato. Mara noticed he didn't have much on his plate – no meat and barely any vegetables. "I don't care what Ricko's parents let him do, Willem, you're not going anywhere near the quays – especially not at night."

A sheet of paper flashed in front of Mara's face as Annelies held it up. Mara blinked in surprise, leaning back a little. "Mum! Look at the drawing I made! It's of you, Mummy."

Helen smiled at her daughter, taking the drawing carefully between two fingers. "Oh, Annelies. That's wonderful, darling! I'll put it on the fridge after dinner."

Will banged his knife and fork against the table so suddenly that it made Mara jump. "This is stupid. I'm not eating in here any more. I'm going to my room."

"Fine." Jan's mum sighed as her eldest son grabbed up his plate and cutlery and stormed out of the kitchen. "Make sure to bring your things back and wash them when you've finished!" she called as he vanished down the hallway. "And don't leave them—" Her words were cut off by the *slam* of a door. "On the carpet again," she finished, looking round at the others with a wry grin.

"So. Mara." Jan's dad – *Vincent*, Mara tried to remind herself – looked at her, with one eyebrow raised. "I'm sorry for the noise."

"It's usually a bit quieter when it's just Dad and me," Mara said and Vincent smiled warmly.

"Speaking of which. How has your father been lately? Prior to what happened last night, I mean, of course," Vincent said, taking another forkful of potato. He ate slowly, swallowing carefully.

Mara tried to answer but found the words were stuck. "He's… I don't know. Working more. He seemed worried," she finally managed to say. A sudden feeling of dread, heavy and hard, filled her up and she put her cutlery down on her plate. "All he told me was to find Lenny and I tried to do that but…" Mara blinked. *Dad's fine*, she told herself severely. *He's fine!*

"Except Lenny's gone too," Jan said, looking up at his father. "Isn't he, Dad?"

Vincent frowned, looking thoughtful. "He seems to be, yes. There had been rumours that someone had been spotted near Lenny's tunnel shortly before he vanished, but I don't know if they're true. It's hard to tell."

Mara looked up at him. "Do you think he's all right?"

Vincent shrugged. "I have no idea. I'm more concerned with why the Tider didn't know one of his network had gone dark."

Mara looked at Jan. "What's 'gone dark'?"

"Disappeared," Jan answered with a shrug, before taking a large mouthful of potato and peas.

"Why does my dad have a network? A network of what?" Mara asked, turning to Vincent.

Vincent blinked, as though her question took him by surprise. "Well. We keep an eye on his Time Dumps," he said. "That's the basic answer."

"Time Dumps?" Mara pushed her plate away, all appetite gone.

"Where your dad stores the Time he harvests from the Warps," Jan said.

"I'm going to start the clearing up," Helen said, leaning over to pick up dishes and serving bowls. "Come on, Annelies. Give Mummy a hand."

The little girl hopped down from her chair and hurried to her mother's side, bringing her own plate and cutlery with her. "Good girl," Mara heard Helen say as they made their way to the sink, Annelies chatting happily as they worked.

"My wife doesn't like this sort of talk," Vincent said, looking away from Helen and focusing on Mara. "She prefers to stay out of it as much as she can."

Mara nodded. She looked back at Vincent. "So that tunnel *was* full of Time?"

"Didn't you know?" Jan said, looking puzzled.

Vincent leaned his elbows on the table and folded his arms. He gazed at Mara. "How much do you know about what your dad does?"

Mara took a deep breath. She reached down to feel around inside the pockets of her father's coat. A moment later she put her father's watch and his notebook carefully on to the table. "He had a handbook too, which explained some things," she said before swallowing hard. "But it's gone now."

Jan looked at the watch and the notebook, his eyes alight with curiosity. "What are these for?"

Mara picked up the watch and popped it open. She angled the face so that Jan and Vincent could see it. "He left these with me. I just know I've got to keep them safe. Dad always had these things somewhere close."

Vincent looked at Mara, his face soft with sympathy. "They're the tools of his trade, I guess you could say," he said. He smiled at her kindly before looking back at the objects on the table. He frowned slightly. "He didn't leave the hourglass?"

Mara shook her head. "Why?"

Vincent pushed out a sigh. "It's a dangerous thing

for someone else to get their hands on," he said quietly, looking back at Mara. "I expect that's why Gabriel felt it was safer with him."

"What does it do?" Mara's voice wobbled a bit as she spoke.

Vincent gave her a sober look. "It's … a record," he began. "Or a map, maybe." Mara watched as he searched for the right words to try to describe something that seemed impossible. "The sand inside it isn't *sand* as we'd know it. Instead, it's made up of one second from every Warp ever harvested. It's a link between the Tider and his Time and if the hourglass ever fell into the wrong hands, it could potentially give access to all the Time that's ever been saved. I think Tiders wear it to remind themselves of the gravity of their duty." He gave a soft chuckle. "Or perhaps it's simply to look good."

"What's the watch for?" Jan asked.

Vincent took in a deep breath. "Well, I don't know all the details. But I believe it's something like this. That watch tells the Tider where Time is running out of kilter. So it helps him to pinpoint where, or *when*, the dangerous Warps are, the ones that need urgent harvesting, and with the exception of the face that tells time in the present moment, it only begins to run whenever a Tider is approaching the location of a Warp. That's why Tiders usually live life on the move – they're always Warp-hunting. Though they don't normally avoid people as much as Gabriel does." He paused. "Being Tider is a big job. Nobody manages to harvest every Warp – they might manage to get most of the significant ones, with any luck, but nobody can be expected to get them all. So Warps exist from hundreds of years ago, say, because a Tider in the past couldn't, or didn't, harvest them.

"There's only one Tider at a time, as far as we know. Perhaps in the early years one was sufficient but it's certainly not enough nowadays. Could I see it again, please, Mara?" She tilted the watch. Vincent nodded, as if something he'd seen confirmed his thoughts. "Yep. It looks to me like the largest face, here, reads the exact time – year, month and day, down to the second – where a Warp has formed. That's the one that only runs in a Warp's presence. And then this face –" he pointed at the one Mara had thought was a stopwatch – "measures how much Time the Tider manages to harvest, which would be something he'd have to record meticulously in his notebook, along with where that Time is stored once harvested." He paused, frowning again as he pointed at the watch. "Who owns the hair?"

Mara turned the watch back towards herself, looking at the hair. "Some of it's mine," she answered. "The rest belongs – or belonged – to my mum."

"Ah," Vincent said, his eyes brightening as they widened. "The Stitch."

"What *is* that?" Mara said, looking at him. "Dad never explained it to me."

"It's – and this is going to be a very basic explanation, you understand, because I'm not fully sure I get it myself – it's a way of stepping through Time very quickly, a lot like a needle being pushed through a piece of cloth and then pulled out again. That's why it was given the name 'the Stitch'. You've heard of the phrase 'A stitch in time saves nine'?" Mara shook her head while Jan nodded. "Well. It's a saying. It might have come from the Tider's work – maybe a long-ago Time Tider decided to name the process after the rhyme. Who knows. In any case, the Stitch enables the Tider to momentarily step out of their own time and place and into another, for the sole purpose of harvesting a Warp. Warps come into being at the moment of a person's premature death, you see? Which means they can only be harvested from that exact moment. And so Tiders can dart into history and then back out again, like a needle. Normally, the process takes only a second or two."

Mara nodded, remembering how her father had vanished. "And they sort of ... disappear while they're doing it?"

Vincent nodded. "I believe so."

"But what's the hair about?" Jan said, wrinkling his nose in confusion.

"To use the Stitch safely, a Tider needs three things,"

Vincent began. "First, to keep their own timeline clear in their minds – the time they belong to and the time they want to go to. Usually, looking at the watch is enough to manage that, as it not only pinpoints the location they want to travel to, but it also allows them to see, down to the second, what time it is at the moment of departure. Then they need something that reminds them of a great pain or a great loss. Something that makes them wish they could step out of Time or go back to a previous time, before that pain had been made real. Something worth stepping out of the flow of Time for, basically." Vincent raised his eyes and his gaze met Mara's. "And the last thing, the final leg in the Tider's triangle, is a token of something they love so dearly that it's worth coming back for. Something that symbolizes their future or the Time they have yet to live through."

Mara turned the watch around again. "My hair," she whispered, looking at it. "So that's why Dad wanted it."

Vincent gave her a kind smile, but his eyes were sad. "He may be the Tider," he said. "But more than that, he's your father. And he loves you, Mara. Remember that."

The Time Tider's Handbook, Introduction:
Walk your own path.

Chapter Seventeen

A ringing car alarm was keeping Mara awake. She lay on the floor of Annelies's bedroom, which was next door to the one Jan shared with Will, staring at the ceiling. Annelies, her duvet tangled around her lower body, was muttering softly in her sleep.

Mara sighed quietly and tried to get comfortable but the sleeping bag was too tight and too hot – and there was just too much *noise*. Voices shouting and traffic on the road and cats yowling… How did *anyone* ever get used to this? Finally she gave up on trying to sleep and sat up instead. The sleeping bag pooled around her waist as she drew in her knees and hugged them, letting her head fall forwards against the shiny nylon fabric.

After a minute, she looked up. Annelies had a small

bedroom but it was pretty. Mara couldn't even imagine how it would feel to have your own space, a room with a door you could close, in which everything belonged to you. There were pictures stuck to the walls all around – drawings, mostly, done by Annelies herself – and interspersed with them were randomly placed luminous stars, which gave the room enough light for Mara to see Annelies's small chest of drawers in one corner, her bookshelf in another and the window, with its blackout curtains, in the middle.

The door to the hallway was open a crack and dim light shone through. Slowly – and as quietly as she could – Mara began to pull herself out of the sleeping bag. She was wearing an old nightshirt belonging to Jan's mum and she pulled it straight before opening the bedroom door and creeping out into the hallway. Jan's flat was in a T shape. To get to the bathroom, Mara had to walk down the hallway past Jan and Will's room, keeping the kitchen on her left, and then go right, towards the front door. The bathroom was on the left. If she walked straight across at the kitchen, instead, she'd end up in front of Helen and Vincent's bedroom door – and she wanted to avoid that.

She reached the bathroom at just the same moment that the kitchen door opened. Helen stepped through from the brightly lit room, a glass of wine in her hand – but she was looking back at Vincent, who was behind her. Mara ducked into the bathroom, hoping they hadn't seen her. She didn't quite close the door, peering out through the crack just long enough to see the couple disappearing into the living room, speaking to one another in low voices. Neither of them even glanced in the direction of the bathroom and Mara let out a silent breath as she locked the door.

She padded to the sink and pulled down the string that switched on the light above it. Her face was pallid in the strange glow. She stared at her reflection, examining the hollows beneath her eyes, the blotchy rash across her chin, the lankness of her hair.

"You need to get out of here," she whispered to herself. "Before you get stuck." She closed her eyes for a moment. *Or before you get put somewhere you can't unstick yourself from.* Mara opened her eyes again, wondering what Helen and Vincent were discussing. Was it her? Were they asking one another what on earth they were going to do with her? Mara tightened her lips. Nobody got to decide things like that. *Nobody but me.*

Quickly as she could, she made use of the loo before scrubbing her face with the dampened corner of one of the towels, which made her feel more awake. She clicked off the light and crept out of the room, hearing the low buzz of adult voices as she drew near the living room. Mara tiptoed close enough to listen.

"Gabriel's job," Helen scoffed, behind the door. Mara pressed herself against the wall, focusing on the words. "It's hardly a *job*, is it? I don't like anything to do with it. You know that, Vincent. And Jan's uncomfortable with it too. He tries not to be, for your sake, but the whole thing – the Tider, the concept of Warps, the lot of it – scares him. The less we have to do with it, the better."

Mara closed her eyes. She'd been right, but the thought didn't give her any comfort. *There's nothing else here for me.* She scurried past the living-room door and turned into the corridor that led to Annelies's bedroom. *Every minute I stay here is a minute I could be looking for Dad. I've got to get dressed,* she told herself, *and find a way out.*

The door to Jan's room was pulled open just as she passed it, and Jan stuck his head out. His curls were even messier than usual, and one of his eyes was stuck shut with sleep. "Hey!" he whispered hoarsely. "What are you up to?"

"Nothing," Mara muttered. "Go back to bed."

Jan opened both eyes and looked at Mara properly. "But what's wrong?" he said.

"Nothing!" Mara hissed. "Leave me alone!"

Jan recoiled. "All right. Sorry for asking." He retreated into his bedroom. Mara shook her head, squashing back her urge to call him back out, and inched into Annelies's bedroom. The little girl was sound asleep, one leg sticking out of her covers, and Mara bent to settle her warmly under her duvet again before standing and pulling off her borrowed nightshirt. Her clothes were folded on top of Annelies's chair – Mara was glad, again, that she'd convinced Helen not to put them in the wash overnight. She dressed, her urge to leave growing.

She closed Annelies's door behind her as she made her way back out into the corridor – but Jan was waiting.

"Right. Tell me what's happening," he said, keeping his voice low.

"Nothing you need to worry about," Mara answered, her gaze darting behind him, over his shoulder, in case either of his parents should emerge from the living room. If they did, she'd have no chance of reaching the front door.

Jan shook his head as he tried to think. "Where d'you think you're going at this time of night?"

"I don't care!" Mara replied, her whisper hoarse. "All I know is my dad's not here and staying here isn't helping me to find him."

"Come on," Jan said, but his eyes were worried. "Let's ask my dad for help in the morning."

"Let's not," Mara said, pushing past him. "I know when I'm not wanted. And anyway, I wouldn't want to *scare* you, or anything."

"Hey!" Jan said, hurt and embarrassment making his face contract.

Mara turned on him, putting her finger to her lips. She shook her head and Jan seemed to subside a little. Then she rounded the corner, walking slowly. The murmur of the TV seeped out through the living-room door, and she tried to relax. *Almost there...*

Jan appeared at her side as she reached the front door. Quickly, quietly, he undid the safety chain. Then he slipped a large key into the lock and it opened with a stiff-sounding *pop*.

Mara nodded her thanks and Jan stood aside to let her pass. She glanced back once as she stepped out but Jan didn't meet her gaze. He stared at the pattern of the carpet instead, and then closed the door silently in her face.

The Time Tider's Handbook, 1/B/iv: Never allow yourself to be distracted from the importance of your calling. Do not fall prey to sentiment, emotion or regret. Never misuse your office or your tools by allowing personal feeling to enter the Stitch alongside you...

Chapter Eighteen

Anger propelled Mara down the stairs of Jan's building and out through the open gate. It sped her feet down the alley that led to the road, keeping her going despite the fear that pulsed through her – the fear of cars swishing past, on their way to who knew where; the fear of people creeping out of shadows. It forced her on, her steps quickening as she walked down the pathway with the river on her left, back towards the bus stop where she'd been attacked with the milkshake earlier that day.

Had it only been a few hours ago? Tiredness and confusion were making her thoughts fuzzy. As well as that, she was carrying a deep ache, a strange feeling she wasn't sure she knew the name for. *Stupid*, she told herself. *Stupid! Trusting people is stupid.* She shook her head, shoving all thoughts of anyone except herself and her dad, and how they were going to be together again, out of her mind.

The bus stop had just come into sight on the far side of the road when she heard the steps behind her. The skin on Mara's neck tightened but she didn't look back. Instead, she quickened her own pace, trying not to break into a run. *Not yet.*

Beneath the footsteps was ragged breathing, drawing closer and closer. Whoever it was didn't seem to care that Mara could hear them approaching – they were making no attempt to hide. Which meant they were probably huge and strong and they thought Mara would put up no resistance… Mara's lips tightened as she pulled in a deep breath through her nose. *I'll show you how well my dad taught me to fight.* Inside her coat pockets Mara's hands folded into fists, and she pulled them out as she spun round, ready to land her first punch.

Her roar sputtered out as she blinked, confused, at the person who was following her. In her imagination, Mara had turned the pursuer into a huge shadow-creature, hulking as a bear, but in fact they were much smaller.

Much smaller and much less bear-like and a lot more Jan-shaped.

"Hold on," the figure gasped, trying to catch their breath. They staggered into the light of the street lamp that Mara had stopped beneath and bent forwards at the waist, resting their hands on their thighs. Mara recognized the curls right away.

"What are you *doing*?" she hissed. "You don't just *follow* someone at night, you idiot. I almost *decked* you. For, like, the second time in less than twenty-four hours."

Jan peered up at her. "You what?"

Mara turned around. "Go home," she muttered over her shoulder.

"No – wait. Hang on!"

Mara looked both ways briefly before crossing the road. *Past the school*, she told herself, trying to ignore the sound of Jan scrambling after her, *then up the hill, through that housing estate...* She felt sure she could find her way back to the derelict house where she'd parked the van but she tried not to think about what she was going to do once she got there. *Where am I going to go?*

"Mara!" Jan whispered loudly. "*Mara!*"

Mara whirled on the spot. "Why are you following me? Won't your *parents* be angry if they spot you missing? Wouldn't want to make Mummy and Daddy upset now, would we?"

Jan stopped a few metres from her, sucking his lower lip. "Don't be like that," he finally said.

"Like what?" Mara wrapped her arms tightly around herself. She looked away from him, blinking hard. "Listen. Your parents really *will* be upset when they see you've gone.

Right? I'm not being … whatever. I'm grateful and they're nice people and all. So go home. Thanks for coming after me, I guess? But I'm doing this alone." She turned again and started to walk away.

"Where are you even *going*?" Jan said, scurrying after her. Mara glanced to her left and saw that he'd fallen into step beside her, his large dark eyes nervous as they flicked around. "I mean, it's not like you've got anywhere to be. Is it?"

Mara buried her face in the collar of her coat. "None of your business," she muttered.

Jan kicked at a discarded can in the middle of the path and it clattered away into the darkness. Somewhere, a dog began to bark. "Let me help you, all right?" he said, walking a little closer to her. "Let me come with you."

"Sure," Mara said. "Because you're going to be loads of use."

They'd reached the taco shop Mara had stopped at earlier and she felt a momentary kick of triumph as she realized she'd found her way back. *Turn to the left up here and then it's a straight run*, she told herself. Already, she could see the lights of the huge bridge over the river. Beyond it was the road back to the van. The road home.

Her thoughts had been so busy that she hadn't noticed Jan taking something out of his pocket. Finally she noticed he had something in his hand – something he was awkwardly trying to show her.

"What's that?" she muttered, curiosity overcoming her. Jan mumbled something and Mara frowned. "What?"

"My dad's," Jan said, handing the object to her. It was cool to the touch, unfamiliar in Mara's hand. A phone, its face smooth and black. "He has all his contacts in it." He paused, licking his lips. "Some other members of the network, things like that. Maybe someone knows where Lenny's gone."

They paused beneath a street light and Mara looked at the phone. She'd barely ever touched one before and she had no idea how to use it. It was a small, shining rectangle of darkness, smooth and vacant and anonymous. She pressed a button on the side and the face lit up, displaying the time and date. Her eyes opened wide.

"Wow," she said, her hand trembling a little as she pushed it back towards Jan. "I mean, I don't want to break it. How did you even get it?"

Jan shrugged. "My dad keeps it in the pocket of his jacket," he said. "It was hanging on his chair in the kitchen. I hope he won't notice it's missing for a while." He looked away from Mara, down into the darkness. "Anyway. Look, let's keep moving."

He began to walk, but Mara pushed him back gently. "Jan, you can't come," she said, meeting his gaze. "I mean, I don't even know what I'm going to do. Where I'm going to go." She paused, taking a thoughtful breath. "You need to go home."

Jan's face hardened with determination. "I'm not afraid," he said, sticking out his jaw. "I'm not! And I want to help."

Mara sighed. "I know you're not afraid."

"And I have the phone, don't I? We can use it to find out where to go next. Get a message to your dad, maybe. Find out where he's gone, even! So you *do* need me."

Mara stared at Jan for a moment, trying to figure him out. "Jan, why do you even want to come? I mean, we're not friends. You don't know anything about me. I don't get it."

Jan tossed the phone lightly from one hand to another, avoiding Mara's eye. "It's just … my dad's talked about this stuff all my life. I used to be scared, maybe, but not any more. It sounds so cool, right? I *so* want to be a part of it. But he's never allowed me to. It's too *dangerous*, I'm too *young*, blah-blah-blah…" He trailed off. "But then it comes knocking on my door." He looked back at Mara. "I want to prove to him I can handle it. That I'm ready. And maybe he'll train me or whatever."

"*Train* you? In what? Babysitting Tiders?"

Jan cracked a grin, and Mara felt something inside her shift a little as she watched him, like an ice cube beginning to melt. "Well, yeah. Basically," Jan said, putting the phone in his pocket and straightening his shoulders.

Mara snorted in amusement, even as she felt a jolt of tiredness course through her. "I just need to find my van, get a good night's sleep and think about all this stuff in the morning."

"And there's the van thing too," Jan continued. "I have *got* to see this van."

Mara rolled her eyes. "Oh yes. It's *super* cool. Just wait until you check out the rooftop jacuzzi and the gold-plated taps in the bathroom."

Jan's mouth dropped open. "D'you really have all that stuff?"

Mara snorted. "*No*, idiot." She turned and began to walk away. "Come on, then. We're closer to the van now than we are to your house. When we get there, I'll give you a guided tour and then I'll take you home. If we're lucky, your parents won't even realize you've been gone and we can do without the police being called and all that stuff."

Jan scurried after her. "Hold up. You mean, you can actually *drive?*"

Mara looked sidelong at him. His face was alight with excitement and she couldn't help but grin back at him. "You'd be amazed at some of the stuff I can do," she said.

"This is going to be *excellent*," Jan said, his smile a mile wide, as they hurried on into the dark.

The Time Tider's Handbook, 1/B/v: There may be those who will seek to use your office for their own ends. You must beware of this and guard against it at all times...

Chapter Nineteen

Jan's mood brightened the further they walked. He swaggered along beside Mara, his hands thrust deep into his pockets, a delighted grin on his face.

"Imagine living in there," he said, as they passed the fancy housing estate. It was imposing in the darkness, the street lights dotting their way up the wide main avenue into its depths. The houses were like giants, with their eyes shut, slumbering quietly side by side. They each stood apart, surrounded by a neat patch of lawn and a paved driveway, separated from one another by ornate metal fences.

"I can't even get my head around living in a house, let alone ones like those."

Jan looked surprised for a minute and then his face settled into a thoughtful expression. "Have you *never* lived in a house, then?"

Mara shook her head. "If we did, I don't remember it."

Jan nodded. "I just thought maybe you were living in a van for *now*. Or that maybe you were waiting to get a new house or something like that."

Mara raised her eyebrows as she looked at him. "Nope. The van's home for Dad and me. I think it's always been that way."

Jan was silent for a minute. "I guess it's like my dad said. Time Tiders need to move around." He shrugged. "I just didn't think it had to be, like, a *permanent* thing."

"Dad enjoys the freedom. And never having to worry about things like who might be looking for us," Mara answered, thinking of her dad standing against the lights of the vehicle that had been pursuing them, his voice ragged as he told her to drive. "Not that it ended up helping," she continued in a lower tone.

Jan gave her a friendly elbow bump. "We'll find him," he said quietly. "Don't worry."

Mara raised her eyebrows at him as they stepped into the shadows beyond the reach of the street lights. "You mean, *I'll* find him. You're going home in a minute, remember?"

Jan sucked his teeth. "Sure, sure, whatever," he muttered. Mara smiled to herself at the resignation in his voice. He had everything – why would he leave it all behind to come with her?

They crunched over the gravel around the dark, derelict house, and then Jan grabbed Mara's arm. "Hold up a sec."

He pulled his dad's phone free and tapped the screen once or twice. Then a bright beam of white light burst from the back, throwing a wide, shining circle all around them. Mara blinked and looked away from it, her eyes dazzled by the sudden illumination.

"Torch function," Jan said.

"Impressive," Mara muttered, squinting.

"Follow me, then," Jan said, using the phone to light the way ahead. The sharp shadows thrown up against the trees by the torch made the branches look like they were moving, and Mara's heart lurched at the sight. She looked away, focusing on the back of Jan's head, and so when he stopped suddenly, she almost walked right into him.

"What's wrong?"

"Is that … it?" Jan said, holding the light high. Mara saw the white glow as it reflected in the dark back window of the van, the single window that remained. But instantly she saw something else. The other window pane – the one that had been broken – now gaped emptily into the night again. Her temporary fix, the blanket she'd tucked into place, had been torn down and was nowhere to be seen.

"This can't be happening," she whispered.

"What?" Jan turned to her, his face creased with confusion.

"Someone's been here," Mara said, the shock of it making her jaw hurt. She hurried around the side of the van, her feet *kssh-kssh-kssh*ing in the gravel as she went. The light bobbed around as Jan hurried after her, trying to hold the torch up so that Mara could see – but it was clear even without the torch that Mara was right.

The driver's door had been wrenched open and was sticking out, its window smashed with a brick that still lay beside the pedals. Mara held her breath as she approached, afraid of what she might see, but when she got close enough it all became painfully clear. Slashes had been made in the upholstery of the seats and some of the yellow-orange foam stuffing had been pulled out. The floor mats had been ripped up. The odds and ends box had been ransacked and the glove box was hanging open, attached only by one hinge. Mara looked down into their living quarters, which were lit up by the automatic bulb that came on when the driver's door was opened. Her blankets had been tossed around and so had her dad's. Her books were ripped to shreds, thrown all over the blankets, and her sketchbook had been stamped on and torn. The box containing her dad's glass apparatus, marked with his initials, was gone. The cupboard doors swung open – the lock had been cracked in half, and their crockery was all over the floor. The 'silverware drawer' had been tipped up and the box smashed. The table looked like someone had tried to yank it off the wall but it had held. The stool, however, had been reduced to splinters. Her dad's watchmaking equipment was strewn around the floor. And his pile of road maps had disappeared without a trace.

Mara felt Jan's hand on her arm, and realized she was crying. A huge sob burst out of her and she covered her mouth with her hand, trying to get her breathing back under control.

"It's all right," Jan said. "It's going to be OK."

Mara turned to him. "It's *not* going to be OK," she said. "I did *exactly* what my dad told me and just *look* at what's happened. There's no Lenny, your dad doesn't know where he's gone and now someone's *trashed* my *van*!" She kicked the nearest tyre, yelling in frustration.

"Does the engine still run?" Jan asked quietly. "If it can still go, that's good. Right?"

"And how far am I going to get with *two* busted windows and the seats all slashed to bits?" Mara wiped her cheeks, searing anger filling her up. "There's no way I can try to hide it anywhere. All I need is one busybody to ring the police and then the game's up."

She reached into the van and shoved her hand down beneath the driver's seat, which had been pushed right back. There was no sign of the bag. Mara's gaze fell once again on the small shelf above the table where her dad's maps had once been. *They took the maps and the glass tubes and the Keepers and the bag*, she thought, trying to get things clear inside her head. Suddenly, the contents of her pockets felt very heavy. *It's almost like they were looking for something...*

"It was the people who took my dad," she breathed, looking at Jan. His hand, still holding the phone with its circle of white light, trembled. "It wasn't just someone looking for money or food or whatever. The people who took my dad – they did this."

"How can you be sure?" Jan said. He glanced around, his eyes huge, before staring back at Mara. "Look – I'll call my dad. All right? I'll phone him and he can come and pick us up. He'll help. I know he will." He began tapping at the screen again, frowning at whatever he was scrolling through, before a realization dawned.

"What?" Mara said. Shock was setting in, making her shiver. Her thoughts were skidding around inside her head, clanking and clattering off one another. "What's wrong?"

"I'm trying to ring Dad's phone using Dad's phone. Like an *idiot*," Jan said. He sucked his teeth, shaking his head as he continued flicking the screen up and down. Mara caught a glimpse of names, a long list of them, zipping past Jan's fingers. "Mum keeps hers on silent in the evenings, once work's done. No point ringing her. I'll have to try phoning Will and getting him to tell Mum and Dad where we are. Which'll be *great*." Jan shook his head. Finally he settled on a name and touched it with one finger, and Mara watched as he put the phone against his ear. She could faintly hear the *brrr-brrr* of a ringtone, which seemed to ring and ring until Jan ended the call in frustration.

"Either he's not answering," Jan said, "or his is on silent too."

"Look, just get in," Mara said. "I'll try the engine. Hopefully we'll get back to your place and then we can find somewhere to stick the van." She sighed. *And then tomorrow I'll wake up and none of this will be any better. Dad will still be missing. The van will still be trashed. And I'll still have to find some way of making it all make sense.*

Jan turned off the torch and tucked his dad's phone into his pocket. Then he climbed into the van while Mara busied herself lifting up the brick and tossing it away into the trees. She climbed in herself and pulled the seat forwards before fishing out the key and fitting it into the ignition.

"Here goes," she muttered.

The great engine roared into life. Mara and Jan turned to look at one another, their eyes filled with relief. Mara looked back out through the windscreen as she flicked on the headlights. They flooded the area in front of the van with bright yellow light, showing the weed-tangled gravel, the back of the crumbling house – and the car, quietly parked facing the van, with two people sitting in it.

The Time Tider's Handbook, 1/C/i:
Guard also against your own vanity and
conceit; allow yourself to be content with
a small, unremembered and unremarkable life.
Do not seek glory. Do not seek fame.
Above all, do not seek wealth...

Chapter Twenty

"What the…" Jan began. "Who are *they*?" The people in the car sat motionless, their eyes covered with dark glasses. Mara couldn't tell if they were men or women or anything else about them.

"No idea," she muttered in reply, quickly putting the van into reverse gear. Just as she began to move, the flash of approaching headlights dazzled her from the rear-view mirrors. She stopped the van and muttered something under her breath that made Jan's head pivot. He looked over his shoulder just in time to see a large black van, much sleeker and newer looking than Mara's own, come rolling up behind them.

Mara looked from one mirror to the other, at a loss for what to do next. She looked out through the smashed pane beside her – all she could see were trees, thick with shadow, and beyond that, the unknown. Could they make a run for it? What would they meet when the trees thinned out – more empty land, or a wall they wouldn't be able to climb? Cold hard fear gripped her at the thought of leaving her van behind – her *home.* The thought of pushing open the door and abandoning everything she'd ever known… Was there room to swing the van round?

"We've got to move!" Jan cried, tearing Mara out of her thoughts.

But it was too late. Mara pressed the accelerator and pulled at the steering wheel, doing all she could to turn – but as her headlights fell against the tree trunks, someone stepped out in front of her. A person – a man – with his hands up, palms out. Mara braked so hard, she and Jan were thrown forwards in their seats.

She sat behind the steering wheel, panting fast, as though she'd run a race. Jan, beside her, was flicking through the lit-up screen of his dad's phone. Mara heard the *brr-brr, brr-brr* of the ringtone as he tried, one more time, to get through to Will.

"It's Van der Meer, state your business at the beep," came the tinny sound of Will's voicemail greeting. "Oh, for *God's* sake," muttered Jan, hanging up.

Mara looked around. The van was surrounded. Adults stood, some casually leaning on other vehicles, others with their legs wide and their arms folded, and there was no room for them to move. Not unless she was willing to accelerate over people, knocking them aside like bowling pins, and hope she could squeeze past the larger van – but before she could fully think through this plan, a voice cut through her thoughts.

"Come on now," the voice said – a woman's, warm and amused. "There's no escape, as I'm sure you can see. Step out of the van, please."

"Oh my God," Jan whispered, shoving the phone into his pocket.

Mara gripped the steering wheel even more tightly. "Where's my father?" she shouted, knowing her voice would carry through the broken window.

There was a pause before the reply came. "He's … safe."

"I want to see him!" Mara shouted.

"There's no need for that," said the man who was standing in front of Mara's van. He took a few steps towards it, removing his dark glasses as he came. Mara frowned hard as she stared out at him. There was something familiar about his face, his walk … something about the way his hair flopped over his forehead, just so… "Come on," the man said, smiling coldly. He tucked his glasses into a pocket. "Let's talk, me and you."

Mara stared at him. He wasn't as old as she'd initially thought – hardly even a grown-up. And there was something so recognizable about him, like he'd stepped out of a half-formed memory or a dream. "I don't want to talk to you," Mara said. "The only person I'll talk to is my dad."

The young man shrugged, as if she'd said something completely obvious. "We can take you to him."

Mara shook her head, irritated and disbelieving. "Who *are* you? How do you even know my dad?" Her breath hitched. "Are you a Clockwatcher?" This question was met with a rumble of chuckling laughter from some of the gathered adults.

The young man pushed open his long coat and shoved his hands deep into his jeans pockets. He wore a plain black shirt, plain black shoes – nothing eye-catching. And yet Mara couldn't take her eyes off him. He was like something that might pounce on you as soon as you stopped looking at it.

"Your dad's pretty famous. Didn't you know? Rather well thought of, in certain circles." The young man smiled at her coldly. "Less well thought of, naturally, in certain others. The question is not so much how I *know* him, but rather how I could possibly *avoid* it."

"You're lying," Mara said, trying to keep her voice from shaking.

The young man's smile faded until it was replaced by a stare as hard as steel. "Have you never wondered why you've lived most of your life on the edges of society, like

174

cockroaches scuttling from one corner to another? Did you never question why your father chose to raise you in the back of a van, refusing to allow you to go to school, never bringing you to the doctor, keeping you from all the little joys that any child should be allowed to have?" He took one step closer to the van and Mara gulped. Their gazes were locked.

"Have you ever been to a funfair, Mara?" the young man continued. His voice was low but Mara could hear him clearly. "Or to the beach? Have you ever tasted ice cream? I bet you've never been to a birthday party. Or even had a birthday party of your own. Never had presents or wrapping paper or ribbons."

"Stop," Mara whispered, through teeth clenched so hard she felt they might crack.

"Well." The young man blinked and looked away, breaking his stare, and Mara felt her body sagging. Her relief didn't last long. "Your father can be blamed for many things, but I'd never call him stupid. Everything he did had a reason. It's unfortunate that you've been raised this way, but your father had good cause to keep you – and himself – under the radar. I mean, living the way you do is a perfectly valid choice, isn't it? Life on the road, free as a breeze." He looked back at her, frowning slightly. "I wonder whether you've ever had a choice, Mara. Wouldn't you like to have a choice?"

"I'd like to choose not to have to listen to *you*. Just tell me where my dad is," Mara said and the young man chuckled. He looked away from her and gestured to the other adults.

"Get them out," he commanded, in a clipped tone.

Mara turned to Jan, eyes wide. "Lock your door!" she shouted – but it was too late. A man was already yanking the passenger door open and Jan swore as he was lifted out of his seat. "Jan!" Mara shouted, lunging after him – but someone reached in through the broken driver's door window and grabbed her legs before she could wriggle away.

"Not so fast," said the person who'd restrained her, and Mara looked back to see a man wearing a dark, close-fitting cap, his hands firmly clamped around her ankles. Mara tried to kick but the man simply took a firmer grip on a fistful of Mara's jeans. She twisted her body, bending at the waist as she reached for his clamped-down hands, slapping and scratching, but another adult appeared at the window – a woman, who pushed herself through the smashed pane to grasp Mara's coat. Together they hauled her out through the window, and before she knew it she had been flung on to the gravel beside her van. The man kept a tight hold of her collar while the woman pulled open the door of the van and switched off the engine. She yanked the keys out of the ignition and tossed them into the waiting hands of the familiar-looking young man who'd suddenly appeared before Mara.

She stared up at him as he crouched in front of her, his head cocked to one side, toying with the keys. Mara fought the urge to spit.

"I'm not really into all this…" he gestured around with the keys, "*drama*. Right? We don't really need to make this any more difficult than it's already been. Why don't you just come quietly and get this over with?"

"Did you t-take my father?" Mara asked, her teeth chattering with shock and rage.

"I'd say it was more like this – your father gave himself up." The man gave a tight, pitying smile. "He showed a bit more common sense than you."

Before Mara could answer, she heard Jan being pulled around the back of the van, his feet skidding through the gravel. As she turned towards the sound, Jan was chucked down beside her, landing in an awkward jumble. "You all right?" she whispered. He nodded but didn't look at her.

"Ah, the gang's all here," the young man said, tossing Mara's keys away into the darkness as he stood up. Mara heard them land in the gravel nearby. "Now, if we're ready? Let's move on out."

Mara and Jan were hauled to their feet and the young man turned to the large black van which had blocked Mara's exit. "Just tell me who you are!" Mara shouted at his back. "Tell me who you are and what you want with me and my dad!"

The young man stopped in his tracks for a moment before turning. He had a strange, scornful expression as he looked at Mara. "Maybe you should ask your friend there how well known your father is and about some of the things he does. You might find young Mr Van der Meer has some interesting answers for you." Beside Mara, Jan gasped. "And as for who I am?" the young man continued, his scorn deepening into a sneer. "Let's just say, there'll be plenty of time to talk about that where we're going."

Before Mara had a chance to reply she felt herself being dragged forwards, side by side with Jan, towards the anonymous black van.

The Time Tider's Handbook, 1/C/ii:
Never forget the true meaning of your calling.

Chapter Twenty-One

"This is not happening," Jan muttered for the twentieth time. "Seriously. It's not. Right? It couldn't be."

"You're not helping," Mara replied.

They were in the back of the black van. Unlike her own van, which had been turned into as cosy a home as could be managed, this van was purely a vehicle for fast and uncomfortable transportation. As Mara looked around at the bare metal walls and the immovable grid that stood between her and Jan and the front of the van, where the driver and two passengers sat in silence, she felt her hope shrivel up inside her like a dried pea. The adults hadn't responded to their shouts or pleas or even their threats. Jan and Mara had long since given up making any noise and now they sat muttering quietly to one another.

"You need to tell them this has got nothing to do with me!" Jan insisted. "Right? They need to take me home, right now. My dad's going to *lose* it."

"I will! But – that guy. He knew your name." Mara clenched her fingers around the metal grid, using it to steady herself as the van bumped over some rough ground. "He *knows* you, Jan."

"Yeah, well, I don't know him," Jan was quick to retort.

"Is he a Clockwatcher? I mean, does he know your parents? How else would he know about all this stuff?"

Jan looked away. "I don't know. It's all too weird. I mean, my parents aren't Clockwatchers – they're just part of the Tider's network. They're not the same thing. The Clockwatchers are more … *official*, I guess."

"What was he saying earlier, when he told me to ask you…" Mara paused, swallowing hard. "To ask you why my dad's so well known? My dad's not well known. He hardly ever even lets people see him in daylight. We don't know *anyone*." Mara rubbed at her chest, which had begun to ache, and Jan took in a deep breath. He sighed it back out.

"Your dad's power is pretty scary, yeah?" Jan began. "Nobody really likes the idea that there's this…" he waved his hand about as he thought, "*Chosen One,* or whatever, who gets to poke his way through Time. Even if it's to fix things, or to make stuff better for everyone, which is what he mostly does." Jan kept his eyes on Mara as he continued. "So there *are* people who know him. Or know of him, at least. And some of them are on his side – and some of them aren't."

"You're talking about the Clockwatchers now, right?" Mara said in a quiet voice.

Jan shrugged. "Yeah, them. And people like my dad, who aren't technically Clockwatchers but who sort of do the same thing – keep an eye on your dad and what he does. I mean, they're *friends*, and my dad always talked about yours as though he was the best guy on earth, you know what I'm saying? But at the same time, he kept his distance. He might have helped Lenny guard the Time your dad had stashed but he wasn't inviting himself round to your van for dinner, let's say."

Mara pressed her lips tight. "You said, he 'mostly does' good stuff. My dad." She paused, hardly able to form the words she had to say next. "But – what else does he do? The not-so-good stuff."

Jan scratched his chin, glancing around the inside of the van as he tried to think. "It's not like he did it very often," he finally began, staring at a point behind Mara's right ear. "Or that's what he always told Dad."

"OK," Mara whispered.

"But – sometimes, when he needed money and when my dad or someone else in the network couldn't afford to lend him any more … then, he'd have to do what he had to do." Jan met Mara's eye.

Mara trembled, waiting for him to continue.

"The Time your dad saves," Jan said. "It's not *his*, not technically. Right? It belongs to other people. Even if they're long dead, it doesn't matter. It's Time they should have had. Days, months, *years* sometimes, that a person should have lived through – except something happened to prevent it. But it's Time that can still be used. Time that hasn't been lived. Spare Time, if you like." Jan tried to grin, but the look of devastation in Mara's eyes made it fizzle out.

"Please, Jan," she whispered. "Just tell me."

Jan stared at the floor. "There are people who buy Time from your dad," he said. "People who are rich, I guess. I don't know how much he charges for it." He shook his head slightly, glancing up at Mara. "But whenever your dad needed money, he'd sell a bit of Time, whatever he had on hand, for whatever he could get. And whoever bought it could just … add it to their own life. So you can sort of imagine how much he could charge for that. People do whatever they have to when they're up against it."

Mara stared at the floor between her feet, speechless. *So that's what he was selling, that day in the field*, she told herself. *Nothing illegal, just like he said.* She thought of the cups of tea and cakes and the things they'd had to save up

184

for over the years, the clothes and shoes and necessities they couldn't get from charity. It all made sense. Her dad's furtive 'jobs'; the strange places they'd had to stop in order for him to 'meet a mate, won't be a minute'; the fact that, whenever her dad needed money for something, he was always able to get it. And he'd never explained how. She began to blink quickly again as her eyes filled with tears. *And he did it to take care of me.* "But it's wrong," she said, her voice a hoarse whisper. "It's wrong to sell Time that doesn't belong to him. It's not his to sell."

Jan nodded. "Exactly. So that's where the Clockwatchers and the network come in. We're there to sort of keep an eye on the Tider, to check he's not going off and selling huge chunks of Time – because apparently that would be a *very* bad thing for, like, the universe, and stuff – and to try to look after him enough so that he doesn't have to." He shrugged. "I guess we didn't always manage it too well."

"And everyone knows about this?"

"There are, maybe, fifty people in the whole country who know who your dad is. Most of them would know about this stuff. But fifty's not all that many, right?"

"Fifty people who know more about my own dad than I do," Mara whispered.

"Look, he *couldn't* tell you," Jan said, sitting forwards. "He wanted to keep you out of all this. He did his best." Quickly, Jan corrected himself. "I mean, he's doing his best. He's going to keep doing his best. OK?"

"How much Time has my dad saved?" Mara asked him. "How many stashes are there, like the one in the tunnel?"

Jan blinked, raising his eyebrows. "I've got no idea," he said. "I mean, the Time stashed in some of those places goes back years. It's not all your dad's, if you know what I mean. Tiders have been using the same Time Dumps forever."

Just then, the van they were travelling in made a sharp turn, throwing Jan off his seat and on to the floor at Mara's feet. She reached down to help him up and they met one another's eyes. Jan's fear was mirrored in Mara's face.

"Where are we?" Mara whispered, hauling Jan up on to the bare wooden bench beside her, where they huddled tight. There were no back windows in the van, just metal panels, and the only light came from a tiny bulb in the ceiling. Outside, it was still dark, but the children turned towards the front of the van. Looking through the gaps between the driver and the passengers, they could see the van's headlights shining against people, other vehicles – and the wide-open door of a huge warehouse, which seemed to be full of nothing but darkness.

The driver pulled the van to a halt and cut the engine. As the passengers opened their door and climbed out of the vehicle, the driver – the woman who'd first spoken to them, back at the derelict house – turned to face the children.

"I trust you enjoyed your chit-chat back there," she said. "But now it's time to talk business."

The Time Tider's Handbook, 1/B/iii:
Remember the daily practice of your skills.
Your tools will help you focus your abilities but
you must be capable of mastering the Stitch
with nothing but your will, if need be...

Chapter Twenty-Two

Mara and Jan were pulled out of the back of the van and marched towards the large warehouse. As they approached the huge dark doorway, someone already inside switched on the overhead lights. The bulbs were long and fluorescent, coming on row by row, popping and buzzing as they warmed up, and in the far corner one flickered irritatingly, on-off, on-off. Mara tried not to look at it.

"Finally!" The voice was one Mara had heard before. She snapped her head round to face it. The young man was striding in through the doorway to their left, and he ushered Mara and Jan forwards as though he were asking them in for tea. "Come on. It's much more comfortable inside." He tilted his head thoughtfully. "Well, *much* is a relative term, I suppose."

Mara opened her mouth to respond, but the person dragging her dug their fingers painfully into her armpit, which turned her words into a yelp. All she could do was allow herself to be brought deeper into the warehouse, following the young man, with Jan by her side.

Eventually they reached some sort of room – an office, Mara supposed, as soon as the young man clicked on the light. The bulb gave a softer glare than the lights outside and Mara could see there was a desk in one corner, with two moulded plastic chairs in front of it and a battered-looking swivel one behind. A machine topped with a large plastic drum stood in the other corner, a stack of paper cups on top. Beside this machine (a water fountain, as she soon worked out when one of the other adults began to fill cups and place them on the desk) was an easel with sheets of paper clipped to it and a collection of coloured markers in the tray beneath.

The young man settled himself in the swivel chair and gestured for Jan and Mara to be deposited into the plastic ones. As soon as Mara was seated, the woman who'd had a painful grip on her arm finally let go. Mara rubbed the sore spot, glaring up at her.

"We're all here," the young man said, looking between Mara and Jan with a cold grin. When he got no response, he began gesturing at the cups of water. "Go on, then. Drink up! I didn't blow the budget on this place only to have the hospitality go to waste."

Jan and Mara shared a glance, and Jan reached out for his cup. He took a sip, then a longer gulp. Mara left her cup where it sat and the young man gave her a sardonic look, as if to say *suit yourself*.

"You can't keep us here," Mara said, annoyed to hear the words stumble out of her mouth much more quietly than she'd intended.

The young man quirked an eyebrow. "Beg your pardon?"

"You can't keep us here," she said, in a louder, clearer voice. "So let us go. We haven't done anything to you. This is *criminal*. It's not right!"

The young man squinted at her. "I guess you take after your mother," he finally said. "Thea, wasn't it? Very sad, how all that turned out." He shook his head, pulling his lips tight against his teeth.

Mara's blood thundered in her ears. "How … how do you—"

"How do I know about your mum? Oh, common knowledge. To anyone with an interest in this business, at least." The young man sat back a little, keeping his eyes on Mara. "It's no big secret that your peace-and-justice-loving mother came a cropper, all those years back. And all because your dad couldn't control the situation."

Mara's teeth clenched. "Don't speak about her that

way," she said, the words tight.

"But it is true, isn't it?" The young man leaned forwards again, lasering in on Mara's eyes with his own. "Your mother's death. It was your father's fault."

"It was the Clockwatchers!" Mara shouted. "*They* killed Mum. And you're one of them!"

The man gave an infuriating laugh. "Oh, no," he said, shaking his head and settling back into his chair. "I'm not. I don't think they'd have much in common with me at all, actually."

Mara frowned, struggling to understand. "But – who are you, then? Why are you doing all this?"

He gave a thin smile. "I'm just a person with an interest in Time and who's spending it," he said. "I'd like to make sure the proceeds are flowing in the right direction, so to speak. They've been stuck in one place for far too long."

Mara blinked at him. "What are you trying to say? Are you saying my dad's *rich* or something? I live in the back of a *van*," she spat. "Which *you've* wrecked."

"Ah, yes! That brings us neatly back to the issue at hand," the young man said. "Your van. Which, as you point out, my people had to search, perhaps a little roughly." He spread his hands and shrugged as though in apology, then folded them neatly on top of the table. "We were looking for some things. A pocket watch. A notebook. I'm sure you know what I'm talking about. They weren't in your van, and your dear old dad wasn't able to produce them from his person when I asked him – and I used my *best* manners too." He raised one hand to casually scratch at his face. "So that means you've got them. Or if they're not on you, chances are you've hidden them somewhere. And –" he gave a terrible grin – "you might be persuaded to tell us where."

"But – what…" Mara began, her fists clenching. "Those things are Dad's! You've got no right to take them."

The door to the office opened behind Mara and Jan and they jumped in surprise. Mara turned just in time to see a woman enter the room, short and strong-looking, dressed in khaki trousers tucked into heavy boots, a long-sleeved shirt on top. Her hair was pulled into a tight bun. "Vik," she said, addressing the young man. "There's a problem."

"Hello, Mother," the young man – Vik – replied, his tone light. "Pleasure to see you. Great timing, as ever."

The woman's mouth twisted in irritation. "He's *gone*," she snapped. "Before we could wrestle the hourglass from him, he skedaddled. Typical of the man."

Vik's eyes widened in genuine surprise. "What? Gone where?" He pushed his chair back from the table and began to get up.

"Into the Stitch. Where else?" The woman's gaze flicked to Mara's face. "This is her, then?"

"Where's my dad?" Mara said, fear grabbing her throat.

"Are you talking about him?"

"The one and only," the woman sneered. "At the first sign of trouble, he vanishes. Don't you know that by now?"

"But…" *Gone? Into the Stitch? How?* Mara's thoughts roared. *He doesn't have any of his equipment! And where – or when – has he gone? Why on earth would he do that?*

"Search her," the woman snapped, clicking her fingers at the people standing in the corners of the room, the people who'd forced Mara and Jan into their seats. They sprang forwards, and in a blink one of them had a hold of Jan. They made short work of emptying his pockets, throwing his dad's phone on to the table. It skidded off, landing on the carpet with a *thump*.

"Wait! Hang on!" Mara shouted, but it was too late. Her arms were grabbed from behind and before she could kick out at anyone, the woman – Vik's mother – had ransacked her coat pockets. From one, she pulled out nothing more interesting than the tin box containing the photo of Mara's mother, which she opened and tossed across the table in one smooth movement.

Mara yelled in anger and fear as the woman's questing hand dug into her deep pocket. When she took her hand out, it was holding the notebook, still stuffed fat with banknotes. She tossed it to someone else and Mara watched as they caught it, her eyes overflowing with rage-filled tears. Then the woman rummaged in Mara's pocket once more and this time she found her prize. With a cry of triumph, she pulled forth the pocket watch.

"Time and tide may wait for none," she said, looking up at Mara before focusing on her son. Mara could hear his excited breathing in her ear as he listened to his mother's voice. "But they're going to start waiting for us. Yes, indeed, they are."

The Time Tider's Handbook, 1/C/iii:
Do not let yourself be separated from your task.
Remember what lies upon your shoulders
and do not fail...

Chapter Twenty-Three

"Can you please sit down?" Jan said mildly, as Mara marched past him for the twentieth time. She hadn't stopped pacing the room since they'd been locked into it, who knew how long before. There were no windows, just a bare light bulb hanging from the centre of the ceiling giving off a weak light. The only furniture was a four-drawer filing cabinet placed against one wall and a chair with a wonky leg, so Jan was sitting on the floor.

"No, I *can't* sit down," Mara snapped.

"Look, it's going to be OK. Right?" Jan said. "When my dad—"

Mara whirled on the spot to face him. "When your dad *what*? When he magically figures out where we are? When he comes stamping in here, demanding someone give him back his little boy?" She stopped, balling her hands into fists. "Look, nobody is coming for us. My dad's … *gone*. Your dad? Has no idea where we are. And they've taken the phone." She dropped to her haunches, a sudden thought bursting through. She looked at Jan, whose eyes were round with fear. "Maybe… Do you think they took Lenny? Whoever these guys are? Is that what happened to him? And if they know Lenny…" She left her thought unfinished.

Jan's mouth dropped open. "You mean … you mean, they might go after my family?"

Mara got to her knees beside him. "I'm sorry. OK? Listen, I'm sure your family's fine. Your parents must have noticed we were gone, right? So, as soon as they did that, they probably cleared out of the house. I'm sure they got somewhere safe."

"But – what if they didn't?" Jan's voice sounded hollow. "What if they just went to bed and my dad didn't check for his phone or my mum didn't peek in to see if we were all asleep, or—"

"How long has your dad been doing this stuff? I mean – helping my dad."

Jan shrugged. "I reckon he was a bit older than Will when he started."

Mara nodded. "Right. Well, then, he knows what's what. Doesn't he? Your parents aren't idiots, Jan. As soon as they spotted something was up, they'll have done whatever they needed to so that Will and Annelies were safe." She paused, pressing her lips tight. "But it means we've got to get out of here on our own."

Jan blinked and looked at her. "Get out of here?" he whispered. "How?"

Mara sucked hard on her cheeks as she thought, glancing around the room. "We don't have much to go on, eh," she said. Her eyes fell on the filing cabinet. Its handles were speckled brown with rust and one drawer was missing entirely but its corners looked dangerously sharp. "How heavy is that, d'you reckon?"

Jan blinked at her. "No idea," he said. "What are you thinking?"

Mara pushed up her sleeves, a determined look on her face. She walked towards the cabinet, sizing it up. It came up to her chest, the paint completely worn away around its edges. Carefully she braced her feet and grasped it, front and back, before gritting her teeth to push. The cabinet wobbled as it shifted forwards, heavy enough that Mara almost lost her grip on it. Jan stood up and rushed over to help. Together they managed to right the cabinet and when it was steady, Mara looked at Jan excitedly.

"OK. Stand here," she said, pointing at the floor in front of the cabinet. Jan turned on the spot cautiously, staring at the patch of floor.

"What am I supposed to do?"

"Lie down. Just sort of *flop* on to the floor, like you'd fallen there."

Jan gave her an incredulous stare. "What?"

Mara stabbed him through with a piercing, impatient look. "*Please*," she said. "Just get down on the floor. Jerk around a bit too, if you can."

Jan snorted. "Maybe I should froth at the mouth, for extra effect," he said. Awkwardly he dropped to the linoleum-covered floor and lay there.

Mara grinned. "Could you? That'd be fantastic." Then she hurried to the locked door. She glanced back at Jan. "Ready?" she mouthed.

Jan gave her a thumbs up. Mara turned back to the door and steadied herself before filling her lungs.

"*Help!*" she screamed, as loudly as she could. "Help, please! Help me!" She waited a moment or two but nothing happened. Then Mara tried again, even more loudly. "Help! Come *on*!" She banged on the door. "He's *dying*! You've got to help him. He needs a doctor!"

"Put a sock in it!" came a voice from the other side – a woman's voice.

"Please!" Mara called, straining her voice with what she hoped would sound like despair. "It's Jan – my friend! He's collapsed! He's *shaking*. He's having a seizure or something. Please, you've got to help him."

There was muttering from the far side of the door and Mara felt a stab of panic. *There's more than one of them*, she thought. *I didn't plan for more than one…* A faint jingling sound came through the keyhole and Mara heard the grind and click of the lock being undone. She stood back a little as the door was pushed open and then a woman made her way through. Someone else – a teenage boy Mara didn't recognize – hovered in the corridor behind her. "What on earth's all the fuss about?" said the woman, glancing around the small room.

Jan, in his corner, thrashed like a landed fish. He made a gurgling noise which sounded strange enough, Mara hoped, to convince even the most hard-boiled adult that he really was in distress. The woman sighed deeply and turned to her colleague. "Go and fetch the first-aid box," she told him. Then she glanced at Mara, her eyes suspicious and filled with warning. "Just in case."

The boy nodded and strode away as Mara and the woman walked across the room.

"Oh, thank you," Mara said, hovering at the woman's back. "He just – I don't know, *collapsed*, right there, and started kicking about. I don't know what's wrong."

The woman frowned and got down on one knee beside Jan's wriggling form. "Does he have any allergies?" she asked Mara, without looking up at her. "Do you know if he's diabetic?"

"I-I don't know," Mara answered. "I don't know him well enough to know any of that stuff."

Jan groaned piteously, making a sound that was halfway between a roar and a retch. The woman recoiled a bit, looking like she was afraid he might throw up on her. "Right, then," she muttered, putting her other knee to the floor beside Jan. As she busied herself taking his pulse and checking his temperature, using the flat of her palm against his forehead, Mara quietly got into position beside the filing cabinet. She glanced at the door, hoping the boy wouldn't come back too soon, and braced her legs. She knew she had to time it just right – give Jan long enough to get up and out of the way but give the woman no chance to dodge the heavy, falling cabinet. *She looks old,* Mara thought, her eyes sketching the woman's back. *Dad's age, at least. She won't be able to move fast.*

"Now," she muttered.

"What was that?" the woman said, distracted.

"Now!" Mara called, and Jan got the message. As the woman turned, realization dawning in her eyes, to see what Mara was up to, Jan bolted out from beneath her hands and rolled to his feet. Mara heaved with all her strength, and the filing cabinet toppled. It smacked the woman to the ground, flattening her beneath its weight. Mara grabbed the lopsided chair as they ran for the door.

They raced into the hallway, Mara holding the chair in

front of her like a battering ram – and they crashed right into the young man, who was returning with the first-aid kit and a roll of bandages. Mara shoved the chair at him, legs first, and the boy dropped the things he was holding, raising his arms to protect himself. He lost his footing and collided with the wall, while Mara and Jan hopped over him and continued running, desperately scanning ahead for any sign of the way out.

The Time Tider's Handbook, 1/C/iv:
Time chooses those who are equal to this burden. Do not doubt yourself. If you were called to the tools, you are fit to wield them...

Chapter
Twenty-Four

Mara and Jan stopped at a corner, their breaths ragged and their hearts hammering, trying to get their bearings.

"Anyone after us?" Jan said, and Mara glanced back the way they'd come.

"Doesn't look like it," she said, wondering how badly injured the woman was – and whether her colleague had stopped to help her or if he'd thought to raise the alarm first. "Not yet, anyway."

"We've got to keep moving." Then Jan's body stiffened, and he turned to look at Mara. "Over there," he said, indicating with a jerk of his head. "Look! There's that stupid office where they took our stuff."

Mara looked. Jan was right. Across a gap of perhaps six metres stood the doorway to the room they'd been dragged to when they'd arrived. The door was ajar, and through the slatted blinds on the window they could see no trace of anyone moving, nor any lights. To the left of the office door was a pile of old pallets. Past that was a door to a storeroom and then the back wall of the warehouse.

"That means the main door has to be to the right," Jan said, peering in that direction.

Mara followed his gaze. People milled around the warehouse entrance and van engines idled. "Oh, goodie."

"Come on," Jan whispered. "We can't stay here either. Someone will be along any minute."

Keeping low, they crept out across the gap, looking left and right before ducking into the shadows behind the pile of pallets. Silhouettes moved against the light in the wide warehouse doorway as people unloaded vans, stacking the cargo against the walls. The low rumble of the engines was barely audible from where they were hidden. "Crates," Mara whispered. She turned to Jan. "Like the ones Lenny had. In the tunnel."

Jan nodded grimly. "They're full of Keepers," he whispered back. "So, whoever these guys are, they've already started stealing the Time from your dad's hiding places." His eyes widened. "You were right. That's what's been happening to everyone. The members of the network – Lenny, and everyone else. I bet this crew's been nobbling them, or whatever, and stealing their stashes. No wonder everyone's been going dark and the network has started to collapse." He sagged a little. "I wish I could tell Dad."

Mara turned back to the door. Clouds of exhaust fumes hung in the air, illuminated by headlights. People barked orders or laughed or talked, standing in clumps of two or three, while others worked to unload the crates. She gulped to see weapons strapped to some of the adults – long guns and night-sticks and other things she couldn't even name. The longer she looked, the more she knew: *all this has to stop*.

"I can't let Vik do this," Mara said, her gaze hopping from crate to crate. She imagined the whole warehouse stacked floor to ceiling with Keepers full of Time and the thought made her shiver. *Is he going to sell it? All of it?* "All those lives. They're not his. They're not *anyone's* now, but that doesn't give him the right to make money from it. It's horrible to make *money* from other people's pain."

"Too right," Jan said quietly. Mara turned to look at him. He met her eyes for a moment before looking away.

"And I'll make my dad stop doing it too," Mara said. "I promise."

Jan looked back at her gratefully, with a quick half-smile. "That'll make my dad's job a lot easier."

Mara tried to think. "Where are we going to go when we get out of here?" She searched Jan's face as though looking for the answer but he seemed as confused and scared as she did.

"I wish I still had my dad's phone," Jan said, glancing

towards the office where it had been taken from him. Perhaps it was still in there – along with Mara's photo of her mother. She knew better than to hope her father's watch and notebook would be there too – she knew Vik would have taken those and kept them for himself. *I'll get them back*, she promised inside her head. *Don't you worry, Dad.*

"What would you do with your dad's phone?" Mara asked, frowning, as she peered out from behind the pallets, wondering how on earth they were going to get past all those people and out of the door.

"There's got to be *someone* in his contacts who could help us," Jan said.

"Who? Like, someone in the network?"

Jan licked his lips nervously. "I was thinking maybe someone else. Someone from the Clockwatchers."

Mara turned to him, hardly able to believe what she was hearing. "*What?* They *hate* my dad." She took in a deep breath, which somehow felt painful in her chest. "And my mum's … my mum's *dead* because of them."

"I know," Jan said, his eyes clouded. "But they're the only people I can think of who know what they're doing – and who might be able to help us." He swallowed. "They won't want to see the entire network collapse, either. Trust me. And this?" He glanced up at the doorway. "This would make them sick." He met Mara's eye. "If you're trying to stop it, they'll help you."

Mara looked back at the Keepers being unloaded. Her head felt like someone was squeezing it and her thoughts were crashing too quickly to be followed, but she knew they didn't have much time. She knew her dad had avoided the Clockwatchers at all costs – but her dad wasn't here now. *He's run away*, Mara thought bitterly. *Again.* "So it's just me," she whispered.

"What?" Jan whispered back.

She turned to him. "You need that phone," she said. "Right?"

Jan shrugged. "It might help."

Mara nodded. She took one last look around and then darted out of hiding, making for the office door.

"Mara!" Jan's whisper was more of a hiss but Mara ignored it. Keeping low, she ran to the door and dived through it, scanning the small room as quickly as she could. On the table was the tin containing her mother's photograph, its lid open, the image visible. Mara jumped to grab it, shoving the photo into her pocket as her gaze fell on the floor beside the table.

Mr Van der Meer's phone, quiet and black, still lay on the carpet. Whoever had thrown it there must have forgotten it.

Mara ducked to pick it up, her heart thundering. As she had expected, there was no sign of her father's notebook, or his watch – all that was left in the room now was the water fountain, the flip chart, the random furniture – and, Mara saw, a battered-looking rucksack chucked in one corner. Without thinking, she grabbed it too, shoving the phone inside and zipping the bag closed before making for the door again.

She skidded round the side of the pallets, falling into Jan's panicked grip. "I got it," she whispered. "I got the phone."

"So now what do we—" Jan began.

His words were cut off by the noise of an alarm, like a drill digging into their ears, and their panicked gazes met.

The Time Tider's Handbook, 1/B/v:
Question the motivations of those who would
seek to help you, and if you encounter those
who seem to know you, and who flatter you with
smiles, be even more carefully on your guard...

Chapter Twenty-Five

Mara's gaze fell on the door to the storeroom, which was a few metres away. "Come on," she whispered hoarsely. "In here!"

Jan was too scared to argue. They scurried towards the door and pushed it open, vanishing through it as quickly as they could, but as soon as they were inside Jan's fear bubbled over.

"We can't stay in *here*! Where are we going to hide? They'll find us!"

Mara looked around. All she could see were shelves filled with boxes, mops stacked in the corner, a pile of old, broken furniture – and, high up, a rectangular window. She had barely registered it was there before she'd made her decision.

"Come on. Up! We need to climb." She began to pull furniture into place, dragging a folding table which sagged in the middle into position beneath the window. Jan rushed to help, his teeth clenched with effort. Mara found a three-legged chair and placed it on top of the table, wedging it against the wall to keep it from giving way beneath their weight.

Then Mara looked up, trying to assess the gap between the top of the chair and the window. "Can you make that?" she whispered, glancing at Jan.

He licked his lips. "I can try."

Mara gave a decisive nod and climbed up on to the table, struggling for balance on the rickety surface. Breathing quickly and shallowly, she built up her nerve. Then she leaped for the chair. She'd barely landed before she'd jumped off it again, reaching for the windowsill high above. Her fingers wrapped around the handle of the window and she got one elbow on to the sill, digging the toes of her trainers into any foothold she could find in the rough concrete wall – and then she was up.

Mara fought with the handle of the window as, below her, Jan began to climb. It seemed like an age later, though it could hardly have been more than a few seconds, before she heard the *crack* of the stiff hinge beginning to move. Gratefully, she slung one leg out of the window before reaching down to help Jan. He was coming, though more slowly and awkwardly than Mara had, and as she looked back she saw him fighting to keep upright as he stood on the chair, flailing around for something to grab.

"Give me your hand!" she whispered. As she hauled him up, his kicking feet knocked against the chair. He'd barely made it to the window, straddling it like Mara was doing, before the whole structure collapsed – first the table folded in on itself with a groan, bringing the chair with it, and somehow the falling objects managed to knock over one of the free-standing metal shelving units, bringing it down with a *crash*.

On their perch high above, Mara and Jan stared at one another. Then, wordlessly, they took it in turns – Mara first – to swing their other leg out through the window before dropping into the weeds and undergrowth below. It was a long drop but neither of them hesitated.

Sounds of shouting burst out through the window. Mara and Jan realized their pursuers would very quickly work out exactly how they'd made their escape, and they began to run.

Mara raced, her long-legged strides putting her well ahead of Jan, towards the front of the warehouse. She scanned the road, which led away from the warehouse into nothing but darkness, and her resolve faltered as she struggled to decide what to do. Breathlessly, Jan followed, his head swivelling from side to side as he checked for pursuers, catching up with Mara as they reached the corner of the huge structure. She'd stopped there, crouched low, hidden behind a pile of crates.

"What are you *doing*?" he hissed into her ear. "You're running right back to where we came from!"

"Stop! I need to think," Mara snapped back.

She knew they didn't have long. Crates of Keepers were stacked all around them, and outside the open warehouse door was a parked van, its back doors wide. More crates were inside it. Beyond the arc of light thrown out by the warehouse, the night was dark. Mara squinted down the road, which still led away into the unknown. *But it has to beat staying here.*

"Hey," Jan whispered. He nudged Mara in the side, pointing towards a nearby crate with a half-busted lid. Inside they could see rows of small glass vessels, their lids gleaming in the light. "We should get some. Keepers, I mean. To show the Clockwatchers. You know, to sort of prove who you are. To prove what they're doing here."

Mara pulled off the backpack. "Good idea," she said. Quickly, Mara and Jan took three Keepers each, placing them carefully inside the bag. "What happens if they break?" Mara whispered, as the glass vessels *clink*ed gently together.

"Bad stuff, I guess," Jan replied. Then he reached into the backpack again to pull out his dad's phone. "Can you keep watch for a second? I want to take a few photos too. You know, extra proof." He shrugged. "It can't hurt."

Mara nodded, peering around the crate and into the warehouse. Everyone seemed to be gathered together at the centre of the room. She could see Vik shouting orders, his face red with irritation. Beside her, she heard the faint *click* of Jan's phone as he took photos of the crates and Keepers all around.

Jan glanced at Mara. She seemed completely distracted, her head turning this way and that as she assessed the best way forwards – so he took his chance. He reached into the broken-open crate and pulled out two more Keepers, but these two didn't go into the backpack. Instead, he shoved them into his trouser pocket, barely managing to get them hidden before Mara turned back round to face him, wide-eyed. Instantly, he knew what had spooked her. There were voices approaching – and fast.

"We've got to move," she said. Jan blinked the guilt out of his eyes as he nodded in response. He clutched the backpack to his front as they made a break for it, running into the darkness beyond the warehouse, trying to dodge the light – but as soon as they did, a voice rang out.

"There they are! I see them." Heavy, running footsteps closed in on them from behind, and Mara spared a glance over her shoulder. Some of Vik's people had been searching the scrubland beside the warehouse, but now they were on their trail. Jan yelped as someone near the front of the pursuing group raised a pistol. "Stop!" she shouted.

Mara grabbed Jan's collar and dragged him along, fear making her legs feel tangled up. Behind them, the van they'd seen with the open back doors roared into life. Its headlights threw a wider arc of brightness after them, making it harder for them to hide – and then the van started moving.

Mara's breath tore through her lungs as she ran. Jan's eyes bulged with terror. *We're not going to make it!* Mara thought, the words screaming through her brain – and then all she could hear was a terrible noise of smashing glass and something that sounded like a rush of wind. Mara stumbled, turning back towards the warehouse just in time to see what looked like a huge bubble forming in the air, growing massively large in the space of a heartbeat. Then the sphere seemed to burst, or at least vanish. For a moment, nothing happened, and then there was a silent explosion of energy that seemed to envelop everything in its wake – and it was growing larger with every second. Mara felt sick to her core, her heart throbbing painfully as she got to her feet again and pulled Jan to his, starting to run once more. She knew they had to get clear of this *thing*, out of its range, before it swallowed them too.

"What's happening?" Jan shouted.

"The crate of Keepers," Mara gasped in reply. "It fell

out the back of the van."

"No way," Jan said, turning over his shoulder to look back.

"Keep running!" Mara called. "It's a Warp. We've got to get out of its way."

After a few moments in which all they could hear were their own gasps, they finally stopped. Mara was so tired and out of breath that she could hardly see – but the Warp was holding steady, a strange distortion in the air all around the warehouse. Her senses buzzed, her teeth rattled in her head, and then she turned away. Jan was on his knees on the tarmac beside her, the rucksack still clutched to his front. Mara collapsed beside him, her stomach heaving – and then she threw up. Jan rubbed her back as they crouched side by side, their bodies trembling with exertion.

Mara wiped her mouth on her sleeve and looked at Jan. He met her eye.

"Come on," he whispered. "We have to keep moving."

The Time Tider's Handbook, 1/B/vi:
Remember, too, there may be those whose motives are pure, and from whose knowledge you may draw support. These people may not come in the guises you expect...

Chapter Twenty-Six

They picked themselves up again and started running, throwing glances back at the warehouse over their shoulders every few steps. The Warp appeared to be holding, and there was no pursuit – for now. Mara's legs began to ache and her chest felt raw. She slowed to a halt, out of breath.

"Hey – wait," she gasped, and Jan skidded to a stop a few steps in front of her. As he turned to make his way back, Mara straightened up and looked around. "Where are we?" She stared through a chain-link fence into the yard of yet another dark, locked-down warehouse. A security light popped on as she moved, and a sign instructed them to BEWARE OF THE DOG, but nothing stirred. It was so quiet, all she could hear was the faint hum of the intermittent lights overhead, their glow harsh and comfortless, and the sound of her own breaths. The pavements were narrow, the road pock-marked with potholes and puddles.

Jan folded his arms tight across his body and tucked his chin to his chest. "Like an industrial estate or whatever." He jerked his chin up for a second, looking around. "Down by the water somewhere, I'd guess." He glanced at Mara. "So what now?"

"Now we find the Clockwatchers," Mara said after a moment.

"You sure?" Jan's voice was quiet.

Mara nodded. She took a deep breath and released it slowly, but couldn't speak.

"Let's go back to my place," Jan said, after a thoughtful silence. "Just … to see if we can find any clues."

Mara looked at him. "But that's the first place Vik will look for us," She'd been leaning on the chain-link fence for support and now she pushed herself away from it and started to walk. Jan fell into step beside her, quietly sucking his teeth. "I get it," she continued. "I mean, if I were you, I'd want to do the same thing." She gave him a sidelong glance. "But now that you're with me, it's not safe for you to go back."

"Yeah," Jan muttered hoarsely.

"I'm sure they're OK," Mara said, the words heavy on her tongue. Both of them knew there was no way of knowing whether Jan's family were OK – or whether *they'd* be OK when the Warp ran out, and Vik and his gang got free. She turned to look over her shoulder, but there was nobody behind them. She was filled with regret at the Warp she'd had a hand in accidentally creating but she also hoped with all she had that it would contain, or at least delay, their pursuers for long enough to let them get clear.

They walked on in silence until, finally, they came to the front gates, which were locked with a chain. Jan held them apart as Mara squeezed through the gap and then she did the same for him from the other side. They came out on to a deserted road, lit by a few lonely looking street lights. Neither direction appeared to lead anywhere.

"I wish I had a map," Mara whispered, shivering a little in the cool, early morning air.

"Oh my God, I'm an idiot," Jan muttered, pulling the rucksack round and unzipping it. He shoved his hand in – carefully, so as not to disturb the glass Keepers inside – and pulled out his dad's phone.

Mara stared at it. "Actually, I don't think we should ring anyone, Jan," she said, her words coming out in a quick jumble. "Just in case word gets back to Vik about where we are or whatever."

Jan sucked his teeth again impatiently. "Not going to ring anyone, dope. But there's a map we can access. On the web." He glanced up. Mara followed his gaze, even though she had no idea what they were looking for. "Assuming we have signal out here, that is," Jan continued, pressing a button on the side of the phone. It woke up, the screen bright in the darkness, and they both looked down at it.

Jan pressed a button and the screen changed, opening up into something Mara recognized. Roads, train tracks, rivers, buildings, all from a bird's-eye view. Jan used his fingers to enlarge the image. "There's the river," he said, angling the phone so Mara could see. "Right?"

She leaned in. "Looks like it. How do you move this thing?"

With the fingers of his free hand, Jan scrolled the map around. Mara started in amazement. "Wow," she breathed, giving him an excited look before staring back at the map. "Go east," she said. "From the river."

Jan snorted. "East. I have no clue which way's east." He handed her the phone.

Mara stood with the phone in her hand for a moment or two, looking around. "Elevation over there," she muttered, glancing at a tree-covered hill on the far side of the road, which rose into the distance. "And the gradient dips in this direction." She looked down the road to their left, which curved around to the right down a slight hill. "Which means – we're probably here." She used her fingers to enlarge the image as she'd seen Jan doing and handed the phone back.

"Milltown Meadows Industrial Estate," Jan said. "It's

miles from my place."

"But at least now we know—" Mara began, before her words were interrupted by a soft *ping* from the phone. Jan stiffened in surprise, before looking up at her.

"Did you press anything on the map? Like a pin icon or a button or anything?"

Mara gaped at him. "I – what?" She shrugged. "No. I don't think so."

Jan stared at the phone again. "Someone's dropped a pin," he said, before looking up at Mara's confused eyes. "It means someone's shared a location with us. Or with this phone." Jan looked down at the phone again before reaching out to touch the screen with one trembling finger.

Mara watched as the map moved suddenly. The image whizzed past before settling again, and a red teardrop-shaped icon hovered slowly over a location that didn't look familiar to either of them.

"Derrinfield," Jan muttered. "Wherever that is."

Mara looked at the map. She could see a train line, a canal, the whirls of roundabouts, and a large-ish town, its streets like capillaries in a leaf.

"How did this happen?" Mara said. "I mean, you said someone shared this location. Who?"

Jan looked at her. Mara could see the confusion and worry in his eyes. "Will's phone," he said. "But the time-stamp on it is ages ago – like, a couple of hours after we left my place last night."

Mara frowned. "But why would Will do that?"

"That's just it though." Jan looked back at the screen. "It came from Will's *phone* but that doesn't mean it was Will who sent it. It could've been anyone."

Mara considered this. "Could it have been your dad?"

Jan blinked and then nodded. "It might have been his only way of telling us what to do," he said.

Mara looked back at the map again. The pin icon still hovered patiently. "But it could also be someone leading us into a trap, right? I mean, what's here?" she asked, knowing nobody had the answer. Jan used his fingers to zoom out. Mara saw Port Ross, and she calculated the distance between it and where the pin had been dropped. Whoever, or whatever, was in Derrinfield, they'd need to cross half the country to get there.

Jan shut the phone off and shoved it into the bag again. "Standing here talking isn't helping, that's all I know," he said, slinging the bag on to his shoulder as he started to walk. After a pace or two he turned back. Mara, frozen to the spot, was watching him. "What's the matter?" Jan asked.

"This is hopeless," Mara said. "We can't *walk* there. My van's busted, and I can hardly steal another one. How are we going to get there?"

Jan gave a sudden grin. "We're going to improvise."

226

The Time Tider's Handbook, 1/B/vi:
And above all, trust in Time to aid you.

Chapter
Twenty-Seven

As they walked, the sun rose over the river. Finally they reached the outskirts of Port Ross.

"Come on," Jan said, heading for a pedestrian crossing just up ahead. He scanned the road, but traffic was quiet as they hurried across.

"What's your plan?" Mara said.

"I don't suppose you've got any money?"

Mara blinked, remembering how it had felt to watch her father's notebook get taken from her back at the warehouse – and knowing there were banknotes folded up inside it. "No," she answered dully.

"Didn't think so," Jan said, digging a hand into his jeans pocket. He pulled out a card wallet with a bank logo on it. "Lucky, then, that I'm *loaded*." He paused, shrugging. "Well, not loaded. But anything's better than nothing, right?"

They stopped in front of a bank. Mara kept watch up and down the street as Jan put his card into the ATM. "I've only got a fifty euro limit," he explained, as he keyed a code into the machine. "But it should be enough to get us there." He threw Mara a glance. "I hope," he continued quietly.

Mara looked away as Jan stared at the ATM. She checked up and down the street, looking everywhere for signs of movement. It was still early enough that the wide pavements were mostly empty, but she felt an itch inside her to keep moving, to get out of sight.

"Are you nearly ready?" she asked Jan, at the same moment that he muttered something angrily under his breath. "What's wrong?" she asked.

"Stupid machine! It's eaten my card," Jan said, making a fist and bashing the ATM screen. Mara leaned around to read the words on it. *Card processing error*, it said. *Please contact your bank branch.*

"So what does that mean?"

"It means we're stuffed," Jan grouched, giving the machine one last thump. He turned away from it and began to stride up the street.

"Can't you get money from somewhere else?" Mara said, jogging after him. "Inside the bank, maybe? If we go in and explain, once it opens—"

"I'd need my parents with me," Jan interrupted bitterly. "They don't just, like, hand over cash to kids."

"But we have to get out of here," Mara said.

Jan stopped suddenly, stepping into the shelter of a shop front. He pulled his father's phone out of his pocket and quickly pressed a couple of buttons. Mara heard the *brrr-brrr* of a ringtone, and then Will's familiar voicemail greeting. Jan muttered, irritated, quickly selecting another number from the list of contacts in the phone. This time it was his mum's, but her phone went straight to voicemail without even ringing.

"I don't know who I can call," Jan said, blinking quickly as he scrolled through the contacts. "I don't know any of these people. I don't know if they'd help us or if they ... if they'd send us right back to Vik or whatever," he said. He looked Mara in the eye. "I don't know what to do."

Mara held her hand out and Jan passed her the phone. She'd watched him skim the contacts list often enough that she knew how to do it by now. With her thumb, she scrolled through the list of names.

LENNY, she finally saw. She met Jan's eye and he nodded. Taking a deep breath, she pressed the phone icon beside Lenny's name and the line began to ring. Surprised, they looked at one another, breaths held.

The line was picked up at the other end, but nobody spoke. All the children could hear was someone's soft breathing and the sound of weeping.

"H-hello?" Mara said, after a moment. "Could I please speak to Lenny?"

"He isn't here," came a woman's voice, rough with emotion. "How did you get this number?"

"I'm – er, I know the Tider?" Mara said. "And I was hoping—"

"All that stuff got him killed!" the woman shouted. "I never want to hear about the Time Tider again, as long as I live!"

"I'm sorry," Mara said, looking at Jan desperately. "But we really need help, and Lenny was my dad's friend."

The woman sniffed, gathering her voice to speak again. "I know nothing about this stuff, kid," she finally said. "You want help, you'd better go to the people who usually had Lenny's back. Timewatchers, Clockwatchers, something like that. And you'd better hope your luck is better than my Lenny's."

"Do you know if—" Mara began, but with a *click* the call disconnected. She handed the phone back to Jan.

"Lenny's dead?" Mara's voice was heavy.

Jan looked stricken. "He was a good guy," he managed to say.

Mara slumped against the wall and closed her eyes. Her head pounded with exhaustion. "Do you think we can trust the pin thing is from your dad?" She looked at Jan.

He shrugged.

"Doesn't look like we've got much of a choice." He twirled the phone in his hand as he spoke. "I mean, if the pin had been dropped by Vik or one of his crew, they wouldn't have needed to follow you to your van, right? They'd just have waited for us to spot the pin, and ambush us in Derrinfield. So, chances are, it *was* Dad. Or Will, doing what Dad asked him."

Mara nodded. "Then we've got to get there."

Jan chewed his lip thoughtfully for a minute, staring down at the phone screen. Then his face brightened. He exited the contacts list and began to scroll through his dad's apps. They meant nothing to Mara but finally Jan landed on one. "This might work," he said.

"What is it?" Jan turned the phone so Mara could see.

"It's a bus pass," Jan said. "Like a ticket on his phone. Dad sometimes goes to his hospital appointments on the bus if Mum's not there to drive him. So he's got this pre-paid pass. Maybe the bus will let us use it."

"His hospital appointments?" Mara asked.

Jan's face clouded again. "The phone's at forty-eight per cent," he said, darkening the screen again and shoving it into his pocket. "Come on. Let's go."

"Forty-eight per cent what?"

"Battery, of course," he replied, looking incredulous. "And I don't have a charger."

Mara shook her head. Only one thing Jan had said in the last few minutes had made sense. "Why does your dad need to go to hospital?" she asked, as they set off once again.

"I don't want to talk about it," Jan said, frowning.

"But I just wondered—"

"I *said*, I don't want to talk about it!" Jan turned to her and they stopped in their tracks as they stared at one another. "Jeez, Mara, take the hint, right? He's sick! Now leave it."

Jan strode off again. Mara hurried after him. "Sorry," she mumbled.

"Whatever. Let's just get to the bus station, OK? And hope Dad has enough credit on his app to pay for us both."

Fifteen minutes later they found themselves beneath the awning of a bus stop. The bus, bright in its red-and-white livery, rumbled patiently as passengers queued to board, and Mara huddled close to Jan as they joined the line.

Finally they climbed the steps of the Dublin-bound bus. Jan held out his dad's phone to the driver's console beside the steering wheel, and it gave a cheerful *bip*. Mara glanced at the ticket machine readout: *One adult fare, Single*. Jan threw Mara a relieved look as they clambered past the driver – but before they could walk down the aisle, the driver stuck one large arm out to block their path.

"How old are you pair?" the driver said.

Jan glanced at Mara. "Um. Fourteen. Both of us."

The driver raised his eyebrows. "Right."

"It's true!" Jan replied, giving Mara a nudge.

"Yes," she piped up. "Absolutely. Fourteen. That's me."

"I can't carry kids under thirteen unaccompanied," the driver told them, looking from Mara to Jan with a beady eye. "So youse had better be telling me the truth."

Jan cleared his throat. "We are."

The driver settled in his seat again. "Youse owe me money too," he remarked, looking at his ticket machine. "You've paid one adult fare, but there's two of youse."

"Oh, come *on*," Jan said.

"One adult fare is fifteen euro," said the driver. "Youse are eight euro each, which adds up to sixteen euro. Right?"

Jan muttered as he dug around in his jeans pocket. He brought forth a handful of random change, along with some bits of fluff, sweet wrappers and a paper straw. He counted through the coins, dropping them one by one on to the driver's tray, until the fare was paid.

"Go on," sighed the driver, dropping his arm.

"Yeah. Thanks," Jan muttered.

"And a pleasant journey to you too," the driver said.

They found seats, and as Mara settled in, Jan sorted through the remainder of his coins. "We might have enough to get the rest of the way," he said, shoving the money back into his pocket. "If we're lucky," he muttered, as the bus started to move.

The Time Tider's Handbook, 1/B/iii: Do not misunderstand your role. It is not to benefit those who already have more than enough, nor to disadvantage those with too little, and let none convince you otherwise...

Chapter Twenty-Eight

They passed the journey in silence. Mara, half-asleep, watched the countryside rolling past outside the windows, streaked through with rain that started to fall just as they left Port Ross. Jan picked quietly at the upholstery of the seat in front.

"I'm starving," he finally said, after they'd been travelling for well over an hour. Mara's own stomach gurgled in reply.

"Do you know how to get to Derrinfield from Dublin?" Mara said, turning to him.

Jan shrugged. "Nope."

"Let's have a look at the map again. Maybe it has bus routes marked on it or whatever." Mara shuffled forwards in her seat as Jan pulled out the phone.

"Forty-six per cent," he muttered. He brought up the

map and handed it to Mara.

She used her fingers to move the image around. "Looks as though there's a train? Or a tram, maybe. There's a stop about five hundred metres from this place your dad wants us to go to." She enlarged the map again, peering at the street name. "Grattan Terrace," she read. "Looks like it's a row of warehouses, or industrial units, or something. Not residential, anyway." She absorbed the map, feeling the route settle into her memory, and handed back the phone.

"I wish I could do that," Jan said, locking the screen and putting the phone away. "Just look at a map and sort of *know* where to go."

Mara shrugged. "I'm used to it, I suppose. Dad and me did it all the time."

Jan gave her a sympathetic look. "You worried about him?"

Mara nodded. "I can't stop wondering what happened. I mean, that woman back at the warehouse said he'd gone into the Stitch?" She kept her voice low. "But how could he have? He didn't have any of his … kit, or whatever. The watch, or the notebook, or anything like that."

Jan shrugged. "Either she was lying or it's possible to do it without all that stuff."

"I suppose. And why would she lie?" Mara let her gaze drop to the pattern on the seat in front. After a moment she pulled herself away from it to look back at Jan. "But another question is *Why did he do it?* Why couldn't he have stayed? I needed him – and he wasn't there. He never is." She blinked hard, staring out of the window.

"He's got a tough gig," Jan said kindly, after a minute. "A big job and nobody who can really help. Or fully understand. I'm sure he's doing his best, and whatever he does, I'm sure he has his reasons."

Mara nodded, turning back to her friend. "Yeah. Maybe. It's not much fun being his kid, though."

Jan smiled and gave her a shoulder nudge. "Hey. It's not much fun being a kid in my house, either. If Will's not knuckling my head or hiding my socks, then Annelies is screeching about her crayons being in the wrong order or keeping everyone up half the night. And Mum and Dad?" His smile faded a bit. "Things haven't been peachy there for a while, what with … what with Dad's illness and all."

Mara pulled her lips in tight for a moment as she looked at Jan. "I hope he'll be OK," she said.

"Yeah. Cheers," Jan replied, but his smile was sad.

Mara looked away for a few silent moments before turning back to him. "So, do you have any idea what's in Derrinfield?"

Jan shrugged. "Nope." His face fell into a worried frown. "I'm wondering why Dad didn't send a message or even try to phone us. I don't know why he just dropped this random pin and expected us to know what to do."

"Maybe that's all he had time for," Mara said.

His eyes met hers. "Do you mean … someone really came for them?"

Mara shrugged, one-shouldered. "You said your dad's been doing this a long time. Why did he get into it in the first place?"

"He met your dad at some rally or something and they became friends and it all went from there. Tiders always build a network, people to help, y'know? It takes years but it's sort of an ongoing process. You can't ask too many people, and you've got to choose the *right* people, who you can trust and who can sort of … fly under the radar. People who nobody pays any attention to." Jan paused, licking his lips as he tried to find the words to continue. "The Tider's supposed to work closely with the Clockwatchers. But mostly Tiders want their own people too, their own network of allies. And for whatever reason your dad and the Clockwatchers have major trouble seeing eye to eye. So he had even more reason to build a network. Folk who mightn't be as hard on him as the Clockwatchers, who wouldn't ask so many questions." He tried to grin, but it was short-lived. "So I guess my dad helps out because he thinks your dad's a good guy. He helps because he thinks your dad's job is hard and important and too much for one person to do alone. He wanted to look out for him as much as possible."

Mara nodded. "So your dad knows what he's doing," she said. She leaned in towards Jan, urging him to believe her. "When he found us gone, he knew just what to do. He knew that wherever I was, you were with me, and he knew enough to figure out that whatever we were doing, it had something to do with Dad. He probably decided to get your mum, Will and Annelies out of there before Vik tried to come after you – and maybe he's still coming. But he's done what he can to help us. He trusted you to be sharp enough to follow the map." She paused, swallowing hard, trying to believe the words she was saying. "It's all going to plan, OK? Just as your dad hoped it would."

Jan looked away. "*Nothing's* going to plan," he muttered. "Things haven't gone to plan since he got sick. *None* of this is what he wanted. It's not what any of us wanted." He turned to Mara, furious. "And there's no way he wouldn't have phoned to find out if I was OK or to tell me what to do. If he only had time to drop a pin, that means he – and my family – were taken. And they're in danger. And I don't know what to do or how to help them or…" Jan's words were lost as he pressed his fists against his eyes. Mara reached out awkwardly to try to comfort him but he jerked away from her. She let her hands fall into her lap.

"We've just got to try to get to Derrinfield," she said after a minute. "Whatever's there, your dad must have felt sure we'd be OK." She leaned in closer, whispering into

Jan's ear. "So you *are* doing something to help them," she said. "You're doing exactly what your dad wanted you to do."

Jan sat in a crunched-up ball, his face hidden. Finally he sat up, scrubbing at his cheeks with the ends of his sleeves. "Right," he said, his voice thick. "OK. It's going to be OK. Isn't it?" He turned to Mara and she nodded.

"Yeah," she whispered, hoping it was true.

"How much further is it?" Jan said, peering out of the window. They were in the city now, passing large houses and shopping centres and wide junctions, cars and trucks and other buses everywhere they looked. The pavements were filled with people, the leaves were thick on the trees. *All this normal, ordinary life,* Mara thought, *just going on, not even knowing about me or my dad or any of it.*

"Imagine," she whispered, running a finger down the inside of the window glass. "If my dad doesn't come back. If there's no Time Tider any more. Imagine what will happen to all these people."

Jan swallowed. "What ... what *will* happen?"

Mara shuddered as she thought about the words she'd read in the handbook, now mush at the bottom of Whiteharbour Bay. "If the Warps aren't gathered in, Time doesn't flow right," Mara said. "People disappear – like, the Warps swallow them up, I guess. And if things get really bad? Time just *stops*. People probably stop dying, which *sounds* good. But they stop being born too." She turned to him. "Imagine being in pain – but forever? If Time stopped while you were suffering, your pain would never end." She stared into Jan's wide-open eyes. "Something my dad had, like instructions he got when he became Tider, said that they are all that stand between humanity and its destruction."

Jan blinked. "I think I see now why my mum didn't want much to do with any of this stuff," he said.

Mara cracked a small grin. "Clever lady," she replied.

"I wish I'd stayed clear of it too," Jan continued, gazing past Mara and out through the window.

"Something I meant to ask you, actually," Mara said, making Jan's gaze flick back towards her. "Why were you there, down at the tunnel? Y'know, when I met you. If you knew Lenny and the crew were gone already, what were you doing?"

Jan's face froze for a moment. "I – er. Oh, you know. I sometimes go down there, just to get away from stuff at home. Nothing major."

Before Mara had time to ask him anything else, the bus driver's voice burst out of the speaker overhead. "We're here, folks," he announced. "Dublin city centre. Don't forget your bags and baggage!"

The Time Tider's Handbook, Introduction:
Be steadfast. Do not shrink from your duty.

Chapter
Twenty-Nine

Dublin bus station was ten times bigger than the one in Port Ross. There were at least twenty gates and over each was an LED screen showing the names of the towns the buses passed through. None of them was Derrinfield.

Jan asked a security guard in a high-vis jacket for directions to the tram stop. As they left the bus station, they passed a newsagent's; Mara pilfered two sad-looking apples from a fruit stand right by the entrance. She quickened her pace to catch up with Jan as he vanished through the bus station doors.

The tram stop was easy to find. A route map was fixed above the screen at the ticket machine and they quickly worked out which line they needed. Jan fed the last of his coins into the slot and the machine started to groan and hum as it printed their tickets. "It's twelve stops away," Mara said, studying the map as she took a large bite out of one of the apples. It tasted mealy and grim, but it was better than nothing. Jan looked surprised as she handed him the other apple but he took it without complaint.

"It won't take long," Jan assured her, as the sleek, silver-bodied tram pulled up to the stop. "These things are fast."

Mara watched the city whizz by. Some of the narrow, graffitied streets looked familiar, and she wondered if she'd ever been here with her father. Eventually the houses grew larger and the streets wider, and the tram zipped over a wide motorway bridge. Something in the flow of traffic caught Mara's eye. She blinked and sat up straight as she stared down at the roaring lanes beneath them.

"What?" Jan said.

"Vans," Mara replied. "Three of them, in convoy. Big black ones."

Jan leaned over to look too but the tram had already sped across the bridge. He turned to Mara. "Vans – like Vik's?" His voice was barely above a whisper.

"I mean, they're just vans, right?" Mara whispered back. "Could be anyone."

Jan gave a tight, worried nod. He sat back in his seat, picking nervously at his fingers as he looked out of the far-side window, the view outside whooshing by.

Mara tensed as their stop approached. They stood, and

together she and Jan made their way to the carriage doors, which opened with a *hss*. They followed the gush of people on to the platform and into Derrinfield. Mara stopped for a moment to get her bearings, orienting herself with the map inside her memory. Ahead of them was a roundabout with a large stone monument in the middle surrounded by huge tubs of flowers. To their left was a church set back from the road at the end of its yew-lined drive. To the right was a granite-fronted library, its windows bright, alongside several shops and a small police station. Mara swallowed hard. Too many places for black vans to be parked, for Vik to be hiding…

"C'mon," Jan said, pushing past her. "Let's move."

As she hurried after him, Mara tried to stay calm. There was no doubt in her mind that the vans they'd seen from the tram were Vik's. All she could do was hope that the pursuit was still far enough away to let them get to safety. *Safety*, she thought, her face twisting in disgust. *Dad would kill me if he knew I was doing this.* But she knew there was no other choice. The network her dad had so carefully built had failed – Vik had broken it and they couldn't trust what was left. So all that remained now was the Clockwatchers, the gatekeepers, the enemy, the reason her mother was dead. Mara swallowed hard as they crossed the road and she traced their way down side streets and alleys almost without thinking, the map bright in her head. The air grew quieter with every step.

Mara felt her skin prickle suddenly as they walked. She reached out to grab Jan's sleeve and pull him to a halt. "What?" he said, turning to her.

"I just … hold on," Mara muttered. "Something's wrong."

Jan looked around. "I don't see anything."

A flicker of movement in Mara's peripheral vision made her jump. She turned as a man, dressed in jeans and a jacket, came striding round a corner. When he saw the children, he stopped for a moment before picking up his stride again, as though nothing were amiss. After a few steps he turned to look at them. His gaze was hard.

"Run," Mara muttered, her grip on Jan's sleeve tightening. They tore back down the street they'd just come up and Mara yanked Jan to the left, where an unfamiliar alley lurked. She opened her senses, hoping to feel the crackle of a Warp, but there was nothing – at least, nothing big enough to give them shelter. She shook her head. *I can't do that, not any more*, she told herself. *I've got to get out of this on my own now.*

The alley led to a pub car park, which was mostly empty. Mara and Jan crouched, gasping for breath behind one of the few cars that was there, keeping watch in all directions. "He looked like an ordinary guy," Jan said, once he could speak. "But he was definitely one of Vik's."

Mara nodded. Her throat was dry from exertion. "And where there's one, there'll be more. We've got to get to the Clockwatchers without being spotted."

Jan fumbled the phone out of his pocket. He called up the map of Derrinfield and handed it to Mara. She scanned the town's layout, trying to work out as many possible routes as she could. There was nothing direct and nothing that didn't involve far too much exposure. *Unless we cut through...*

She pushed the phone back to Jan. "Right," she muttered, getting ready to move. "Follow me, OK?"

Jan nodded and then they were running, keeping low. They reached a gate at the car park's far end, which Mara scaled easily. She straddled the top, reaching down to help pull Jan up, and they dropped into a laneway behind some houses, filled with wheelie bins and rubbish. They picked their way down it, emerging into a wider street with cars and shops and people.

"Come on," Mara whispered, urging Jan forwards as they dashed across the road. An archway led to a shopping arcade and Mara kept hold of Jan as they tore through it, dodging shoppers and buggies and children.

"There's a woman, over there!" Jan gasped, and Mara saw her too, leaning against a wall nearby – her gaze was trained on them both and she was poised to follow. Mara dragged Jan into a bustling supermarket, aiming for the thickest crowd.

"Don't run," she gasped. "Just walk. Don't make a fuss."

Jan nodded, keeping his gaze steady as he followed her through the aisles. Mara's head moved constantly as she searched, and finally Jan felt her grab his hand as she took off, making straight for a huge pair of swinging double doors at the back of the shop marked *Staff Only*.

"What?" he hissed. "We can't go in here!"

"Just *trust* me!" Mara whispered back, as they burst their way through.

"Oi!" someone called, but Mara didn't waver as they ran through the supermarket's storeroom. High, deep shelves all around were packed with goods, while to the left stood several huge fridges. They dodged a slow-moving forklift and ran for the loading bay, through massive doors which were standing open. A lorry was beeping as it reversed right outside the door and Mara ignored the angry shouted warnings as they darted past it. They sprinted across another car park, much busier than the last one, and Mara heard Jan's breath tearing through his lungs along with the rattling of the Keepers in his backpack.

Mara leaped for the wall at the back of the car park and reached out to help Jan up. "We've got to walk along the top," she told him, her chest heaving. "Can you do that?"

Jan nodded uncertainly, and they got to their feet. Mara watched carefully as they went. This wall eventually ran around the side of the industrial units along Grattan Terrace, and if they could make it into the laneway behind the units, they should be safe…

"Mara!" Jan shouted. She stopped, turning to see three adults emerging from the supermarket's delivery-bay doors, looking around in confusion. One spoke into a walkie-talkie.

"Get down!" Mara hissed. They dropped flat on their bellies before pushing their lower bodies off the top of the wall and taking their weight on their arms while they let their legs dangle out of view. All Mara could hear was the noise of Jan's trainers scrambling for a foothold, and her own rapid breathing as she did the same, hoping she could keep her grip. Keeping her head as low as possible, she peered over the wall. She saw the irate supermarket employee emerge from the storeroom, red-faced with anger as he challenged Vik's cronies. Their raised voices carried across the car park as the employee insisted they get off his delivery bay, and while the adults argued, Mara looked back. She caught Jan's eye and they nodded. *Be ready.*

Their pursuers disappeared back inside and Mara and Jan wasted no time pulling themselves back up to the top of the wall and getting to their feet again. They ran, arms wide for balance, until Mara spotted a pile of cardboard boxes and rubbish bags heaped against the wall, right behind a warehouse. She reached back for Jan's hand. He pulled the rucksack around to his front and then they jumped, landing heavily amid the trash.

"Ow," Jan moaned, as they pushed their way out.

"Don't be a baby," Mara muttered, helping him stand.

"And you can both stop right there," came a voice. Mara whirled on the spot and Jan fell to his knees, his arm clutching the rucksack tight. They saw a woman, her face half covered by a scarf and her long black braids in a topknot. She held a pistol pointed right at them. A door was open behind her, with several more adults emerging through it.

Mara and Jan instantly held up their hands. "That backpack," the woman barked at one of her people, indicating towards Jan with the barrel of her gun. "Take it."

Jan looked around, but he barely had time to move before the nearest adult yanked the bag away. "Hey!" he shouted, as the man who'd taken it stepped back a little and pulled the top open. Mara licked her lips nervously as she watched him peer inside, and then he stiffened with surprise. He muttered something to the woman beside him, holding the bag to let her look in.

Straight away, she turned to face the woman with the gun.

"Boss," she said, reaching a hand into the bag. "You've got to see this."

The woman with the gun turned her head, irritated, keeping the weapon pointed at Mara and Jan – but her eyes bulged with shock when she saw a Keeper, full of swirling Time, being lifted out.

Her head snapped back round to Mara and Jan. She pulled down her scarf and looked more closely at the children. "Where did you get this?" she demanded. "Do you have any idea what it is?"

"We don't have to tell you anything!" Mara shouted back.

The woman put the gun into a hip holster and settled her jacket over it. She regarded Mara and Jan coolly, her head tilted slightly to one side.

"Who are you, anyway?" Mara said, lowering her hands.

"I might ask you the same question, young lady," the woman began.

"D-don't tell them anything, Mara," Jan said.

"Mara," the woman repeated, looking back at her. "Now that's interesting."

"Nice work," Mara said, throwing Jan an acid glare.

"Do you know where you are?" said the woman, folding her arms.

"Someone left us a map," Mara replied. "We hoped it would lead us somewhere safe." She paused, looking at Jan. "We were even hoping the person who left it for us might be here."

The woman's eyes flicked towards Jan, whose face was taut with hope. "I'm sorry," the woman said, and she sounded genuine. "But nobody has arrived here before you." Jan's expression crumpled and the woman looked back towards Mara.

"Please," Mara said. "Are we safe here?"

The woman unfolded her arms and held out her hand for Mara to shake. "That remains to be seen," she said. Her grip was firm and her skin was warm. "But for now, let me say I'm pleased to make your acquaintance. My name is Pearl and this is the Clockwatcher compound."

Mara nodded, swallowing hard against her fear. "Then I've been looking for you."

The Time Tider's Handbook, Introduction:
Be ever wary.

Chapter Thirty

Mara cradled a warm cup of soup in her hands, carefully watching Pearl over its rim. The woman sat in a nearby armchair, one leg draped across the armrest while the other beat an impatient tattoo on the floor. Jan quivered on the sofa to Mara's right, picking skin from the edges of his fingernails and trying not to look at the adults stationed in the shadows of the room.

"Anything else you need?" Pearl asked Mara, one eyebrow raised.

Mara shook her head. "No, thank you." She put the cup down on a nearby table.

Pearl swung her leg to the floor and leaned forwards, fixing Mara and Jan with a look. "In that case, let's talk."

Mara and Jan exchanged a glance and then Mara began

to speak. "I think you probably know who I am."

Pearl smiled. "Yes, little Tider. I know you. Or I should say, I know *of* you. Your father, on the occasions I've met him, often spoke of you."

Mara blinked. "Did he?"

Pearl chuckled, turning her focus to Jan. Her dark brown eyes narrowed slightly. "It's you I'm not so sure about."

"I'm Jan," he began. "Van der Meer. Vincent's son. And Helen's."

Pearl's expression cleared. "Ah, yes. Your father's in the network. Am I right?"

Jan nodded. "Yeah." He coughed. "I mean, yes. Ma'am."

Pearl gave a quiet snort of amusement. Then, "Did Vincent leave you the map?" she said, glancing between the children.

Mara nodded. "We don't know why he wanted us to come here," she said. "But we were looking for the Clockwatchers, anyway. We … sort of need your help."

Pearl sat back into her chair. Her amusement faded, leaving behind nothing but caution. "Is that so?"

"I don't know how all this works," Mara began, gesturing around with one hand. "I mean, my dad didn't teach me much. Nothing, really. I suppose he thought I didn't need to know." She pressed her lips together, clenching her hands into fists for a minute. "And then he went and *vanished*, and I don't know what to do."

Pearl looked interested. "He vanished?"

Mara looked up at her. "Into Time," she said. "To escape from … from a man called Vik. He's been stealing Time, raiding the Dumps, stockpiling it in a warehouse. He kidnapped us too. We got away but he's following us." She swallowed nervously. "He's coming – we barely got away."

Pearl regarded her calmly. "I have people all over," she said. "We'll see him before he gets close enough to do any damage." She tightened her lips. "And I'm used to dealing with his sort." Mara and Jan exchanged a nervous look.

"So he's the one who's been causing us all so much trouble, eh?" Pearl continued. "This Vik. Picking apart the network, targeting our people?"

Mara nodded, shrugging. "He wants to sell Time – I mean, in a *big* way. Like, much more than my dad ever did." The words were out of her mouth before she could stop them, and instantly Mara wished she could stuff them back in.

"It's all right, Mara," Pearl said kindly. "We're aware of your father's doings."

"Hey! It's not like he did it all the time," Mara said, heat building up inside her chest. "Only when we were desperate. What else was he supposed to do?"

"But that's where it begins," Pearl said, raising one hand

to quell Mara's words. "It always begins with 'just a little' or 'I only need some money to buy food', or, or, *or*. And next thing you know, we're all back where we started, with Tiders tearing holes in Time and Warps forming out of control and people – ordinary people – suffering, dying, going missing, running out of Time because a Tider has stolen it." She stopped, leaning forwards again, her brown eyes boring into Mara's own. "Do you know why the Clockwatchers were founded, Mara? I suspect nobody has ever told you."

Mara shook her head. "I want to know," she said.

Pearl frowned. "Ah, but do you?" she began. "I guess we'll see." Pearl ran her hand over her face and Mara suddenly noticed how tired she looked, but before she had time to think about it, the woman had begun to speak. "For centuries of human history, Time governed us and not the other way around. We woke when it grew light, we slept when it grew dark, we planted our crops when the sun was at a certain height in the sky and harvested them when the world around us told us the moment was right. And then came the bells and the clocks and the machines, rousing us while it was still dark, lighting our way to work throughout the night, making us eat not when we were hungry, but when a man-made thing, with its cogs and wheels and ticking hands, told us to. And Time began to separate from us – or rather, we began to separate from it."

She paused, and Mara waited for her to continue. "And this separation, this gap between the reality of Time and our clumsy human ways of measuring, chopping, labelling and giving a value to it, was like a whirlpool forming in a river, a stoppage in its natural flow."

"A Warp," Mara whispered.

Pearl gave a quick, approving nod. "Exactly so. The first Warps were the worst – whole villages disappearing into dust, people going missing and returning a day or a week later, having aged twenty or thirty years, or not coming back at all. Stories and legends were told about it in every culture, all over the world. Calendars had to be reset, wars were fought, which made everything worse…" Pearl sighed. "But Time provided the solution. Time appointed a Tider, someone with the ability to use the Stitch to walk between the Warps, someone who could mend Time's fabric or, if you like, clear the flow of Time's river to allow it to move properly." She gave Mara a strange look, one that was sad and resigned. "But, people being people, it didn't take long before they managed to abuse the power of their office."

"You said *Time* appointed a Tider," Jan said. Pearl flicked her gaze to him. "I don't get it. It's not … alive, is it? Time, I mean? How can it, like, *think*, and make decisions?"

Pearl thought for a moment. "It's not alive, in the sense that you or I are," she replied. "But it is *reliant* on life. Time requires an observer – something living – for it to exist. So before the first tiny wriggles of life in the universe, Time was a static, unchanging thing. But as soon as there were creatures being formed, living and dying in their turn, Time began to flow. Then, as more complex life began to be *aware* of the passing of Time, the connection between living things and the Time that flows around and through them grew stronger and stronger. Perhaps, over the aeons, Time has absorbed some of the aspects of a living creature. All I can say is: Time facilitates things that help it to work smoothly – like water, which always takes the easiest and quickest course from one point to another. Sometimes, this means people will find themselves doing certain things – going to a particular field and digging up strange objects that they've never seen before, yet somehow know how to use." She paused, gazing at Mara. "Or following a map they've been given in order to end up in a place they've never been, yet somehow know they've got to reach."

"Tell me the other bit," Mara said quietly. "The stuff about Time Tiders abusing their powers."

Pearl sighed. "That's a long and painful story."

"OK," Mara said. "But I think I need to hear it."

Pearl's eyes were steady as she gazed at Mara. "Imagine you're a queen," she began. "To whom money is no object. Imagine you have a son. Your heir. The most precious baby that has ever been born. You love him more than you can bear. And now imagine your baby has a disease that will take his life before he learns how to walk." She paused and Mara knew what was going to come next. "Now imagine a person comes to your palace in the dead of night, dressed in swirling robes, holding mysterious objects, *powerful* objects – a watch, an hourglass, a book – and tells you that he can give your son all the Time he needs to grow old and grey. Imagine how much you would pay for that."

"I'd pay anything," Mara whispered.

Pearl nodded. "And so it has been, over and over again. Tiders bear a huge responsibility. Their work is unsung, unseen, unknown and absolutely vital. Without them, Warps would form uncontrollably, whirlpools in the river of Time which suck everything down into the deep, never to return. But it's a lot to expect of a person, this task of harvesting the universe's most precious and valuable resource and then ... doing *nothing* with it." Pearl's lips tightened as she searched for her next words. "There has never been a Tider who has not succumbed, at some point. Your father is by no means the worst, but not even he is immune to temptation."

"How bad was the worst, then?" Jan said. Mara looked at him. His eyes were round as coins.

Pearl considered his question for a moment. "There will always be people willing to supply, if there are people willing to buy – particularly if the buyer will meet any price, and in these situations it is always the poor who are disadvantaged and the rich who benefit," she said. "Tiders have always surrounded themselves with those who want to help or be involved somehow in the business of saving and sharing Time – the network, essentially. Mostly, this is a good thing; it gives Tiders support that the Clockwatchers, sometimes, can't provide. But at other times, it has helped to elevate Tiders to the inner circles of powerful, rich people, people who willingly exploit whatever they can in order to get what they want. And in centuries past, there were people – *poor* people, desperate people – who would willingly offer their lives to be harvested by Tiders, in return for a cut of the profit, and Tiders who knew exactly what sort of person to target. The vulnerable, those with no better choice than to sacrifice something vital in exchange for their next meal."

Mara frowned. "But – I don't understand. Tiders only harvest from the moment a person dies, right? So how can the dead person take a cut of any money?"

Pearl looked at the floor as she replied. "Each of us is born – or so the theory goes – with a store of Time inside us. That store, our life, is slowly being used up with every breath we take. And if our Time store is empty when we die, then we pass on peacefully to whatever, if anything, comes next. But when we die with Time still left inside us? That's when problems arise." She looked up at Mara. "When Tiders have to harvest this unused Time, they use the Stitch to travel to the moment of death and then they scoop up the Time before the Warp starts to disrupt reality. But sometimes… Well. There were unscrupulous Tiders who weren't very particular or careful about when they began the process of harvesting a dying person's Time. Some of them harvested seconds or minutes or *hours* of a person's life, Time they should have had. And that led to further irregularities."

"Whoa," Jan said, holding out his hands. "You're talking about *killing* people. Ending their lives before they should have run out."

"Yes," Pearl answered. "I am. And I'm also talking about Tiders who learned to harvest from the living. Such Time fetched a particularly high price. It requires great skill to harvest it, of course, which accounts for some of its cost, and unfortunately there are buyers for whom the thought of using Time taken from a living person is so thrilling that it means money is no object." Pearl's face twisted in distaste. "Tiders charged accordingly."

"But what happened to the person?" Mara said, barely able to hear her own words through the rushing in her ears. "The person being harvested from?"

"If they allowed too much Time to be taken from them or if they were forced to give too much, they would die," Pearl replied, her eyes on Mara.

"Is there, like, a *limit* on how much Time you can take?

I mean, to add to your own life?" Jan asked.

"Theoretically? No," Pearl replied, turning to him. "But truthfully? We don't know. Endless Time is not the same as endless health. And you can still be killed." Pearl grimaced. "There *was* a Tider, once, who aimed to make himself immortal. The Clockwatchers of the time ... dealt with him. Severely, I'm afraid to say. The situation hasn't recurred, as of yet."

"Wow," Jan breathed. "So it could happen again?"

Pearl paused, looking back at Mara. "It's always a concern."

Mara dropped her gaze to her hands, lying in her lap. She thought about her father's hands – hardworking, kind, talented hands, hands which held hers, hands which drew lines on maps and rested on the steering wheel of their van – and then she imagined those same hands doing some of the things Pearl had just described. Her insides felt like they were being stirred about by a huge, sharp-edged blade and she was afraid that if she sat for a second longer on this sofa, she would throw up.

She scrambled to her feet and pushed her way out through the door, and when she began to run she didn't think she'd ever stop.

The Time Tider's Handbook, Introduction:
Do not fear the truth.

Chapter Thirty-One

"Mara," came Pearl's breathless voice in her ear. Mara felt the woman's arms wrapping around her, slowing her. "Please. I know this is hard." Pearl paused to gasp in a breath. "But it's not hopeless."

Mara pushed Pearl's arms away, slapping at her hands. She whirled to face the woman, her eyes filled with tears, and Pearl's face was soft with sympathy. "Leave me alone!" Mara sobbed. Her voice echoed strangely around the large, empty space they were standing in. Behind them was a concrete slope which led, Mara assumed, up to street level; where they were standing now looked like a large underground car park. Lights buzzed overhead, their sound grating, setting Mara's teeth on edge.

"So much has been done in the past, Mara," Pearl said,

dropping her arms to her sides and taking a step back. "Our founder was a person whose brother gave too much of his Time, his *living* Time, to the Tider of his day, and we aim to stop things like that from happening again. Our original twelve members passed their duty to their descendants, and sometimes we recruit the best people we can, if we need to, and we've – *mostly* – been on good terms with Tiders going back centuries now. We were never your father's enemy, Mara." Pearl paused. "Our job is as vital as his. We don't have the power to harvest and we can't use the Stitch, but our task is to supply the Keepers, to help guard the harvested Time and keep it safe and accounted for." She gazed steadily at Mara. "And that's why I wanted to show you something we've been working on."

Mara hiccupped back a sob, staring at Pearl. "What?" she whispered.

Pearl dropped to one knee, looking slightly up at Mara as she continued speaking. "A place where we can store harvested Time safely," she said. "A place to keep the Time secure, which won't be accessible by any one person on their own. A centralized location instead of having hundreds of ill-secured places where Time has been dumped. In the past, using the Keepers and relying on an army of volunteers to guard them, the responsibility handed down from one generation to the next was the best that could be managed. But we can do better now."

Mara wiped her cheeks. They were raw from her tears and the roughness of her hands. "What is it?"

Pearl gave her a quick smile. "We're calling it a Timelock," she said. "It's basically an underground bunker made of reinforced concrete. We've been working for years to get it going – gathering money, getting official permission, all the usual business." She rolled her eyes. "We had to make up some excuse about it being a storage facility for waste products. They'd think we were off our rockers otherwise." She smiled again and this time Mara returned it, a wobbly, short-lived grin. "But it's the lock that's the best part. It's biometric – you know what that means?"

Mara shook her head and Pearl continued. "It means that the lock needs a scan of someone's eye or their fingerprint – and only a handful of trustworthy people can open it. There's a physical key too, but four people will always have to be present before the lock can be opened. The idea is, of course, that it's never going to be opened. It's there to store and that's all. There should be no reason to ever remove any of the Time stored inside it." Her face clouded over with worry. "But, naturally enough, we need the Tider to be on board with us to make it work."

Mara focused hard on Pearl. "I need to ask you something first."

Pearl blinked in surprise, sitting back a little. "Sure. Anything."

Mara steadied herself before she spoke. "Did you know my mum?"

Pearl's mouth opened. "I – er. Well, not personally. But I knew of her. Why do you ask?"

"Because … wasn't she … didn't she *die* here?" Mara blinked hard.

Pearl's eyes shone with sympathy. "Not here, no. In a place like this one, maybe. I know she … lost her life during a disagreement between the Clockwatchers and your dad. It was an accident, Mara. Someone had a gun and tempers frayed, and your mum – she was in the wrong place at the wrong time. I know your father blamed himself for the fact she was even there at all." Pearl looked away, as though the words she wanted to say next were somewhere hidden in this vast, empty place. "We'd called a meeting to ask your dad to do something like I'm asking you now," she continued, her voice low. "One of our members had designed something he called the Time Bomb, a device he said would actually *destroy* harvested Time. Your father wasn't convinced it would be safe. He said, with good reason, that while destroying harvested Time was *possible*, if there was so much as a stray second, a second that had been taken from a person's life instead of their unused Time, and if that ended up being detonated, it might set off a chain reaction which would cascade through Time and space itself. Some of us agreed with him, others didn't. Anyway, he wasn't happy with the idea of Time being stored either, and put beyond anyone's use, even his own."

Mara sniffed. "Why?"

"I guess he felt his authority – or maybe his credibility or trustworthiness – was being undermined or dismissed," Pearl began, looking back at Mara. "But I reckon, mostly, he was scared he'd never be able to sell Time again. He needed to feel like he had something he could support his family with and he felt like we were asking him to give that up, but we weren't." She gazed kindly at Mara. "Your dad's made things very tough for himself by wanting to do things without us. His job is hard enough. I really wish he hadn't made it harder. And it's clear, over the past few years, that he hasn't been coping. He's leaving work undone; he hasn't been travelling to gather Warps abroad. Things are getting dangerously out of balance. And whatever's been going on, we just want to help."

"He's been running from you all my life," Mara said. "He told me there were people after us. Every minute of every day. He meant you. So how can I trust you if he couldn't?"

Pearl paused. "Remember that story I told you? About the queen and her baby son?" Mara nodded and Pearl continued. "Well, now imagine that when the robed, mysterious figure arrives in her palace to offer her the Time her baby needs, that the Time has been stolen from *you*. So somewhere else, maybe hundreds or thousands of years in the future or in the past, your life – *your* life, Mara, which should be yours and yours only – was stolen, in order to allow someone else to live instead. Does that seem right?"

Mara shook her head. "But my dad doesn't do that," she mumbled.

Pearl sighed again, reaching out to hold Mara's arms. Her touch was gentle and warm. "It's all part of the same picture, sweetie. Your dad sells Time that has never been lived through – fine. Is there any real harm in it? Maybe not – but it's still wrong." Pearl paused, trying to find the right words to continue. "The world has changed so much since Tiders first came into being," she finally began. "The job was always too great for one person, but now? It's impossible. Things need to change. The Clockwatchers want to help. We're all on the same side, Mara."

Mara thought for a long minute, letting her eyes slide closed. Her mind filled up with the Warp that had formed when she'd made her escape from Vik. *All that Time belonged to real people*, she told herself. *They all lost their lives before they should have – and nobody has the right to make money from their pain.* She opened her eyes to Pearl's patient face. "I just need to ask one more thing. What happened to them? The people who … killed my mum. Are they … are they still Clockwatchers?"

Pearl's lips tightened and her eyes darkened, like she

was reliving a bad memory. "I wasn't a senior Clockwatcher then," she began. "But I know the person who smuggled in the gun was expelled right away and turned over to the authorities. An investigation was carried out into how the situation was allowed to happen. A few months later there were several more expulsions, and we all received training on de-escalating those sorts of scenarios. We refresh that training every year." She met Mara's eye. "I deeply regret what happened to your mum. It shouldn't have happened and I'm sorry. But you won't have to deal with the people involved. I promise."

Mara's insides boiled with indecision. Pearl seemed sincere but her father's fear was at the top of her mind, impossible to ignore. She thought about how terrified he must have been after her mother's death – and how broken with grief. She understood why he blamed the Clockwatchers for all of it. *No wonder he was on the run,* she thought, a dart of sympathy flaring in her chest. *But I've got to do things differently now.* "I want to help," she finally said.

Pearl's face relaxed. "That's great news." She settled again, looking serious. "And while we're on this subject, I need a favour."

"If it's about what was in Jan's bag—" Mara began.

Pearl hooted out a laugh. "No flies on you, little girl!" Her brown eyes danced with amusement and Mara couldn't help but grin. "That's exactly what I wanted to ask." Pearl's expression sobered as she continued. "We've only had a few seconds, here and there, to test our Timelock. We actually bought a little Time from your dad a while back – he didn't know he was selling to us, of course, and we couldn't afford much. We're also in the process of emptying the few Time Dumps we know of around here but we haven't finished yet. It would've been great if you'd had your dad's notebook, so that we could have found the locations of all the Dumps … but there's nothing we can do about that, is there?" Pearl gave Mara a kind look. "So to have so many Keepers arrive on our doorstep? It's a huge opportunity for us. I mean, *probably*, the Timelock will work fine. But I was hoping…" She let her words trail off.

"You want to use the Time to test your … thing," Mara said. "Yes. Let's do it."

Pearl held up her palm and Mara gave her a high five. Then Pearl pushed herself up on to her feet again, gesturing to their right. Mara looked – all she could see was a dark passageway. "It's this way. I've had some of my crew drop the Keepers down for us already."

"I'll get Jan first," Mara said and Pearl nodded. Mara jogged back towards the room. Jan was standing in the doorway, looking like he'd wanted to follow her but had become stuck on the threshold. "Hey," Mara said as she drew near. "We've got to do something for Pearl."

"I don't like any of this," Jan muttered.

"Your dad sent us here," she reminded him. "So he must trust Pearl. Can you try to trust her too? She needs us."

Jan looked at Mara. "Why aren't they here?" he whispered. "My family. I thought they'd be here."

"I bet they're coming," Mara said.

Jan looked away, nodding, as though trying to convince himself to believe her. When he looked back, his eyes were clear, dry and filled with purpose. "Right," he said. "Let's do this." He moved, instinctively putting his hand over his pocket. The Keepers were still there, safe and unbroken.

"Everything OK?" Mara said, glancing curiously at him.

Jan shook himself back to his senses and gave her a quick, reassuring smile. "Everything's fine," he said, following her out of the room.

The Time Tider's Handbook, 1/B/xi: The Time you will save must be treated with as much respect as those from whom it has been stolen. Your role is to lay the Time to rest, to guard it with your life, and to ensure its safe-keeping...

Chapter
Thirty-Two

Pearl led Mara and Jan down the corridor towards an ordinary door, which opened into an ordinary-looking room where two Clockwatchers were sitting in front of a bank of computer screens. Each screen, Mara saw, was connected to a camera. From this room, the Clockwatchers could see the street outside, the yard at the back (including the rubbish heap she and Jan had jumped into) and any vehicles approaching, as well as every inch of their underground compound.

"No wonder you knew we'd arrived," Mara said, looking up at Pearl. She gave Mara a quick smile, then looked back at her colleagues. She cleared her throat gently.

One of the Clockwatchers turned round. When he saw Pearl, he jerked to attention. "Commander Sangare," he said in a loud voice, while nudging the other Clockwatcher. She spun in her chair and both she and the young man got to their feet.

"Ichika," Pearl said to the young woman, who nodded in acknowledgment of her name. "Harry. This is Mara Denbor and her friend Jan Van der Meer."

The younger Clockwatchers grinned at them. "Good to meet you," said Ichika.

"I'm going to demonstrate the Timelock to our guests. All right?" Pearl said, her tone brisk.

"Of course, Commander Sangare," said Harry. His hand went to his belt, where a security fob was hanging. It looked like a small red circle made of plastic. Pearl pulled a similar fob out of her own pocket and together, the two Clockwatchers walked to the right, where a more secure-looking door was set into the wall. There was a sensor on either side, set widely apart, so that there always had to be two people operating the door at the same time.

"Three, two, one," Pearl counted down, and then she and Harry lifted their security fobs to the sensors. With a tiny *beep,* the large metal door unlocked, its bolts retracting with a muffled *thump.* Pearl nodded her thanks to Harry as she pulled open the door and the younger Clockwatcher resumed his seat in front of the cameras. "Come on, you two," Pearl said, holding open the heavy door as she ushered Mara and Jan through.

"So, *Commander* Sangare, huh," Jan said, as soon as the door *thunk*ed shut behind them.

"Someone's got to be in charge around here. It might as well be the one with the brains," Pearl replied, looking amused.

"Is this it?" Mara said. They were standing in a room, its walls grey and featureless and smooth: a concrete box. It was lit by spotlights in the ceiling which activated as soon as they stepped inside. Against the back wall, someone had placed the rucksack. All that was in the room besides it was an iron panel in the wall, which didn't look like a door but had a spinning lock in the centre anyway. Beneath the spinning lock was a plastic box, its sides thick, which protruded from the metal panel. Its top was open, allowing for something fairly small – a Keeper, Mara realized – to be placed inside it. She wondered what would happen when Pearl did exactly that and figured she would find out soon enough.

"This is it," Pearl answered in a reverent-sounding voice.

"Where's the biometric bit?" Mara asked, looking around. Her eye fell on a dark screen in the wall, two metres or more to her left. It was like a computer set to sleep mode, only a little smaller, at adult head-height. Instinctively, she turned to the other wall – a similar panel was set into it. When Mara turned to look at the back of the room, she already knew what she'd see – a third grey screen, this one set lower to the ground, waiting for its moment to ping into life. Pearl watched Mara put the answer to her own question together inside her head. "Those screens are the biometric lock. Right?"

Pearl nodded. "Exactly. If this Timelock were ever to be opened, three people – and not just any people, but senior Clockwatchers, myself included – would have to be present at each of those locks at the same moment for the security measures to override. A fourth would need to then physically open the seal, here." She rested a hand on the spinning lock as she looked at Jan. "As I've already explained to Mara, of course we never expect to *have* to open the Lock. It's here to store Time, not to release it."

Jan nodded. "How does it work?"

"You've heard of black holes?"

Jan and Mara blinked in confusion as they stared at Pearl. "Sort of," Jan finally replied.

"Well, the Timelock is similar, in some ways," Pearl continued. "It uses electromagnetic resonators to create something *like* a black hole, a phenomenon that attracts everything in its locality towards it, allowing nothing to escape – light, Time, whatever – but of course it's much smaller than a *real* black hole. We worked for years to create one that actually does what we hoped it would and now – thanks to you both – we get a chance to test it out."

"It's not, like, going to explode or anything, is it?" Jan

said. "And destroy the space-time continuum, or whatever?"

Pearl's mouth tightened as she tried not to grin. "We hope not," she said.

"Cool, cool, OK," said Jan, shoving his hands into his pockets.

"Now," Pearl said. Mara could hear the excitement in her voice. She turned to Mara. "Would you like to do the honours?" Pearl stepped back and gestured at the rucksack, and Mara gave her an uncertain look. "Just choose a Keeper and put it in the box. The Timelock will do the rest."

Mara looked towards the rucksack. She crouched in front of it, balancing carefully as she slid her hand inside. Her fingers reached a Keeper and she pulled it out. "Here goes nothing," she whispered, staring at the swirling nebula of Time behind the glass. She remembered the moment she'd seen a full Keeper like this one in her father's hands, that day in the field. *A Warp full of Time – full of lives – that had ended in so much sadness*, Mara thought. *So much pain…*

"Don't look at it for too long," Pearl warned. The sound of her voice knocked Mara out of her spiralling thoughts. "It can get sort of … hypnotic."

Mara nodded, doing her best to focus, but as soon as she looked back at the Keeper her brain writhed and pulsed inside her head again, just like the Time trapped behind the glass. It ached to be free, Mara knew. It wanted to be loose, to be released, to *live*…

"Mara," came Pearl's voice, calm and commanding. "Put the Keeper in the Timelock, please."

Mara snapped to attention, feeling dizzy. The Keeper in her hand was warm, like something alive. Quickly, before she could rethink what she was doing, she placed it into the waiting glass box. As soon as the Keeper was in place the box began to retract, sinking into the wall, and a piece of the Timelock's mechanism clicked into place over the mouth of the Keeper like a clamp.

Then, in the next breath, the swirling twist of trapped Time was gone, sucked into the Timelock. Inside the box, Mara could see the Keeper glowing red, like the glass had been super-heated for a split second, and then it was all over.

"Argh!" Jan shouted, clutching at his leg. "*Help!*"

Mara whirled towards him. "Jan! What's wrong?"

Jan's breath was coming through his teeth in a pained hiss. On his left leg the fabric of his trousers was smoking, melting away, right where his pocket was – or had been. As Jan jiggled his leg to try to get his skin away from the sudden heat, Mara heard the clinking sound of glass vessels clashing – and then she looked again, more closely.

Jan's pocket disintegrated completely, the material falling to the floor in blackened, twisted lumps. His fingers, blistered with heat, were still trying hard to keep the pocket's contents from falling out, but it was no use. Finally he had to let go.

Two Keepers dropped to the floor, tinkling as they landed. Their glass still held a faint red glow, which began to vanish as Mara looked at them. Thoughts raced through Mara's head too quickly to grasp as she struggled to understand what she was seeing.

"I'm sorry!" Jan said, fear and pain making his voice sharp. "I'm sorry!"

Pearl pulled a glove out of her back pocket and picked up one of the Keepers. She held it up to her face, her brown eyes glowing as she stared at the small glass jar, its spindle empty but still slowly rotating. Then, quickly, she examined the seal on top – it appeared to be undamaged. "But there's nothing inside," she whispered, staring at the Timelock. Her eyes were wide, and her mouth slack with something that could have been surprise – or fear.

The Time Tider's Handbook, 1/C/v:
Do not think that Time is yours to toy with or
mould to your own desires. You are a guardian
of that which is most precious but it does not –
and can never – belong to you...

Chapter Thirty-Three

"Ow," Jan mumbled, as Mara wrapped a bandage around his thumb with a lot more force than the job required. "Could you not?"

Mara swallowed her temper and resumed, trying to take a little more care. "I'm so angry with you, it's amazing I haven't shoved your *head* into the Timelock. See how you like that."

Jan sucked his teeth quietly. "Look, I said I was sorry."

Mara tied off the bandage and glared at him. "Just … why? Tell me what *for*. You'd better have a good reason for this or I'm handing you over to Vik myself." She began to shove the medical supplies back into the first-aid kit. "And after *everything* you said about my dad. I mean, come on! Were you hoping to get a good price for it somewhere?"

Jan's eyes flashed. "Hey!" he snapped. "I wasn't going to *sell* it, all right? So you can get that out of your head right now."

"Well, what *were* you going to do? Give it away? Use it yourself? Just tell me!"

Jan said nothing for a minute. "It's my dad," he finally said, his voice cracking as he spoke. He met Mara's eye. "He's not just sick, Mara. He's dying."

Things began to click together in Mara's head. *Jan didn't want to throw away his life to come with me, just for fun,* she thought. *He's had this planned all along.* "You did it for him," she whispered.

Jan nodded miserably. "That day we met, down at Lenny's place. I wasn't there just for head space, or whatever. I was there because Dad had just been to see his doctors and they'd had nothing but bad news, and I couldn't think about anything else. Like, literally. My brain felt like it was going to burst. And then I realized – the answer could be right in front of me." He paused, giving a humourless laugh. "Right under my nose. I knew Lenny was gone, and that his tunnel had been cleared out. But I thought, maybe … maybe there's one Keeper left. Maybe, beneath the muck, somewhere hidden in a corner, I might find what I was looking for."

"More Time for your dad," Mara said. "I get it."

Jan looked at her sympathetically. "Yeah," he said. "I

know you do." He looked down at his hands. "But maybe it's like Pearl said," he continued. "Maybe my dad's Time is just running out. It's not that he's being taken early. It's just … this is all the Time he gets."

"You don't know that," Mara said.

Jan nodded, looking towards the back of the room as he tried to settle his emotions. "So what now?" he whispered. "I've said I'm sorry, and I mean it. But I get it if you can't trust me, or whatever. I'll just go and sit in a corner and—"

"Oh, give it a rest," Mara sighed. She bumped Jan's shoulder and they shared a grin. "Pearl doesn't want you under her feet, right? So shut it. You're stuck with me."

"I think I'd rather risk the wrath of the commander," Jan muttered.

"Yeah. Well, think of this as your punishment," Mara said, zipping up the first-aid kit.

"I can't believe I snuck into a Time Dump and found the Tider's actual kid already there," Jan said. "It's a bit like – I dunno. Like breaking into a bank vault to find the cops inside it, waiting for you."

Mara raised her eyebrows at him. "I'm not the cops," she said. "But I do agree with Pearl, which is almost the same." She sighed, rubbing at her face for a moment as she gathered her thoughts. "All this Time has to be put somewhere safe – somewhere Vik can't get it. Somewhere it's safe from anyone who might want to steal it, no matter what their reason is. And I have to find my dad, somehow. I need him to agree to all this. But I don't know where he's gone – or *when* he's gone…" Her voice trailed off.

"At least we've got some help from people who have a clue what they're doing," Jan said, at precisely the same moment that a Clockwatcher – a man with a bright blue turban, a neat black beard and a face filled with panic – burst into the room.

"Commander Sangare?" the man said, blinking when he saw two children where his boss was supposed to be. "I – er. Do you know where the commander is?"

Mara closed her mouth. "She's … somewhere… I mean, no?"

The man muttered something under his breath and hurried out. Mara and Jan glanced at one another, eyebrows high and questioning.

"C'mon," Jan said with a shrug.

They followed the man, carefully closing Pearl's office door behind them. There was a meeting room a little way down the corridor, its vertical slatted blinds open just enough for them to see a group of animated adults inside. The man in the turban joined them, taking a seat at the back of the room. Jan and Mara quickened their steps. As they drew near, they could hear raised voices.

"Don't you understand what this means?" Pearl was saying, as she paced back and forth at the top of the room.

"The Keepers were *outside the Timelock* and yet the machine emptied them. So the only logical explanation is the Lock is faulty – there's a leak, maybe, allowing the forcefield to escape. We can't operate it until we get it fixed!"

"But, Commander, the mechanisms are regularly checked and inspected, and we've never—"

Pearl stopped in her tracks and turned on the speaker, a woman with a tight braid down her back. She spoke in a low voice. "I saw what I saw, Shereen," she said, and the woman with the braid fell silent.

Mara and Jan stepped into the room. None of the adults noticed them.

Pearl looked around at her team and began to speak again, leaning heavily on her desk. "Right. So, unless anyone has any further objections, what we need to do is—"

"Pearl?" Mara said, in as brave a voice as she could muster. "I have an idea." Every adult head in the room whirled round towards her and Mara wavered beneath the weight of all those eyes.

Pearl straightened up, folding her arms, looking curiously at Mara. "Well," she said. "Let's hear it."

Mara swallowed, glancing at Jan. He nodded at her to continue and she tried to get her thoughts straight. She closed her eyes, trying to block out everything in the room, and focus on the chain of ideas that was forming inside her mind. The answer was in there, she was sure. She remembered her father's strange apparatus – the glass tubes, connecting one Keeper with another, allowing their contents (*Time*, Mara told herself, *that's what it was*) to flow from one vessel to another. She thought about his handwriting on the pages of the handbook and focused on recalling what her dad had written. *Two minutes' dark added to five minutes' summer Time...* Finally the answer came to her. *He was talking about mixing Time from different Warps together*, Mara realized. *I don't know* why *he was trying to do it, but that's got to be it.* "I don't think the Timelock's broken," Mara said finally, opening her eyes to look straight at Pearl. "I just think the Time in the Keepers was connected."

Pearl frowned. Mara could see the spark of interest in her eyes. "Connected?"

Mara nodded. She glanced around; the adults were still looking at her so she pulled her gaze away and focused on the clock just above Pearl's head as she spoke. "Dad had these glass tubes," she began. "With little rubber stoppers and things to join them together. Whenever I asked him what he was doing, he'd just tell me it was dangerous and I wasn't to touch it. And sometimes, he'd connect Keepers to them. He called it his apparatus. I never knew what it was for." She met Pearl's eye. "I think I know better now."

Pearl looked confused. "What were they for?"

Mara took a deep breath before she began to speak again. "For mixing Time. I think. I read in some notes he made things about mixing January Time with July and how much summer Time you'd need to lighten the darkness of winter. I don't know why he was doing it but I think that's what was happening. And if that's something you can actually *do*, then maybe the Timelock isn't broken. It's not leaking." Mara paused, licking her lips. "Maybe, the Time we were putting into it was from the same Warp as the Time in Jan's pocket, and they were all close enough for it to – *suck* it up, or whatever – at the same time."

"He was Blending," Pearl said, her voice barely higher than a whisper. She looked at Mara and spoke more clearly. "You're sure about this, Mara? Certain about what you saw?"

Mara nodded. "I'm sure. And Vik's people took his apparatus when they trashed our van. All Dad's glass tubes and things are with him now."

"It's an old skill," Pearl said, staring hard at Mara. "Blending Time to taste, to suit the customer. Some people want Time from a particular season. Some want night-Time, or day-Time, or days' worth of sunset. As far as we knew, Tiders stopped doing it over a century ago – they came to an agreement with us, and we expected them to keep to it. It seems they haven't."

Mara felt her mouth drop open. She hadn't meant to

get her dad into more trouble than he was in already. "I – well, I mean, maybe he wasn't—" she began.

"But what you're saying makes sense," Pearl said, talking over Mara. "I think you're right. And it means we have to work even harder to get the Time Tider to come to his senses. All Time-selling has to stop." She looked around at her colleagues, each of them as stony-faced as she was. "Time must never be harvested from the living again and all Time saved from Warps must be stored safely, where it cannot be released to cause further Warps. The only proper solution is to salvage as much Time as we can from the Dumps, as many of them as we can find, and put it into our Timelock as quickly as possible. We've got to get moving on this, without any further delay."

"We need to find Vik's warehouse, then," Mara said, the words sinking into her gut as she spoke them aloud. "Because he's already started raiding the Dumps, and he's way ahead of us." She thought about her father's notebook with a pang of despair. "And he's got a map to all the Time that's ever been saved."

Pearl's face was set. "Well, then. Even more reason for us to get moving."

You've got no choice but to work with the Clockwatchers. You don't have to like them, and you'd better not trust them, but don't fight them. The harder you fight, the tighter their grip. (Note, originally in French, added to The Time Tider's Handbook, dated 1918.)

Chapter
Thirty-Four

Mara sat in the front seat of a large van, feeling sick. Jan was squashed in beside her in the long bucket seat; on his other side was a male Clockwatcher with a box fade and sharp brown eyes. Pearl hauled herself into the driver's seat beside Mara and glanced at the others.

"All right?" she said. Mara turned to her and nodded, while Jan kept his focus on the dashboard.

"Ready to move out, Commander Sangare," the man replied.

"Excellent," Pearl said, starting the van's engine.

Every vehicle the Clockwatchers could lay their hands on had been put to use. They were locking down as best they could, leaving a skeleton staff behind at their headquarters while everyone else available went on the march. Pearl, Jan, Mara and the man – "Gregoire," Pearl had said as she introduced him. "If he starts muttering in French, you know we're in trouble," – were in the last van. It was longer than the others, and Mara knew there were shelves purpose-built in the back, ready to be loaded with crates of Keepers. Even with the Clockwatchers' entire fleet, however, Mara knew they'd only be able to transport a fraction of Vik's stash of Time. *So either we defeat him,* Mara thought, a wave of cold fear washing over her, *or this whole thing fails.*

Pearl whistled through her teeth as she set the van in motion. They were leaving the underground car park behind and heading for the slope that led upwards and out. Gregoire's head swung from side to side as he kept a careful eye on their surroundings. Mara watched silently from her seat at the front of the van. She glanced at Jan, whose face looked strange – it was as if he was fading, like a watercolour painting with too much water in it. *Where's Vik?* Mara thought. *Have they got rid of him?* She felt ill. *Or is he still coming?*

"Cheer up," Pearl said. "Has someone taken your batteries out or what?" She cut a glance at Mara and Jan.

"Vik has a lot of people," Mara said. "And they have guns."

Pearl shrugged. "So do we," she said. "We know how to handle ourselves. We've been doing our job a lot longer than Vik's been doing his. And now that we have you on our team, we actually know where Vik *is*, which is exactly the breakthrough we've been waiting for. So I reckon that puts us one up on him, don't you?"

Mara didn't answer. They were coming near the top of the concrete ramp now, and the floor was levelling off. She could see plastic strips covering the entrance to the compound, still swinging in the wake of the last vehicle that had passed through them. In the daylight, they looked cloudy. She felt her hands squash into tight fists as Pearl drove out and the sudden brightness made her close her eyes tight. She felt the van turn left, towards the road. *Towards Port Ross. Towards Vik's army. Towards...* After that, Mara's thoughts stopped.

For a few seconds, all she heard was the van's engine. Then: "Gregoire," Pearl said, her voice strained. "What's going on?"

Mara opened her eyes, blinking against the light. For a moment, she didn't see anything out of the ordinary – then she and Jan both saw it at the same time.

"Are those ... security barriers?" Jan said. "They're coming up!"

Pearl growled. "I can see that," she muttered.

At the end of the road they were on, right before it joined a larger thoroughfare, six metal pillars, each plastered with black-and-yellow stripes warning of DANGER, were slowly rising, like zombie fingers pushing out of a grave. If they got much higher, the van would be trapped behind them. Mara felt her breath catch.

Pearl accelerated and the van leaped forwards, but the barriers were coming up too quickly. Right at the last second Pearl pressed hard on the brake and the van skidded to a stop, barely missing crashing right into the metal poles. Pearl flung the van into reverse and they spun back towards the compound.

"Commander!" Gregoire shouted, pointing. Mara and Jan looked too. A security shutter was lowering over the entrance, like a metal eye closing.

"What in the seven rings of *Hades* is going on?" Pearl said, as the van screeched to a halt once more. "Who gave this order?"

Gregoire pulled a walkie-talkie out of a pocket and began to shout into it but all that came back in response to his questions was a sea of static.

"Is … is that normal?" Jan said, staring out through the windscreen. Mara glanced at him, then looked in the direction of his worried gaze. A car was emerging slowly from the entrance of a building on the far side of the road. Mara heard Pearl gasp and she looked up. Pearl's eyes were wide with shock and anger.

"Who *is* that? And how did they get through security?"

Gregoire slid his walkie-talkie back into place and

looked at Pearl. "I suspect we may have been breached, Commander Sangare," he said. Then his hand went to the gun he wore in a holster on his hip. He pulled it out and pointed it at her. "In fact, I know we have."

Pearl turned to face him, her shock giving way to pure fury. Then, faster than Mara could imagine, Pearl unclipped her seat belt and launched herself forwards, grabbing Gregoire's gun-holding hand. She drove the heel of her other hand into the bridge of his nose, making him howl in pain. Mara winced as she heard the crunch of Gregoire's bones breaking beneath the force of Pearl's blow. He dropped the gun and Pearl quickly seized it. "Get out of this van," she said, pointing the gun at Gregoire. He had one hand to his face, blood trickling between his fingers. With the other, he reached behind him to open the door.

Mara's breaths felt like they weren't filling up her lungs properly. She and Jan were pressed together, squashing themselves against the seat. Pearl tracked Gregoire with the gun as he walked, hands in the air, towards the slowly moving car. Finally the car came to a stop. One of its back doors opened and a person stepped out.

Mara already knew who it would be.

"Vik," she whispered, trembling as she looked at him. He was wearing a long dark coat and an expression of casual interest, as though he were on a day trip to a place he'd never been before.

"He's a *child*," Pearl said, pointing the gun at him. "How on earth is he doing all this?"

"He's got a lot of help," Mara said. "There's a woman who works with him. His mum, I think." Then, almost like she'd been summoned, Vik's mother exited the car's other side. She gave the van, and its occupants, a triumphant look.

"Ingrid Maxwell," Pearl growled.

"You know her?" Mara stared at Vik's mother.

"Used to be a Clockwatcher," Pearl said, her mouth twisting. "Until we kicked her out."

"What for?"

Pearl gave her a sidelong look, filled with apology. "Possible involvement in your mother's death. We just couldn't prove it." Pearl looked back at Vik. Mara's stomach flipped over as she stared at Ingrid Maxwell, her breaths shallow. *Pearl said I wouldn't have to face the people who killed Mum*, she thought, swallowing an ache. Jan grabbed her hand and held it.

"Hi, Mara!" Vik called, waving at the van Mara was sitting in. She shrank deeper into her seat. "Great to see you! Would you mind telling Commander Sangare to lower her weapon?" He laughed. "We wouldn't want her damaging her lovely high-spec vehicle now, would we?"

Pearl muttered something under her breath. Mara guessed it wasn't complimentary. "You two, stay here," she said before opening the door. She kept the gun trained on Vik as she slid out of her seat and stood, the door in front of her. "What have you done with my people?" Pearl called.

Vik smirked, pushing his hands into his coat pockets. "Some of 'em are my people now," he said. "The others? We let them get far enough away and then we ambushed them. Anyone who survived? Well, I guess they'll have to decide whose side they're on."

Mara's heart lurched. She looked at Jan, whose face was drawn with panic. "There's no help coming," Jan whispered. "It's hopeless."

"Don't say that," Mara whispered back. "It's *never* hopeless. Your family's out there, Jan, looking for you. We can't give up now."

"What do you want?" Pearl shouted, adjusting her grip on the gun. "Let's get this ridiculousness over with."

Vik looked surprised. "What do I want? I thought that would have been clear enough. I want access to the Timelock, Commander Sangare," he said. "I want to *destroy* it. And I want our friend Mara there to come out and teach me everything she knows about using the Stitch. And then I want you and your irritating little Clockwatchers to just…" Vik waved his fingers in the air, as though he were scattering petals into the breeze. "Go away," he finished, fixing Pearl with a cold look.

"Over my dead body," Pearl replied, strengthening her

stance. She took better aim at Vik but threw Mara and Jan a worried glance too. "Get down on the floor, you pair," she muttered to them.

"Oh, I don't think there needs to be a gun battle, Commander," Vik continued, in a chiding tone, before Mara and Jan had a chance to obey. "You'll *lose*, anyway. But in case it helps to decide what comes next? Why don't you say hello to my guests." He turned slightly, indicating something with a nod of his head. The back doors of the car were pulled open and Mara felt Jan stiffen with horror beside her as people were yanked out, blinking in confusion.

A split second later, Mara realized what he'd seen.

"The Van der Meer family," Vik said, extending an arm towards Jan's parents, who stood with a white-knuckled grip on Will and Annelies. "I think you *may* already be acquainted."

The Time Tider's Handbook, 1/A/iv:
Insofar as it is possible, ensure you maintain no
familial ties... Leave no trace of yourself
upon this earth.

Chapter Thirty-Five

"Mum!" Jan shouted. "Dad!" His parents looked towards the van. Mara saw Helen's eyes fill with tears.

"Stay there!" she shouted back. "Do as you're told, Jan."

Vik nodded approvingly. "Good advice," he said. "Excellent advice, Mrs Van der Meer. Or may I call you Helen?" Helen stared at him and Vik laughed.

"Let my children go," Vincent said. "They have nothing to do with any of this."

Vik sucked his lower lip, like he was giving it some thought. "No can do, I'm afraid, sir," he said. He turned back to Pearl. "So, Commander. What'll it be? Unconditional surrender on your part, or me and my people making a bit of a *mess* out here, with all the blood and whatnot, and then taking over your headquarters by force anyway?" He bobbed his head from side to side in mock indecision. "Choices, choices," he said, his voice sing-song.

Mara looked at Pearl. Her rock-solid stance didn't waver for several seconds, and Mara could practically hear her thoughts moving around inside her head – but finally, Pearl's body sagged. She pulled the gun back and pointed it towards the sky, holding up her other hand in a gesture of surrender. She looked at Mara and her eyes were anguished. "I can't risk it," she said.

"Good choice, Commander," Vik said. "Come on out now and throw that weapon on the ground." As Pearl stepped out from behind the van door and kicked the gun away, Vik looked back at Mara and Jan. "And as for you!" He gave a cold smile. "Seems you sold me a dud, Mara. The watch?" He shrugged. "Doesn't work. And what was with those bunches of old *hair* taped into the case?" Vik pulled a face. "*Disgusting.* They went straight in the bin, let me tell you."

Mara gasped. *Mum's hair,* she thought, blinking hard. *It's gone...* Jan's grip on her hand tightened and she tried not to tremble.

While Vik was speaking, some of his crew had emerged from the building behind the car. His mother walked to stand beside him, looking at him proudly. Some others moved towards the van. A couple took Pearl into custody, her face like thunder as they pulled her arms behind her back, while two more came to the open van doors, one at either side. "Come on, then," said the woman nearest to Mara. She looked familiar – and she had a large, colourful bandage on her forehead. "Remember me?"

Mara swallowed hard. It was the woman she'd injured during their escape from the warehouse. She gave a mirthless grin as she saw Mara put two and two together. On the far side, a man was pulling Jan out. He was still holding Mara's hand, and they tried to keep their grip on each other as long as they could – but eventually the adults pulled them apart.

"Looks like we're ready," Vik said, as Jan and Mara were dragged towards him. "Let's get going, shall we?"

Gregoire emerged from the building, his face obscured by a wad of blood-stained padding around his nose. He ignored his former commander as he walked past her, looking a little unsteady on his feet as he pulled a key out of his pocket. He inserted it into a box beside the metal security door that had come down over the entrance to the compound, and as he turned it the door began to rise. The whine of the motor pulling up the heavy door and the clanking of metal were the only sounds Mara could hear.

"Let's make ourselves at home, shall we?" Vik said, striding through once the door was high enough. He slapped aside the plastic strips and made his way down the slope towards the Clockwatchers' compound, surrounded by his lackeys. Mara felt herself being pulled along behind him. She turned, trying to see Pearl or Jan or *anyone*, but they were moving too quickly for that. She blinked as her eyes adjusted once again to the dim interior of the building, the lights in the ceiling popping into life as they walked beneath them. Soon, they emerged into the wide car park where, only hours before, she had agreed to team up with Pearl. It seemed like another lifetime, a different universe.

Vik strode straight to the small office which faced the car park. Mara was jostled through behind him and Jan behind her. "Now," Vik began, making straight for the chair Pearl had been sitting in the last time Mara had been in this room. Mara and Jan were thrown back on to the couch they'd sat on before. They huddled together, staring across at Vik, who looked completely wrong in this place, in *Pearl's* place. "Let's talk. While my people are getting the Timelock opened, I want to know what you can tell me about the Stitch." He gave a tight, unpleasant smile. "Please. And thank you."

"*Why* are you doing any of this?" Mara said, pushing the words out. Her teeth felt like they wanted to chatter and she forced them to stop. "If you had any clue what was going on, you'd *know*. You'd know I don't know anything!"

"You know plenty, Mara," Vik said. "You know more than you think you do."

"I don't!" Mara fought to stop herself from shouting.

"I *don't*. My dad never told me anything. So, whatever I know, I've worked out myself, and most of it is probably wrong. It's *pointless*, all this stupid stuff you're doing. Just let Jan and his family go!"

Vik sat back a little in the chair, his gaze steady. "Family, eh? Family's important to you, isn't it? I think I'm right about that."

Mara blinked at him, confused. "What?"

"I know my mother's important to me," Vik continued, folding his arms as he looked at Jan. "Jan, your family's clearly important to you. Right?" Mara felt Jan nodding beside her. Vik's gaze slid back to her face. "Yes. Family's the thing. We'd do anything for our families, Mara. Wouldn't we?"

Mara stared hard at the young man. Since the first moment she'd met him, she'd known there was something strangely familiar about him – something *haunting*. It was the colour of his hair or maybe the way his eyes narrowed or the angle of his nose. And now there was this odd talk about family… "Who are you?" she whispered, a tremble creeping back into her voice.

"My mother's a Clockwatcher," Vik said, as though he hadn't heard Mara's question. He let his gaze drift, settling somewhere on the wall behind their heads as he thought. "Or she *was*, I guess. She was relieved of her duties a few years back for being mouthy, I think. Or maybe it was because someone didn't like her ideas?" He shrugged and fixed Mara with his stare once again. "Anyway. Long before all that, she was pretty high up in the Clockwatcher hierarchy. Got to spend lots of time with the Tider – no pun intended." He smirked. "They were quite close for a while. Long before he met Thea, of course. Years before his happy family began and then fell to bits, as these things often do."

Mara felt herself begin to tremble. "Just tell me," she said.

"They weren't married or anything like that, my mum and your dad," Vik continued, his voice low. "Just, you know, *together*. Young and in love. And then your dad left." Vik shrugged as if it wasn't important, but Mara guessed it was anything but. "Just ... took off, like he does whenever things get too tough. Mum was heartbroken, of course. And then, a little while later, she realized he'd left something behind."

Mara swallowed. "What?"

"Me," Vik said, staring at her. "I can't believe you haven't worked it out, little sister. I mean, why else do you think I'm doing any of this?"

Mara's heart *thock*ed. She stared at Vik, desperate not to believe what he was telling her, but she knew it had to be true. She'd known, somehow, right from the start. The reason he looked so familiar ... the reason he wanted to take everything her father had, and make it his own…

"Do *not* call me that," Mara said, forcing the words out between her teeth. "I am *not* your sister!"

"What would you prefer? Tiderling? *Usurper?*" Vik leaned forwards a little, staring at her. "Daddy's little girl?"

"Shut up!" Mara shouted.

"Look, my family – they don't have anything to do with you," Jan said. "Please. Let them go. At least my brother and sister. Come on. My sister's only five years old."

Vik flicked his gaze towards Jan. "I was five years old once too," he began. "Five years old and my mother was never home and my father had abandoned me." He looked back at Mara. "Abandoned me to go and find *another* home, a different family. To go and have another kid. One he liked better."

Mara swallowed a bitter laugh. "Yeah? Not so sure about that. My dad doesn't like *me* much, either," she muttered, feeling like something was being scooped out of her insides.

"So you want *me* to feel sorry for *you?*" Vik said, his eyes narrowing. "You've got to be kidding. Did he ever mention me? Talk about me? He never even sent me a *birthday card.* Not once! And he knew where we were. Don't try to tell me he didn't."

Mara looked at her half-brother. His eyes glittered with rage and pain, his jaw tight. "He never said a word about you," she told him. "Not once. It was like he didn't even know you existed."

Before Vik had a chance to reply, there was a muffled *boom* from somewhere close by. Mara and Jan jerked, looking around, while Vik launched himself out of his chair. His eyes were wild as he stared down at Mara. "What's going on?" he snapped.

"How should I know?" Mara yelled back at him. "I thought *you* were the one in charge."

Vik leaned forwards angrily and pulled Mara to her feet. Jan scrambled up to stand beside her, his fists clenched. "Tell me how to use the Stitch," Vik said, dragging Mara so close that she could feel his words spray across her skin. "Even with the tools, I can't get it to work. There's no point in me having my father's watch, the key to the richest seams of Time in existence, with no way of *getting* to them."

Mara took a deep breath, staring into her brother's face. Out of the corner of her eye she saw people moving outside – running back towards the compound entrance – and she tried to squish her panic down. "I have no idea how to use the Stitch," she said, focusing on Vik once again. "Dad never showed me. So I can't help you." She paused, before pushing her face even closer to his. "And even if I *did* know, I'd rather sew my mouth shut than tell you."

With a roar of temper, Vik shoved Mara away. She stumbled, saved from falling only by Jan, who caught her before she landed back on the couch.

Someone knocked on the office door and pushed it open, all in one movement. "Got some trouble up here, sir," the person said. Mara saw him glance at her with a worried look.

"Can't you deal with it?" Vik snapped.

"It's more than I can handle," the young man said. "Sir."

Vik whirled on the spot and stared at him. "Well, what is it?"

The young man swallowed. "It's the Clockwatchers, sir," he said. "Seems we didn't get 'em all. And now they want their commander back."

The Time Tider's Handbook, 1/B/iii:
Balance is key to using the Stitch. Key, too,
is knowing your own worth, your own value...
You are the anchor which holds the Stitch.
If that hold fails, the Stitch collapses...

Chapter Thirty-Six

Vik muttered under his breath as he strode towards the door. "Keep an eye on those two," he said to the other man, jerking his head back in Mara and Jan's direction. "Don't let them leave this room."

The young man nodded as Vik pushed past him and out through the door.

"Hey! What about if we *have* to get out?" Jan shouted. Vik ignored him and kept walking, striding away across the open car park, his long coat trailing behind him like a cloak. He didn't look back.

"Right," the young man said, stepping into the room and closing the door. He faced Mara and Jan, folding his arms. "You pair had better ... go and play, or whatever."

Mara blinked at him. "We're not *babies*."

"You can't keep us in here," Jan said. "I want to see my parents!"

The young man flipped back his jacket to reveal a holster. The handle of a weapon was barely visible inside it. "If you want to try to get past me, little man, be my guest," he said.

Jan sagged, stepping back a little. "If my brother Will was here, he'd—"

"Whatever," the young man retorted, closing his jacket and pulling a chair in front of the door. He flopped into it, looking bored. "Look, I don't want to be here either, OK? I'm missing the fun on account of you pair." There was another *boom* from outside the room and the sound of raised voices.

"What's happening?" Mara asked.

The young man shrugged. "Some of the Clockwatchers got through the ambushes we set up," he said. "They're breaking their way back into the compound, looks like."

"Pearl's not going to let you destroy her Timelock," Mara said, though her voice shook a little as she spoke.

The young man gave her an amused look. "It might not be up to dear old Pearl in the end," he said. He settled himself more comfortably in his chair, stretching out his long legs and crossing them at the ankle as he waved dismissively at Mara and Jan. "Anyway, I'm not here to chat. Go and … do something. Quietly."

"But—" Jan began.

Mara pulled his arm. "Shush," she whispered into his ear.

The young man snickered. "Best listen to your little girlfriend over there, sonny," he said.

"*What?*" Jan spluttered.

Mara hurried around to the back of the broken sofa. She kept her eyes on the young man for a second before ducking down behind it, out of his line of sight. He seemed more interested in what was going on outside the room than he was in guarding the kids inside, pulling apart two slats of the blinds covering the window to peer out through them. Mara grabbed Jan by the sleeve and forced him to the floor.

"I've got to get my dad," she hissed, as soon as Jan was crouched beside her.

"What? But he's *gone*, isn't he? And it's not like he's just popped to the shops, or whatever. He's, like, *gone* gone. Right?"

Mara kept her gaze steady. "Yes. But listen. He went into the Stitch, just … *by himself*, not using his tools. He couldn't have used them because he'd given them to me. So you don't *need* the watch to use the Stitch. Vik thinks you do – but you obviously don't."

Jan blinked at her. "Yeah. If you're the *Tider*," he said. "And you have the first clue what you're doing."

Mara took a deep breath before replying. "I have to *try*," she said. "Vik's right about one thing – Dad does run, as soon as things get tough. He's been running all my life, away from stuff he didn't want to deal with, and he's done it again now. The first chance he got, he disappeared into the Stitch and he didn't even think about me." She clenched her fists. "He abandoned me twice. So I'm going to find him. And he's going to come back here and sort out this mess – the mess he made."

"But – do you even know how to do any of this?"

"Remember what your dad said," Mara replied. "You need three things. Something to step out of Time for, something worth coming back for and something to remind you of the Time you belong to. The Stitch isn't something you need any special equipment to use – it's something *inside* you." As she spoke, Mara remembered the feeling and the sound of the soft places – the Warps – that she had been able to sense all her life, and she remembered the words she'd seen in the handbook her dad had kept for all those years, which she'd destroyed. It had been an accident, Mara knew, but now she wondered: had it happened to clear the way for new rules to be made – new rules about who could be Tider, and about what they could do? *Recognizing a Warp is a basic skill, instinctive to most Tiders.* She stared at Jan, sure of what she was going to say next. "My dad can do it. And I can do it too. I know

I can."

"Yeah. Right. If you say so. But – how are you going to get it to work?"

Mara slipped her hand into her pocket. "I've got Mum," she said, fighting to keep her voice steady as she pulled out Thea's photograph. "I can step out of Time for her. But I need something to remind me of the Time I belong to. I don't have Dad's watch." She wiggled her wrists. "I don't have *any* watch." She looked up at Jan in confusion and his eyes suddenly brightened.

He began to rummage in his own pocket. "How … about … *this?*" he said, pulling free something that had been hidden there. It was a small rectangular card, its corners peeling a bit with age. On it, Mara could see a cartoon drawing of a character she'd never heard of, one with multicoloured flames spewing out of its mouth and a bright red shell on its back. *Strength: 50*, she read, from a box beneath the image. *Magic: 150.*

"Worth a lot, this one," Jan muttered, rubbing one fond finger over the image. "You can give it back, soon as you get home."

"What is it?"

Jan shrugged. "Sort of a swapping game," he explained. "I used to be into it, a few years ago. This is the last one I've got left." He cleared his throat. "Dad gave it to me."

Mara looked up at him. "I can't take this," she said.

Jan frowned. "You can," he said. "It's only a loan, right? And it'll remind you of me, which means it'll remind you of *now*, and you'll be able to come back here, no problem."

She looked back at the card. "I mean – thanks, Jan," she whispered.

Jan shrugged. "Now all's you've got to come up with is something worth coming back for," he said.

"That's the bit I can't figure out yet," Mara said, looking worried. "And it's kind of important."

They sat in silence for a moment or two. More *boom*ing noises filled the air, and somewhere there was the rattle of what sounded like gunfire. They met one another's eyes.

"Don't leave me for too long, right?" Jan whispered, his eyes giving away his fear.

"Unless I can crack this, I won't be going anywhere," Mara said. *I need my dad to come and sort this out*, she told herself. *He needs to tell Vik to stop. He needs to tell* everyone *to stop.*

"Hey," Jan said, grabbing Mara by the arm. She looked up at him. His eyes danced with excitement, and a small smile played on his face. "I've got it!"

"What?"

"The thing you need to come back for. I know what it is!"

Mara rolled her eyes. "Don't tell me – it's *you*, isn't it?" She pulled back a little. "You're not going to, like, *kiss* me

322

now or anything? This isn't a movie, Jan."

Jan looked appalled. "Don't be *stupid*. It's not me you've got to come back for." He jabbed her in the shoulder with one finger. "It's *you*."

She gave him an incredulous look. "*What?*"

Jan leaned closer, staring at her. "You need to come back for *you*. You're the thing worth coming back for, Mara. You've got to come back for your own future. You've got things to do, don't you? I *know* you do. So come back for you." He paused. "Your dad's the grand Time Tider, right? The expert at all this? And *he* thought you were worth coming back for. So if it's good enough for him?"

Mara smiled, determination beginning to hum through her like electricity. "Then it's good enough for me too." Jan nodded, giving her a fleeting, hopeful smile.

Mara settled herself on the carpet. Right beside her was a work desk with a switched-off computer on it. Above that was a painting on the wall of a man in armour passing a lady in a beautiful gown on a twisting turret staircase. To her other side was the back of the old, worn-out sofa, its upholstery ripped. In front of her was Jan, looking worried, and behind him was a tall metal shelving unit, stuffed with papers and envelopes and rolled-up charts and dust. She took in her surroundings, steadied herself and then closed her eyes.

Breathe.

Her mother's face came to life, right before her eyes. Mara could see Thea's curls dancing in the breeze and she watched as her mother blinked, her eyes shining in the light. Her earrings glinted. Her skin smelled of warmth, of soap, of sunshine and the sea. Thea's lips moved and Mara knew her mother was saying her name.

Breathe.

Jan's game card hung in Mara's mind now, spinning gently. It was a precious thing, Mara knew. It was Jan's, and Jan was here, right now, beside her. Here was when she had to come back to.

Breathe.

Mara's heart was pounding in her chest. Her curly hair tickled the back of her neck. She imagined herself as an adult – tall as her father, with a laugh like her mother's, but filled with power all her own. What would she do? What would she be? Mara knew she needed to find out.

Breathe.

A bright blue-white triangle roared into life inside Mara's head and she started in surprise. Its *hum* of power was like nothing else she had ever known and she felt her heart rate quicken with excitement at the sight, its strength and stability, its three points strong. Her mother, her friend and herself. The three things she needed to keep steady in order to open the Stitch. But the triangle was moving, slowly, like an arrow searching for something – a destination. Mara realized she'd forgotten one of the things she needed to work the Stitch. *I've got to tell it* when *I need to go*, Mara said, inside her head. *Hold it steady, and then…*

Mara let her father's face float into the centre of her mind and, without a second's pause, the triangle shifted. Mara felt herself flung forwards like an arrow from a bow, her ears filling with the *buzz* of a Warp – and then she was gone into the Stitch.

The Time Tider's Handbook, 1/C/vi:
Walk lightly among the Warps and
leave no trace of yourself behind...

Chapter Thirty-Seven

Before she had time to haul in a breath, she found herself sprawling on a very different floor to the one she'd left behind. She skidded across stone, the cold biting into her skin and bones, and she didn't stop until she hit a wall. Disoriented, Mara looked up.

The wall was stone too, made from giant blocks. Something that looked like a carpet hung right above her, billowing slightly, and Mara searched her memory for the right word. *Tapestry?* she thought, her mind stretching with confusion. She blinked and looked away. In the far corner of this large room a huge fireplace danced with flames but none of its heat made it to Mara. She'd never felt so cold and so afraid in her life.

Not far from the fireplace was a bed. Someone was

lying in it – and another person was standing over them. A person whose silhouette Mara knew straight away. They held an empty spindle. In the next moment the person on the bed gave a small shudder, and Mara saw her father place the spindle on their chest and set it spinning. Within a moment, the spindle was fat – gold and silver and black and red – and the Tider pushed it inside a Keeper before sealing the Keeper's lid with a gentle *click*. The spindle kept turning slowly inside the jar as the Tider put it into a pocket of his coat, and Mara knew the person in the bed – the small person, she now saw – was dead.

"Dad," she whispered hoarsely.

Gabriel jerked. He glanced towards her, his face haggard and drawn in the light of the fire. He seemed to have grown old, his hair greyer and his beard as unkempt as sheep's wool caught on a barbed-wire fence. "Mara?" he murmured. "How … what? How are you here?"

Mara pushed herself off the floor. Somehow, as she walked towards her father, she couldn't keep her eyes off the child in the bed. "What happened to them? To … to this kid?"

Her father glanced back at the child. Mara was close enough now to see that it was a boy, and as she drew even nearer she saw, hidden in the shadows on the far side of the bed, that a woman sat there, sleeping in a chair. Her face was creased with worry, even in sleep. *His mum*, Mara thought, and her heart overflowed with grief.

"His injuries look as though he fell, maybe from a tree," Gabriel said, his voice low. "Something we could perhaps have healed, in our own time. But here, they proved too much."

"His poor mother," Mara said.

As Mara spoke, the woman stirred in her sleep. "Come on," Gabriel whispered, pulling Mara away from the fireside and into the furthest corner of the room, where darkness lay thick. They could barely see one another, though the firelight shone in their eyes.

"Dad," Mara said, her voice barely loud enough to be heard. "I need you. You've got to come back."

"There's something I must do first, Mara," he replied.

Mara blinked. "Dad, it doesn't *matter*. You can do it later! I've got a brother – did you know that?" She took fistfuls of his sleeves, holding on to her father as though she were a climber clinging to a mountain. "When were you going to tell me?"

Gabriel said nothing for a moment. "I didn't know," he whispered. "I never knew. His mother – she never told me." He looked at Mara and she could see the edge of his face dancing with orange-yellow light. "I swear, Mara. The first I heard of that boy was ... was when he came after me."

"And you ran. Again." Mara's words were choked with

anger. "You didn't *deal* with it. You just decided to *leave*, like you always do."

"Mara," Gabriel reminded her. "Keep your voice—"

"Alphonse?" came a sleepy murmur from the far side of the bed. "A-Alphonse? *Alphonse!*"

"We need to leave," Gabriel said, staring at his daughter. "Now."

"*How?*" Mara hissed.

"Just hold on to me," Gabriel said, gathering Mara into a hug – and in the next breath, as voices shouted behind them, Mara felt her mind fill with the familiar *buzz*. Then she and her father thumped down on to hard ground – but instantly it felt different. Mara lost her grip on her father's coat and tumbled away from him, landing with her elbow in a puddle.

"Ow," she muttered, flipping over on to her front.

"It gets easier with practice," her dad said, from somewhere behind her.

"Where are we?" Mara pushed her hair out of her face. All she could see were trees, with thick undergrowth between them. The day was warm.

"Who knows? I don't even know *when* we are. Unless you've got my watch?" he asked hopefully.

"Vik's got your watch, Dad," she replied, getting to her feet. She turned to face him.

"And you're using the Stitch…" he prompted.

"With the power of my *mind*," Mara replied, waving her fingers in the air on either side of her head.

"There's a first time for everything," Gabriel muttered, as he pulled Mara to the forest floor.

"Hey!" she protested. "What's that supposed to—"

Gabriel turned to her, one finger to his lips, and Mara swallowed her words. A moment later she heard the *thump-thump, thump-thump* of hoofbeats. There was a horse coming, and it was coming *fast*.

Then down a pathway – or a muddy track churned up by feet and hooves and wagon wheels – the animal finally appeared. It was covered with mud splashes, its eyes wild, and on its back sat a skinny young man in a ridiculous hat, a long feather trailing out of it. He wore an elaborate jacket and thin leggings, and his face was drawn with panic.

As he came level with Mara and Gabriel's hiding place, an arrow flew from somewhere further up the path. It struck the young man in the back and he slumped off the horse. The panicked animal kept running, its hoofbeats vanishing up the track, and Gabriel hurried towards the fallen man. Mara dug her fingernails into the ground, her eyes huge with horror as she stared at the scene in front of her.

Gabriel took a Keeper out of his pocket, getting it ready. He opened the lid and removed the spindle, keeping the empty jar close. Then he laid one hand on the man's head, stroking it gently like someone comforting a child. Mara saw the wounded man's chest rising, falling, rising, falling – and then it didn't rise again. Quickly, her father filled his spindle and made it safe inside its Keeper.

More hoofbeats filled Mara's ears. Whoever had shot this young man was hot on his heels.

"Dad!" she called, her voice strained with panic. "Come on!"

Gabriel didn't need to be told. Throwing one glance up the path, he sealed the Keeper, all while getting to his feet and hurrying back to their hiding place. He pulled Mara behind a large tree, just in time to avoid being spotted by the man's pursuer, the bow still in his hands as he reined in his horse beside the body.

"Murderer," Mara said, staring at him. He flicked his gaze towards them and Mara felt her father take a firm grip of her arm.

"Enough," Gabriel muttered before they vanished once more into the Stitch.

This time, things seemed different. Mara braced herself to slam into yet another floor, but there was no floor. There was no *anything*. It felt as though they were floating in the centre of a cloud. All around them was a soft grey light and it was neither hot nor cold. Instantly Mara hated it.

"Where are we?" Mara shouted at her father. "What's *happening*?"

"First," Gabriel said, his tone maddeningly gentle, "you need to calm down."

"Calm down? Calm *down*?" Mara began to tremble. "We just watched someone get *murdered!*"

Gabriel nodded. "Yes. But it happened, Mara, and there was nothing we could have done to prevent it. Sometime in the past, that young man met his premature death in that forest. That's historical fact. My job – *our* job, it seems, now – isn't to interfere with things that have already happened. You've read stories, right? Where people who time travel sneeze at the wrong moment, or something, and next thing you know, they've created a new Black Death which wipes out half the world?"

Mara breathed, the shakes still rattling through her body. "I guess," she whispered.

"Well, that's what I mean. So if we'd stepped out into the path? If we'd stopped that young man? If we'd somehow deflected the arrow?" Gabriel shook his head sadly. "Yes, we might have saved that one life. But who knows what other damage we could have done?" He held up his hand. Between his fingers was a Keeper but there was something different about it. He'd clicked the Keeper's lid so that a tiny hole had appeared in it – a hole just big enough for a thread to pass through. And inside the Keeper, the spindle full of Time was slowly unspooling, growing thin as thread and passing out through the hole.

But as soon as the thread reached the outside, it vanished.

"We aren't here to interfere with history," Gabriel continued. Mara pulled her gaze away from the vanishing thread and looked back at her dad's face. He was focused on the Keeper in his hand, turning it this way and that as if admiring it. "That's not what Time intends. We're here to keep things moving. We're here to gather up wasted Time, like janitors mopping up a spillage." He met Mara's eye. "Time appointed me and it looks like it's appointed you too."

Mara stared at him. "Appointed me to what?"

"You're a Tider," he replied, his expression softening as he looked at his daughter. Mara's thoughts were a jumble. "I can't quite believe it, but you are. It has never happened before, to my knowledge, that a child – and a *girl*, at that – has been chosen, but Time has its reasons for everything. You're a new start, perhaps. Or a better continuation than me." He paused, considering. "There's no way you could have come after me otherwise. You found your way into the Stitch. You *mastered* it." Her father smiled, but his eyes were sad. "I'm extremely proud of you, Mara. Though I really wish you weren't here."

"Thanks," Mara muttered.

Gabriel's smile collapsed. "I mean … I mean, I wouldn't have chosen this life for you, sweetheart. I wouldn't have chosen this life for *either* of my children." His face looked stricken. "I can't explain what's going on. The office of Tider isn't supposed to pass from father to child, but I think … I think, a lot of things are changing."

"That's what Pearl thinks too," Mara said.

"Pearl? Pearl Sangare?" Gabriel's eyes closed momentarily. "So they found you."

"No, Dad," Mara said. "I found *them*. Because I needed help." She took a steadying breath, keeping her eyes on her father's face. "We can talk about this later. But right now? We've got to talk about Vik. He thinks you rejected him, Dad," Mara said. "He thinks you abandoned him."

Gabriel shook his head. "I swear to you, on your mum's memory. I never knew that boy existed. I would *never* have abandoned him, had I known."

"Well, you need to tell him!" Mara said. "He needs to hear it from you. He's going to do awful things, *terrible* things, mostly because he wants to prove he's better than you – that he can control Time better than you can. He wants to be Time Tider, no matter what he has to do. And he wants to prove he doesn't need you. But he *does* need you." Mara stared at her father. "I need you too, Dad. I need you to come back."

Gabriel gave a sad smile. "Time chooses its Tider, sweetheart. Your brother can try all he likes – he can take apart my watch or smash it if it makes him feel better. But

335

if he hasn't been chosen, he can never use the Stitch. He can't harvest Time. None of the power he's looking for can ever be his."

"But if we don't stop him, he'll never leave us alone. He'll *never* stop trying. Unless you talk to him, Dad. Unless you explain the truth." Mara looked back at the Keeper in her father's hands, and then around at the strange space that enclosed them. "Dad – where are we, right now? Are we ... are we in someone else's Time?" She looked back at her dad. "Is this how it feels? To ... to *buy* Time? Is this what people pay you for?"

Gabriel gazed at her, looking weary. "That day, when you saw me making a sale," he began. "You saw the customer taking Time, ingesting it. When people do that, the Time simply gets added to their own life, seamlessly and without them even feeling it. But if a person wants particular Time, which I've Blended to their taste – so summer Time, winter Time, whatever – they can spend it like this, by releasing it and essentially creating, and using up, a custom-made Warp. They can share it with loved ones, just as we're doing now, though that means it gets used up more quickly. When the Time runs out, the customer is returned to their own timeline as though nothing ever happened." He looked down, avoiding Mara's gaze. "And if I'm travelling without my watch, without a particular destination in mind, I'm forced to hop from Warp to Warp at random, harvesting whatever Time I find. So I'm using some of the Time I've harvested to create a little bubble here for us to be safe in."

Mara shook her head. She wanted to rip the Keeper from her dad's hand but she was afraid to touch it. "This is wrong, Dad. And you know it." She stared at her father. "Are we using up Time that little boy should have had? *Tell* me!"

Gabriel looked pained and Mara knew she'd guessed right. She was alive but suspended in a stopped clock, her own life on hold while she lived someone else's. It made her feel sick. *And this is what people pay for...* "Mara, I can't go back yet. I can't. There's something I need to do first before I put all this right. Before ... before I stop your brother, before I put all Time beyond use, before I fix everything." Gabriel put the Keeper back into his pocket and held Mara's arms, leaning forwards so his face was level with hers. She wondered if he was trying to restrain her. "I need to find her first, Mara. I need to find her Time. Then I can let all this go."

Mara gritted her teeth. "*Whose* Time do you need to find?"

Gabriel tightened his grip. "Your *mother's*, Mara. I harvested it, when ... when she died, but then, some days later, I was overcome with grief and I couldn't bear the idea that she was *trapped*... So I took her Keeper to a lakeside and opened it. I freed her. But as soon as I'd done it, I knew

I'd made a mistake." His cheeks were wet with tears, but he kept speaking. "Her Time joined a Warp, and I don't know where it is. I've been searching for it ever since. And I admit, I've been neglecting my duties, failing to harvest Warps that need harvesting, breaking the Clockwatchers' rules, not looking after *you* properly, all because I need to do this. But once I've done it – don't you see? I can live in peace with the Clockwatchers and I can focus on you." He stared at Mara, begging her to understand. "She's out there – or her Time is. I can't bear knowing that someone might *buy* it, might use it for … for *anything*. It should have been hers." His voice stumbled to a whisper. "I have to get her back. And then I can put everything else right."

Mara's eye was caught by her father's hourglass pendant, which had slipped out from beneath the collar of his shirt as he bent towards her. He closed his eyes again, crumpling inside his own pain, and Mara felt the grip on her arms relax a little. "I don't expect you to understand, Mara," he continued, his eyes still closed. "You're just a child. But I have to ask you to leave me be and let me do what I need to do."

Mara kept her eyes on the pendant. Mr Van der Meer's voice played in her memory as she recalled what he'd told her about the hourglass. *One second from every Warp that's ever been harvested*, she thought, remembering how the Keepers in Jan's pocket began to heat up as the Time within them was sucked into the Timelock, because the Time inside them was connected. *If one second is enough for the Timelock to work… If putting this pendant into the Timelock could literally store* all *the harvested Time, from every Time Dump, all at once…* It was worth trying, Mara realized. It *had* to be worth trying.

"Actually, I do get it, Dad," Mara said. "I understand how it feels to know what you need to do and to know you've got to do whatever it takes to make it happen."

Gabriel's eyes popped open and he looked at Mara in confusion. Before he had a chance to say anything, Mara made her move.

She tore her arms out of her father's grip and pulled Jan's card out of her pocket. With her other hand, she grabbed Gabriel's hourglass pendant and gave it a savage yank, feeling the thin leather strap snapping. Then, her eyes on Jan's card, Mara threw herself into the Stitch and vanished.

The Time Tider's Handbook, 1/C/iv:
Do not allow your focus to slip...

Chapter Thirty-Eight

Noise was the first clue Mara had that she'd come back to the right place – and the right time.

"Oh my *God*!" Jan was shouting. She felt him grab her up in a hug. "You … you … *vanished*! Just, like, *gone*! And now you're back!"

"How long?" Mara asked, her words muffled. Her face was pressed into Jan's shoulder. "How long was I gone?"

He pushed back a little from her and stared into her face. "Fifteen seconds? Twenty? Long enough for me to say 'Oh God, oh God, oh *God*' about two hundred times."

Mara couldn't help but laugh but it didn't last long. A *boom* from somewhere close by made the grin fade from her face. "What's going on outside?"

"Who knows," Jan said. His eyes were still wide.

Mara renewed her grip on the hourglass pendant. "Right. Come on, then. We're not just going to sit here, are we?"

Jan spluttered. "What? Have you *lost it*?"

"I've got a plan," Mara said, pushing herself up on to her knees. "Well. Sort of."

"Oh. Brilliant." Jan wobbled his head, his already-wide eyes growing wider. "Nothing I like more than having a *bit* of a plan while you're throwing yourself into mortal danger."

"Just come on and stop complaining," Mara said, getting to her feet.

Muttering under his breath, Jan stood up. The children looked at the chair their guardian had been sitting in – it was now empty, and the door to the office stood open. The young man had clearly done a runner, eager to join the fighting outside. Outside, the car park was empty, and the ramp leading up to street level curved away into the distance. Mara and Jan crept towards the door, their eyes and ears wide to catch any sign or sound of danger.

Just as they reached the door, the largest *boom* yet sent them both sprawling to the ground. A cloud of thick dark smoke billowed down the ramp, filling the underground space with choking dust.

"What's going on?" Jan shouted, coughing out the words.

"Maybe they've got in," Mara called back.

"*Who?*"

"The Clockwatchers," Mara replied, her spirits lifting. "The ones that still follow Pearl, at least."

"Funny how they were the bad guys, not so long ago," Jan said. They peered through the smoke. It was clearing slightly, enough for the children to see shapes running down the ramp and into the compound. Voices seemed to yell from every direction.

"Come on," Mara said, pulling Jan to his feet. "We've got to move."

"This is insane." Jan jogged at Mara's side, his head turning this way and that as he tried to keep watch on their surroundings. "What *is* the plan, anyway? Or whatever we're calling it."

Mara pulled Jan to one side. They flattened themselves against a wall, still mostly hidden by the smoke. "Here's the plan," she said, holding out the hourglass. Even in the semi-darkness its strange silver 'sand' shone, seeming to move and shift inside the hourglass despite Mara holding it steady.

"Your dad's hourglass," Jan said, reaching out one finger to touch the pendant gently. "Right?"

"And if what your dad said about it is true – which I'm sure it is – this is like a key to all the harvested Warps," Mara said. She thought about her father for a moment and what he'd told her about her mother's Time. *There's one second from her Time in here too – which means, if this works, it'll be sucked into the Timelock...* She slid the hourglass back into her pocket, pushing away all thoughts besides the one that was most pressing. "Which means it's valuable to a Tider – or to someone who wants to pretend to be one. I'm going to use it to distract my brother. And then maybe Pearl or someone can ... do whatever. Lock him up, or something."

Jan didn't say anything for a moment. "Yeah. OK. Let's do it," he finally whispered.

"We've got to get to the Timelock," Mara said. "I bet Vik's there – and Pearl too, probably."

Mara and Jan hurried through the corridors. An alarm had started to ring, its shrieking loud enough to be disorienting, and there were red lights flashing at every turn. They kept close to the walls, hoping the chaos would hide them. Adults ran past them in both directions, and as they neared the turn for the Timelock, Mara glanced back up at the room they'd just been in. Someone – one of Vik's people, she had a feeling – burst through the door, followed by several more heavily armed grown-ups.

"That was close," Jan whispered.

Mara stared at him. "But now they know we're gone."

Jan swallowed hard, giving a determined nod, and then he and Mara dashed the rest of the way to the outer door of the Timelock chamber. It was hanging off its hinges and the computer screens that had once monitored the street outside were now smashed and dark. The chairs were empty, with no sign of Harry or Ichika.

But from the room housing the Timelock itself, voices were raised. Even through the thick locked door, Mara and Jan could hear them.

"Vik!" Mara shouted, as loud as she could. She began to beat and kick the door, and after a moment or two Jan joined in. "Vik, get out here!"

For several long minutes, nothing happened. There was silence from the room beyond. Mara kicked the door again, just as a crackling noise from a speaker beside it drew her attention. A small screen above the speaker glowed into life, showing the scene beyond the door. The first thing Mara saw was the Timelock, still sealed, and she breathed a sigh of relief.

But then Vik's face swam into view on the screen. He glowered out at his sister. "There had better be a good reason for this interruption," he told her.

Mara stood back a little, her courage momentarily flickering. The sight of Vik's face, twisted with anger, made her insides churn.

Then Jan was beside her. She turned to look at him. He was scared too, but he gave her a fleeting smile. "Go get 'em," he whispered.

Mara looked back at the screen. "I've got something

you might want," she said.

Vik cupped his hand behind his ear. "Press the button if you want me to hear you," he said in a mocking tone.

Mara frowned, leaning forwards to push down a small black button beneath the speaker. "I *said*, I've got something you might want," she repeated in a louder voice.

"Oh? And what's that? The secrets of the Stitch? The coordinates to the Warp of the *Titanic*? Or have you done a nice drawing you want me to look at?"

Mara stood back from the screen just enough for Vik to see her properly. Then she pulled the hourglass out of her pocket and held it up. Straight away, she could see that she'd gambled correctly. His wide eyes were filled with greed.

Next thing Mara and Jan knew, the security door unlocked with a *thunk* and a *hss*, and was pushed open from the inside. Vik stood there, and behind him were three of his people, each of them guarding a Clockwatcher. Judging by the state of disarray they were in, Mara could see the Clockwatchers had been fighting hard against being used to open the biolock. Pearl was slumped in the corner, with a scowling Ingrid Maxwell standing over her. Mara hoped the commander of the Clockwatchers was simply unconscious.

"Now," Vik said, holding out his hand. "Let's have a look, shall we?

The Time Tider's Handbook, 1/C/vii: Do not lose yourself. Time is vast. You are infinitesimal.

Chapter
Thirty-Nine

"You're joking, right?" Mara said, in a voice that was far more confident than she was. "I'm not going to just *give* it to you." She took several steps back as she spoke.

"Oh yes, I forgot," Vik said, raising his hand and letting it drop again. "You'll want to *negotiate*, won't you? And you'll want something in exchange for this great and wonderful treasure you're trying to pawn off on me."

"Jan's family," Mara said. "You let them go. Now."

Vik shrugged, one-shouldered. "We'll see."

"If you don't, you're not getting this!" Mara's voice was shrill.

"Sweetheart," Vik said, barely able to flatten his gleeful grin. "I think you'll find that whatever I want..." he gestured to something behind the children, making them whirl on the spot, "I tend to get. Whether you like it, or not." Two adults stood behind Mara and Jan, looking at the children with cruel amusement. The man behind Jan cracked his knuckles and reached out to grab him.

"No!" Jan shouted, kicking out. Mara fought just as hard but it was no use. The woman overpowered her, pinning her back with one strong arm, and dragged her in the direction of the bank of computer screens. The man pulled Jan, squirming and shouting, into the Timelock chamber behind Vik.

"Now," Vik said, over the sound of Jan's shouts. "What were you saying?"

"Please," Mara said desperately. *This isn't how it was supposed to happen!* She squeezed her eyes tight as the plan – her half-thought idea of how things would pan out – flashed across her mind like a sped-up movie. *I was supposed to entice Vik with the hourglass … use it to free Jan's family … then somehow wriggle out of actually handing it over and put it into the Timelock instead…* She wanted to roar in frustration, but the woman holding her captive tightened her grip as Mara fought to be free. She opened her eyes again and stared at her brother. "Please! Let Jan and his family go. They don't deserve any of this."

"Toss me the hourglass," Vik said. "Just throw it carefully and I promise you I'll release the Van der Meers." He raised an eyebrow, looking amused. "Including your loud friend here."

"Let him go first," Mara said. "Tell your *soldier* to release him or I swear you're not going to get the hourglass."

"You've never negotiated before, have you?" Vik took a step towards her and Mara desperately pushed against her captor. The woman was too strong and she didn't move an inch. "Usually, it's the person with the most power who gets to dictate proceedings. In this case, I believe that person is me."

"Power? Don't make me laugh. You're not a Tider," Mara said, feeling her legs wobbling beneath her. "You'll *never* be a Tider. No matter how hard you try. So it seems to me that you're not as powerful as you think."

Vik's face hardened. "Who told you that?"

"My *father*. I told him all about you."

"Your father?" Vik looked puzzled. "How did you find him?"

"The hourglass. It lets you go where you want," Mara lied. "It lets you find any Warp, any time." She paused, hoping for the courage to keep going. Her heart was skittering so fast inside her, she feared it would fail. "It let me use the Stitch. I'll give it to you if you let Jan and his family go."

"Give it to me," Vik said. His eyes flashed. "Toss it, right now."

"Jan goes free first!" Mara shouted.

Vik snapped his fingers. The man holding Jan seemed to tighten his grip. Jan groaned in pain, throwing Mara a panicked look.

"If you don't hand it over now," Vik snarled, "there may not be much of him to release."

Mara felt something shatter inside her. She looked at Jan. He'd stood beside her all this way, despite being scared the whole time. He'd tried his best to help, even when it meant losing everything he loved. His eyes begged her not to give in but she knew she had no choice.

"All right," she said, her voice choked. "All right! I'll do it."

Vik put his hand out to catch the hourglass as Mara adjusted her grip to throw. She raised her hand, tossing the hourglass overarm, hating the feeling of it leaving her fingers.

It flew through the air, turning slowly end over end. Mara watched it, its silver sand sloshing about behind its glass sides and its dark metal fittings gleaming in the lights…

But before it landed in Vik's open palm, the air in the room shimmered – barely visibly, but enough to make everyone blink in confusion – and then a person appeared out of nowhere. A man, his greying hair tufting around his head in a way that Mara recognized instantly. He reached up and plucked the spinning hourglass out of the air, catching it before it had a chance to reach Vik, and then he turned and tossed it back to Mara. The woman holding her was too shocked to react as Mara reached for it.

"Dad," Mara breathed, staring at the man.

"*You*," spat Ingrid Maxwell from inside the Timelock chamber.

"Let my daughter go," Gabriel said, staring at the woman holding Mara captive. "Or all that will be left of you is a pile of dust on the floor."

Instantly, Mara felt the woman's hands release their grip. Mara put the hourglass in her pocket and took a couple of running steps in her father's direction, her arms wide – and her father caught her, holding her tight in a one-armed hug. "I knew I'd be able to get back to you," she heard him whisper into her hair. "My little girl, my one constant thing. I'll always be able to find you, no matter when you are." Mara squeezed him even more tightly but after a moment she felt him release her.

"This charade is finished," Gabriel said, turning to Vik. "Release these people and deal with me."

Vik's face tightened into a mask of fury and hatred. "I will release *nothing*."

Gabriel straightened, squaring out his shoulders. "Your argument is with me, Vik. Not with any of these innocent people."

Ingrid Maxwell stepped out of the Timelock chamber,

her face like flint. "So you *do* know his name. Remembered you have a son, then?"

"I don't know what either of you think I'm supposed to have done," Gabriel said, looking from Vik to his mother and back again. "But I need you both to hear me, now. I need you to understand." Gabriel focused his gaze on his son's face. "I did not know about you, Vik. I didn't *reject* you. I didn't know you had ever been born." He paused. "If I had, I would have been there. I would have tried."

"You're *lying*!" Vik shouted. His face began to redden, his mouth pulled tight in a grimace of fury. "My mother told me she wrote to you. She *told* you when I was born. She sent you a photo of me. And she never had a reply!"

Gabriel reached out for his son, his face soft with compassion. "Ingrid always knew how to find me, Vik," he said in a level voice. "She knew my pick-up points, the places where I collect letters, whenever I can. If she'd wanted to get word to me, she would have. I promise you, I never received that letter."

Vik turned to his mother. Ingrid's face was cold. "Mum?" he asked. "What is he saying?"

"So this is how you're going to do it, then?" Ingrid said. "How you're finally going to try to destroy our son."

Gabriel frowned. "Destroy him? That's the furthest thing from my mind."

"Don't give me that," Ingrid snorted. "First, you deny

him the father he should have had. And then you try to ruin his future too." She lifted her hands, making menacing claw shapes with her fingers. "Wriggling your way into his head, trying to make him believe all he loves is a lie." She gave a mirthless chuckle, shaking her head slowly. "You've got style, I'll give you that."

"Ingrid," Gabriel said, taking another step towards them. "I don't know what you're trying to suggest, but—"

"He is *owed* this!" Ingrid shouted, so loudly that Mara jumped in fright. Ingrid's face was twisted with fury. "He is *owed* the power of the Tider. I don't care what you say about how Tiders are chosen – my son is choosing it for himself! You are *not* going to take it from him. And you're certainly not going to give it to *that* snivelling brat," she continued, turning up her nose as she glowered at Mara.

"Mum," Vik said, his voice quiet. "Is he … is he telling the truth?"

Ingrid looked at her son. Her face shook with emotion. "Don't tell me you believe him, Vik? After all this time?" She set her jaw once again, gesturing towards Mara. "Look at his daughter. Look at how he treats her! And you're telling me he could be a *loving* father? Who would have cared for you? Don't make me sick."

Gabriel turned to look at Mara, gathering her in his arms again. "I'm sorry," he murmured. "I'm so sorry. I've made such a mess. You've showed me that." He paused to kiss her head. "I should have lived the time I had with you instead of chasing Time I'd lost."

Mara looked up at him. "Dad? What … what do you mean?"

"I love you. Remember that. And – if you can, one last time – trust me, sweetheart." With one final hug, he turned back to his son. Vik was staring at him, hatred in his eyes and something like disgust making his lip curl. Beside him, Ingrid Maxwell stood, a smirk of triumph on her face.

"Oh, enough of this," Vik snapped, gesturing at his people. "Take him." Nobody moved, and Vik stared around in disbelief at the people who worked for him. Several of them, shamefaced, dropped their gazes to the floor. "So that's how it is," Vik continued, his voice low. "At the first sign of difficulty, you show me where your true loyalties lie." He narrowed his gaze. "He can't *hurt* you. Do you think he's going to suck all your Time away, leave you like empty shells?"

"Vik, this can all be sorted out between us," Gabriel said, taking a step towards the young man who stood in the doorway of the Timelock. Vik turned to face him. "Your mother's right – being the Tider is your birthright. But it's a complicated thing, something you'll need guidance on, something only I can help you with." He took another step. "There's nobody else who can talk you through the delicate details, who can help you avoid the mistakes I've made, who can *teach* you. Please, son. Let me help you."

Vik sliced a glance at Mara. "I thought you said I could never be the Time Tider, little sister," he said. "I thought you said your *father* had told you so. Which is it?"

Gabriel gave Mara a worried look. "Mara was probably mixed up," he said, looking back at Vik. "You've got the watch, haven't you? And the notebook? Now all you need is practice." He took one more step, until he was almost close enough to touch his oldest child.

"Oh, we've got those things, all right," Ingrid said, her voice low. "And they'll stay safe, until Vik cracks them. Only a matter of *time*." She smirked, amused at her own joke.

Vik's expression hardened even further. He folded his arms and strengthened his stance, facing his father down. "Why the change of heart now, Dad? Why are you willing to hand over the keys to the kingdom *now*, when earlier – back in my warehouse – you scurried away into the Stitch so you wouldn't have to talk to me?"

Gabriel licked his lips as he tried to think. He glanced at Mara and then back at Vik. "I – there was something I thought I had to do," he began. "Something in the Stitch that I felt I had to fix before I could deal with things here. But I know now that my children are more important. The *future* is more important than anything I did in the past." He looked at Mara and his eyes were soft with sorrow. "I just wish I'd understood that sooner."

"How very touching," Vik sneered. "You know, I've got this far on my own, Dad, so I don't think I'll be needing your help. I think I'll just pop you all in the Timelock so that when it explodes, all my problems will go up with it. How does *that* sound?"

"What?" Mara shouted. "You *promised* to let Jan go!"

Vik stared at her with cold eyes and then he shrugged. "We don't always get what we want, little sister," he said. He reached into a pocket and pulled out a gun, which he levelled at his father. "In fact, some of us *never* do."

"Wait!" Gabriel bellowed, holding out his hands. "Vik, wait. Listen to me. You've got to listen! You've been manipulated, son. Your mother was *always* able to make people believe what she wanted them to. She's made you believe I hate you, when nothing could be further from the truth." He paused, his voice catching. "Look, I'm going to level with you now, Vik. Ingrid's made you believe you can be the Tider but you can't. What I said, just now, about you simply needing practice? That wasn't true either. Being the Tider isn't something you take. It's something that's given. And it hasn't been given to you."

"He's lying, Vik," Ingrid hissed. "He's been lying to you all your life! The power is in our hands now. We've just got to seize it. Finally we have our chance. This is what we've been working towards, all these years. You're going to be the next Time Tider, son – and the *last* one!" Her eyes looked wild. "Remember our plan. Once we have access to Time, we never have to give it up. Who would forego the chance to live forever?"

Mara felt ill. *The last time a Tider tried to make himself immortal, Pearl said the Clockwatchers had to kill him...*

"This is a mistake, Vik," Gabriel said quietly, gazing at his son. "Endless Time? Sounds good, for sure. But it never works out like that." He looked at Ingrid. "And who really wants to be Tider, I wonder? You or your mother?"

Mara watched Vik's face. Emotions flickered over it, too quickly to read. His eyes filled with unshed tears. "That's enough," he whispered, his grip on the gun wavering.

"It doesn't matter how much you want it," Gabriel continued, moving another step closer, his hands still held out. "You are not, and will never be, the Time Tider. But you are, and always have been, my son. I want to make things up to you. Will you let me?"

Vik's face hardened. The gun steadied. "Make it up to me?" His laugh was bitter. "Ironically, Father, it's much too late for that now." He cocked the gun, the noise awful in the small, cramped space. Even Ingrid flinched, taking a few steps back.

Gabriel turned towards Mara, staring at her with an urgent expression. "Looks like Time is going to fly, my darling."

Mara stared at him. "*What?*"

Her father didn't answer. He just threw an empty Keeper into the air and Mara instinctively reached out and caught it. She glanced at her father's other hand – it held a spindle, poised over his heart, ready to receive its load of Time.

And the next thing Mara knew, Vik's gun retorted with a *bang* and the room became a burst of golden light.

Learn from my mistakes. (Note in Gabriel Denbor's handwriting, on the back cover of The Time Tider's Handbook, undated.)

Chapter Forty

A small but intensely bright Warp opened up inside the room. Everyone – except Mara – turned away from it, shouting in fear. The light was almost too overpowering to see through, but Mara stared into the heart of it, anyway. She saw her father leap for Vik, embracing him in something that looked like a hug, but together the two men fell to the floor.

Then the golden light was sucked into nothingness – and with it, Gabriel and Vik. Mara blinked, her heart thundering as she stared in confusion at the place where her father had been until a few seconds before, her mind filling with the buzz that only she knew how to stop.

She glanced down at her hand, which still held the Keeper her father had thrown to her, and then she closed her eyes. She blocked out the sounds in the room – the screaming of Ingrid Maxwell, the shouting from some of the others, the ringing air of shock all around. Mara quieted her ragged breathing, stilled her mind and got ready.

Her mother.

Thea smiled. Her eyes were warm with pride.

Her father.

Gabriel held out his hand, offering it to her. Mara reached for him.

Jan.

Her friend, in his home, with his family.

Herself.

The Stitch blazed into life inside Mara's head and she felt it pinpoint its destination without delay – the moment, a few heartbeats before, when, Mara realized, her father had harvested Time from his own life, creating a Warp. But a Warp like none she'd ever seen before. This Warp pulsed with golden light, a Warp that contained more than Time – it contained living people too. Mara flickered into existence inside the same room she'd just left, but now she wasn't just Mara, scared and confused and worried for her father. This time, she was the Time Tider.

Everything felt strangely slowed down. Mara looked at her father, and he gazed at her with sadness and pride. He tossed a full spindle towards her, and then he threw himself at his son. The bullet Vik had fired seemed to hang in the air, floating between them. It vanished into the folds of Gabriel's coat as he tackled Vik to the floor. The noise of their confrontation was like a distant roar in Mara's ears, and inside her chest she was aware of her heart slowly beating. The full spindle, wrapped around with gelatinous golden Time, hovered in the air in front of Mara's face and, feeling like her arm was several miles long, she raised the Keeper. As soon as she clicked open its lid, the spindle slid inside, spinning faster than Mara could believe, only slowing when she sealed the lid closed.

And then, Mara felt herself thrown out of the Stitch. Everything sped back up. Her heart *thunk-thunk*ed, her knees ached, Jan was shouting somewhere nearby – and in Mara's hand, there was a Keeper filled with Time. It throbbed and thrashed, like a living thing, like an *angry* thing.

"*No!*" Ingrid shrieked, falling to the floor and scrabbling towards the patch of carpet where, until a few moments before, her son had been standing. She collapsed there, sobbing.

"Dad," Mara whispered, her eyes filling with tears as she looked at the Keeper in her hand. She knew it contained her father's Time – the rest of his life. And that Vik was in there too. She closed her eyes and let her tears fall, fat and hot. *I hope I did it right, Dad. I hope I made you proud.*

"Oh my God!" Jan shouted, and then Mara felt him

fling himself down beside her. His arms wrapped around her and Mara did her best to hug him back with her free hand. "*What* just happened?"

"I think – if I tried to explain, you wouldn't believe me," Mara said.

"Yeah," Jan replied after a thoughtful moment. "You're probably right."

Sudden shouting from the Timelock chamber made both of them look up. Mara's eyes met Pearl's and a wave of hope roared inside her chest. The commander of the Clockwatchers held a weapon, with which she was keeping the remnants of Vik's people at bay, despite seeming dazed from a head wound. Pearl looked at Mara, eyes full of concern, and Mara gave her a quick thumbs up.

"Commander Sangare!" someone called. Mara turned to see the man with the blue turban, his face dirty with something that looked like soot but his smile wide. Behind him came several other Clockwatchers, many of them armed. "We've regained control of ground level, Commander," the man continued. "All hostile forces have surrendered."

Pearl glanced towards the man, satisfaction on her face. "Excellent," she said. "Keep Ingrid Maxwell in custody, please, and ensure she gives up the Tider's tools," she continued, before looking at the subdued members of Vik's team, each under Clockwatcher guard. "Now. Out of here, all of you." She glanced back at the turbaned man. "Khaira, I expect you and your people to guard these traitors until I've had a chance to make the Timelock secure and look after the civilians." Khaira nodded, as his colleagues began ushering Vik's people past him. "I look forward to discussing your defection in great detail," Pearl called after them as they left, looking shamefaced.

As soon as the captives were gone, Pearl crossed the floor to Mara and Jan, getting to her knees to wrap them both in an embrace. "I don't know what to say," she whispered, into Mara's ear. "Thank you."

"My dad's ... my dad's gone," Mara said, pulling herself out of Pearl's arms just enough to show her the glowing Keeper. "He and Vik. They're in here."

Pearl stared at the Keeper. Its light was strange on her skin. "He allowed you to harvest his Time?" she whispered. "*All* of it?"

Mara cradled the Keeper. "He made a Warp out of the rest of his life. I guess he thought it was the only way," she said. "The only way to stop Vik and keep everyone else safe."

"What a sacrifice," Pearl said, gazing sombrely at Mara.

Mara returned Pearl's gaze, a crushing loss wrapping itself around her heart as she remembered what her father had told her, back in the Stitch. "He was looking for her. Looking for Mum. That's what he's been obsessing over,

367

all these years – finding her Time." Mara looked back at the Keeper. "He wasn't just avoiding the Clockwatchers because … because of how she died. It was also because he was afraid you'd stop him from searching for her." She looked back at Pearl. "But you'd have understood, wouldn't you? He's spent years running from you, all for nothing."

"I never blamed Gabriel for keeping his distance, not after Thea's death and our role in it," Pearl said softly. "But I wish he'd told us the full story about why he was avoiding us. If we'd known the truth…" She left the rest unsaid, placing one gentle hand on Mara's.

"So – who's Tider now?" Jan said, staring at Mara. It looked like he already knew the answer.

"Dad dug his tools up from a field, and I found mine in a hidden bag, but I guess it's all the same. I dug them up, just like he did. They found me when I needed them," Mara replied, hardly able to believe the words.

"Time appoints its Tider," Pearl murmured.

Mara looked at the commander. Then she looked down at the Keeper containing her father's Time and her brother's, and her eyes filled with tears again – tears of pride. "I'll be just like my dad," she said, looking back up at Pearl. "I promise."

Pearl smiled. "I know."

*

"Come on, Dad," Jan called. "Put your back into it!"

Mara turned to look, a smile already on her face. Vincent, thin and pale and tired-looking but eager as a puppy – along with Will, who proclaimed that working with the Clockwatchers was better than *Lethal Warfare IV* any day of the week – was helping to haul a crate of Keepers on to the loading platform of a large truck. He was going against Helen's strict instructions to 'take it easy!', but Mara doubted anyone could have stopped Vincent from pitching in. This was the twelfth Time Dump they'd found with the aid of the notebook and the air buzzed with excitement. Mara's eye was caught by a collage of photographs on the wall not far from where Vincent was working – photographs of the members of the network who hadn't been found. Mara couldn't see from here but she knew one of them was of a smiling Lenny, his eyes shining green behind his glasses. Ingrid Maxwell had claimed responsibility for his murder but Mara wondered if she'd really done it or if it had been Vik instead. Ingrid's hatred of Gabriel and the Clockwatchers meant that she couldn't bear the fact that her plan to get revenge on them both, and her cruel manipulation of her son, had come to nothing. She seemed to be claiming any victories she could, however hollow and terrible they might be. Thea's death remained unexplained but Mara was sure that had been the beginning of Ingrid's attempts to destroy her family. *But she failed*, Mara thought. *I am not alone.*

Vincent raised a hand to wave, and Mara and Jan turned back to their own work. They were at a table with Pearl, planning the next mission.

"You see how easy things can be when we make full use of all the tools at our disposal," Pearl muttered, glancing up at Mara with a raised eyebrow.

"Sorry," Mara said, with an exaggerated shrug. "I'm afraid I have *no* idea what you mean." She put her hand into her pocket and pulled out her father's watch, which sat comfortably in her hand. The case, when clicked open, now contained Jan's game card, bent a little to accommodate the curve of the lid. Mara checked the time, and the Time, and then slid the watch back into place.

Pearl's gaze landed on the hourglass around Mara's neck. Among the silver grains there shone one made of gold – the second saved from the Warp her father had created from his own living Time, which had appeared there after Mara had harvested it. Mara saw her looking and she tucked the hourglass back beneath the collar of her shirt.

"And if you'd only let us use *that*," Pearl continued, good-naturedly, indicating the hourglass with her raised eyebrows, "we could all go home and have a nice cup of tea, and that would be that."

"Pfft. Tea's overrated," Mara said, shrugging as she

looked back at the map. All the Time Dumps they'd neutralized so far were marked with a large red X. The other sites they'd discovered were circled in green, and the ones they were hopeful of finding, with the help of the notebook and the remaining members of the network Vik had done his best to unravel, were marked with blue. There were a lot of them. "You know I can't let you put the hourglass into the Timelock. My dad's in there and his Warp's made from living Time. So maybe, one day, I'll be able to get him back."

Pearl shifted in her chair. "And maybe, one day, I'll sprout feathers and you can pluck me and roast me for Sunday lunch," she said, but there was no anger in it. This was a conversation she and Mara had at least once a week, and she'd never managed to get her own way yet. Pearl knew she never would. "All right. Keep the hourglass. What else would we be doing, anyway? It's not like anyone has anything more *pressing* in their calendar, right?"

Mara looked at Jan. He was gazing at his dad. Will had moved to another truck, working to save Time. Helen and Annelies were at home, waiting for them all to get back. *Home*, Mara thought, thinking of her bed, her things in the corner of Annelies's room, the locked box in the living room which contained the Keeper with the rest of her father's Time in it. They'd rescued what they could of her van, and it was now parked in a side street not far from Elysium Towers, but Mara no longer kept the key in her pocket, where it would always be ready to grab. She'd even found herself growing accustomed to the sound of car alarms and other people and the chaos of family life. Come September, Helen said, Mara would be joining Jan at school – she wasn't too sure about *that* but she was excited to give it a try.

She looked back at Pearl, who was regarding her with a wistful expression. Mara shook herself out of her thoughts and back into action. "Right," she said, jabbing at the map. "I reckon we should try here tomorrow. It looks like our best bet for our next Timesaving job."

Pearl smiled at Mara and gave a quick salute. "Yes, ma'am, Miss Denbor." She cracked a grin. Jan joined in, before sitting up and pretending to be serious as Mara rolled her eyes at her friends. "I mean," Pearl continued, her own eyes warm, "whatever you say, Time Tider."

Author's Note

Dear Reader,

Even though *The Time Tider* is a brand-new book, it's actually a very old story – to me, at least. About twenty years ago, I was eating lunch in the café of the university where I was studying and working at the time. I was also reading a book by the French medieval historian Jacques le Goff. (It was called *Time, Work and Culture in the Middle Ages*, and it was very good). Part of it discusses how ideas about time changed when clocks started chiming out the hours, sounding their bells across the fields where people would once have risen and gone to bed with the sun, and eaten when they were hungry. As I was reading, I got thinking about this dual aspect of time and the flash of an idea burst across my mind. *What if there was a gap between the two times ... and what if that gap was filled with the unused Time of all the people who die before they're supposed to ... and what if it was possible to go back and collect that unused Time, bring it to the present day and sell it...*

It was one of the first 'this could actually be a book!' ideas I ever had. It set my imagination spinning, and it's one of the reasons why I became an author.

But having an idea and making a book out of it are two different things. I've tried to write *The Time Tider* many times. It has had different settings, different eras, different secondary characters and different mechanisms for wriggling through Time – but in each of these versions, something about the story just didn't work. So I came up with a setting I'd never tried before: a contemporary one. I knew I finally had the right place, the right time period and the right characters to tell my decades-old tale about Time and the girl who knows she must do something about the illegal buying and selling of it. (The lesson here? *Never give up*).

I'm so glad to have brought this idea from an exciting spark to a finished story, and delighted to be handing it over now, for readers to make it their own.

Time and Tide may wait for none … but will they wait for you?

Sinéad

Acknowledgements

The idea for *The Time Tider* was one of the first ideas I ever had, and I've tried to write it many times over the past twenty years – always unsuccessfully, until now. So the fact that this book exists at all is down to the support I have received from so many people, principally my agent, Polly Nolan of PaperCuts Literary Agency and Consultancy, who has been by my side through the torment of trying and failing and trying again and failing again to write this story. Thank you, Polly – I'm glad you stuck with me.

My publisher, Little Tiger Press, have supported my work for many years now and it has been a joy to publish my previous novels (*The Eye of the North*, *The Star-Spun Web* and *Skyborn*) with them. I'm so glad that *The Time Tider* has finally come together and I'm delighted that it's their logo on the spine. Thanks to the entire team.

Endless thanks to Ella Whiddett, Lauren Ace, Karelle Tobias and Melissa Gitari, all of whom worked with me to shape and edit *The Time Tider*, to tidy up its timey-wimey stuff and to ask the tough questions. Finding the answers to those questions helped endlessly in making this book tick. Thank you all.

To Abigail Dela Cruz and Sophie Bransby, thank you for the beautiful cover art and design. I wish I could live in this book's jacket.

To Susila Baybars and Leena Lane, thank you for catching my goofs and whack-a-mole-ing my repetitions. (Sorry!)

To Margaret McElligott, driving instructor extraordinaire, who has never *once* made me feel like she's heartily sick of me (though I'm sure she is by now); it's down to her that any of the driving descriptions in this book are even somewhat realistic. I'm sorry for being the worst student you've ever taught, Margaret, and I promise you won't be trying to teach me for the rest of our lives.

To the bloggers, teachers and librarians out there (by now, too numerous to mention individually) who give so much of their time, energy, and effort to getting books into readers' hands – thank you. Your work, like the Time Tider's, is often unsung but it does not go unnoticed.

To my family – my parents-in-law, my cousins, aunts, and uncles, my dear brother, my beloved parents and my cherished husband and daughter – without you, I would not be here. Thank you all.

And to you, the reader – and to all the readers who've made my stories part of their story over the years – thank you. I hope you'll always find yourselves in books, and that one day, you'll find a way to tell your own tale. I can't wait to read what you create.

Also by Sinead O'Hart

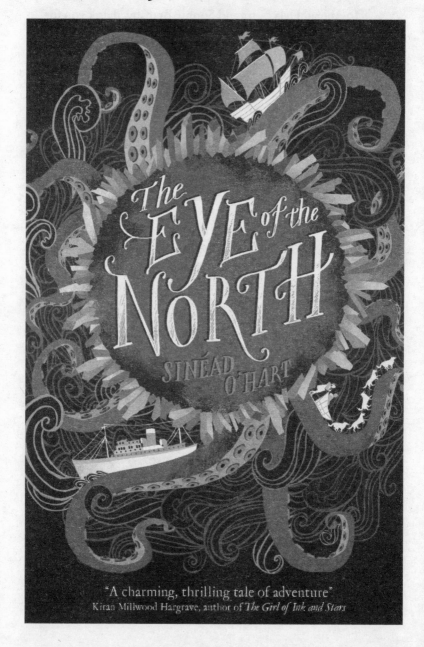

THE EYE of the NORTH

SINÉAD O'HART

"A charming, thrilling tale of adventure"
Kiran Millwood Hargrave, author of *The Girl of Ink and Stars*

Emmeline is prepared for everything – until her parents mysteriously disappear. Fearing for her life, she flees on a ship to France where she befriends a stowaway called Thing. But even he can't help her escape the clutches of the villainous Dr Siegfried Bauer.

Dr Bauer is bound for the far north to summon a mythical monster from the deep. And he's not the only one plotting to unleash the creature.

In a frozen land, with danger at every turn, can Emmeline and Thing reunite in time to save the world? The race is on...

Also by Sinead O'Hart

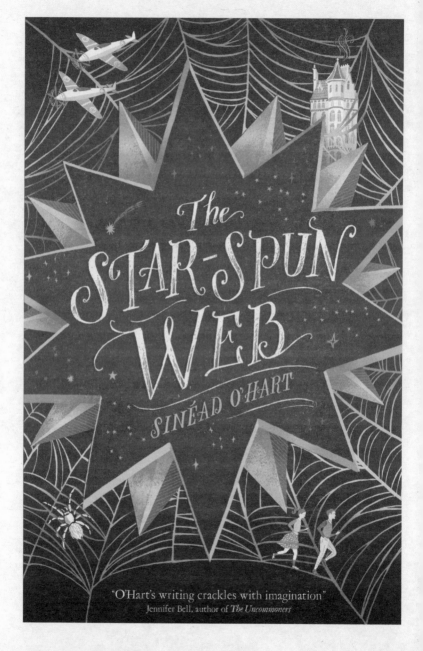

The
STAR-SPUN
WEB

SINÉAD O'HART

"O'Hart's writing crackles with imagination"
Jennifer Bell, author of *The Uncommoners*

Tess de Sousa is no ordinary orphan.
When a wealthy stranger appears at Ackerbee's
Home for Lost and Foundlings claiming to be
her relative, she embarks on a new life with him.
She takes nothing more than her pet tarantula Violet and
a strange device that she was left as a baby.

But far from providing answers to Tess's mysterious past,
it becomes clear that her guardian's interest in her is
part of a terrible plan. With the future of more than
one world at stake, it's up to Tess to stop him...

Also by Sinead O'Hart

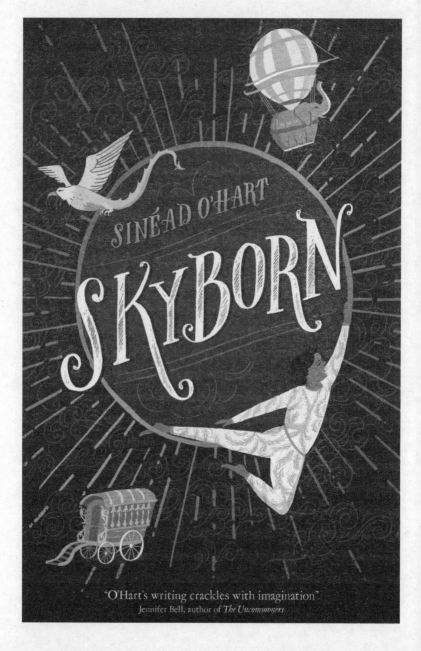

SINÉAD O'HART

SKYBORN

"O'Hart's writing crackles with imagination"
Jennifer Bell, author of *The Uncommoners*

The circus has seen better days, but for Bastjan it's home. He will do anything he can to save it, even if it means participating in a death-defying new act. But when that fails to draw in the crowds, the ringmaster makes a deal with a mysterious man by the name of Dr Bauer.

In exchange for his help, Bauer wants a box that belonged to Bastjan's mother and came from her birthplace – the faraway island of Melita. Bastjan is desperate to keep his only memento of his mother out of Bauer's hands. And as he uncovers more about the strange objects contained within, he realizes it's not only the circus that's in terrible danger…

About the Author

Sinéad O'Hart is a children's author living in the Irish midlands, in a house almost completely filled with books. Her novels include *The Eye of the North*, *The Star-Spun Web* and *Skyborn*. When she's not writing she's either reading, podcasting (with Susan Cahill over at shows.acast.com/Storyshaped), or planning her next book-buying trip.

Follow her on Twitter @SJOHart.